Brown's Sugar

SHE iS series Book 1

Marlee Rae

D1523100

Cover designed by Under Cover Designs

This book is a work of fiction. Names, characters, places, and incidents either are products of the author's imagination or are used fictitiously. Any resemblance to actual persons, living or dead, events, or locales is entirely coincidental.

Marlee Rae
Visit my website at www.MarleeRaeReadsAndWrites.com

Printed in the United States of America

First Printing: May 2023

Chapter 1 ~ Tonya

The comedy show was hilarious; wish I could have said the same thing about my date.

He put his arm around me and asked, "Are you enjoying the show, Tonya?"

I smiled politely and nodded. "Yes, very much so, thank you again for inviting me."

I felt bad because Daniel was a genuinely nice man, but I wasn't feeling him. He was missing the swagger and edge that I loved in men.

"Did I tell you how nice you look? Your outfit is really pretty."

What a drag. "Thank you," I said and inwardly rolled my eyes. This was about the tenth time he commented on my outfit. I mean I was looking fly in my little black short romper, but him calling it pretty was ridiculous.

I wanted to tell him my outfit wasn't pretty, it was sexy. But that would have been rude, so I kept it to myself.

Daniel had served in the Navy with my younger brother, Macon. He was new to St. Louis, and we met by chance while he was visiting Macon at home.

After a couple of phone calls, I agreed to meet him for dinner. The dinner went well but I wasn't intrigued with him at all. I figured I was being hasty, so I agreed to a comedy show. I should have gone with my first instinct and declined any further activity, yet here I was.

Daniel was handsome enough. Not overly tall, but that didn't matter because I was only five-three. He was light skin with a small to medium build. His hair was low-cut, and he didn't wear any facial hair. His skin was beautiful, and I believe his eyelashes were longer than mine.

His clothes were classic but a little too stuffy for the occasion. The black suit, white shirt, and black tie were reminiscent of a limo driver. He was only missing the hat and driving gloves.

By the time the show was over, I was more than ready to end the date. He was sweet and handsome; he just wasn't for me.

He led us into the corridor and stopped at one of the stations to have our phones removed from the pouches. We were required to power off our phones and lock them inside the Yondr pouches during the show.

"Daniel, I need to use the restroom." It was extremely crowded in the venue, but I could not wait.

"Ok, I'll walk you over and then have our phones unlocked."

I nodded and followed him across the crowded corridor to the ladies' restroom. My feet were on fire. Not sure who told me to wear stilettos on a concrete floor.

"Wait here when you are finished. I'll take the pouches to get our phones out," he said.

"Ok." I handed him my pouch and almost ran into the restroom.

By the time I came out, it was still crowded. I leaned against the wall to give my feet a little relief while I waited for Daniel.

I did a little people-watching since I didn't have my phone. The couples were interesting, they were dressed in everything from jogging clothes to floor-length gowns.

After what felt like an hour, Daniel had not returned, and my feet were killing me. The crowd seemed to have thinned out. I looked up and down the hallway but didn't see him anywhere. This was just icing on the cake. I was on a boring date and now he was missing.

The floor was pretty much empty, and security was clearing the area.

"No way this guy left me," I mumbled to myself. He told me to wait outside the restroom and that's where I was.

"Ma'am, you have to head toward an exit," the security guy said as he approached me.

"I was waiting on a friend, but I don't know where he is."

"No one is left on this floor, why don't you try the first floor and the valet area."

"Okay, thank you. Can I borrow your phone?"

He handed me his phone and I tried the only number I knew by heart, my parents' landline which had not changed in years. I figured I could reach Macon and get Daniel's phone number. Of course, they didn't answer so I returned the phone and left the area.

I took the escalator down two flights to the entry-level and waited near one of the main doors. I had no idea where he parked because he dropped me off at the entrance when we arrived.

After more time passed and there were only a few people plus security guards milling around, someone called my name.

"Tonya?"

I turned toward the familiar voice and was a bit spellbound. My high school crush, who didn't even know I existed until a couple of years ago, was walking toward me with a big smile on his face.

Damn, he was fine—medium brown skin, medium but very toned build, and a slightly salted shallow beard.

He was wearing dark brown dress pants, a pale orange dress shirt, and a pair of tannish-colored hard-bottom dress shoes.

"Hey, Dre!" I finally said as he scooped me up in a hug and kissed my cheek.

I wrapped my arms around his neck and inhaled his manly scent that was sprinkled with a heavenly cologne.

"How have you been?" he asked, flashing his pretty white teeth and perfect smile.

"I've been good, what about you?" I probably hadn't smiled this hard all night.

"I can't complain. Look at you with the legs all out and glistening. Girl, you look good."

I waved my hand and blushed. "You are so crazy."

"I just wanted to say hi, I won't keep you. They are clearing us out and my truck is still with the valet. It was good seeing you though." He pulled me in for a second hug, which I gladly accepted. "Who are you here with?"

He looked around and of course, no one was there.

"Well, I guess I'm still on a date," I said, and shrugged.

"What do you mean you guess?" He frowned. "Where is he?"

I explained the story and included the part about him having my phone.

4

"The show has been over for an hour. I don't know where he is but I'm not leaving you downtown alone without a phone."

I tried not to blush because this was the type of man I liked; one that took charge.

A thought occurred to me. "Where is your date? I don't want to inconvenience the two of you."

He shook his head. "No date, I came with a friend from work; she lives on the east side, so we met here. I walked her to her car because the valet line was too long when we first came out. Come on, let's go. You can use my phone after I charge it up some, it's dead."

"Thanks, Dre. I appreciate this, and I hate to leave but I don't know what else to do." I did feel bad about leaving but again, what was my option? I could be looking for Daniel all night without a phone. And the way they were locking the doors they weren't about to have me hanging around waiting.

"Please exit the building!" the security guard yelled out to the last few stragglers, including us.

Dre ushered me out the door and handed the valet his ticket.

"We will sit out front for a few minutes and wait; if he's in there he should be coming out soon."

"Ok," I said.

Dre laughed. "Your feet hurt, don't they?"

I was shifting my weight back and forth on either foot. I didn't realize he saw me.

Palming my forehead, l said, "The shoes match my outfit, ok?"

He looked me up and down. "You look good tonight; I would say the pain is worth it."

I put my hand on my hip. "Only tonight?"

The valet pulled up in Dre's black Range Rover. He opened the passenger door and held his hand out with a smile. "Tonya, you know you're a dime, you don't need me or anyone else to tell you what's already known."

I blushed and took his hand. As he guided me inside, I replied, "Sometimes, it's good for others to confirm."

"Well, let me put it like this. Whoever lost you tonight is a sucka. You wouldn't have been out of my sight for a minute if you were with me. Period." He closed the door.

I had about three seconds to cool off and get rid of this silly smile I had been wearing since he called my name. It was like I was in high school all over again, watching him in the hallways and at the football games. He had so much swag it was ridiculous.

When he got into the driver's side and closed the door, he said, "I'll pull over here where you can watch out for the sucka." He laughed. "How long have you been with this dude?"

He maneuvered the truck to a space where I could see the entrance.

"This is only our second date."

He reached into the backseat and asked, "Do you like him?"

"Umm..."

He chuckled. "That's a no, you took too long. Here you go, these are brand new."

He handed me a pair of socks.

"Why do you have new socks in here? Not that I'm complaining because these shoes are coming off."

"My gym bag is in here. Tell me why you don't like the sucka?"

I took the shoes off and replaced them with the thick socks.

"He's very nice, I just don't think we are a good match."

"He must be boring," he said.

I blew out a breath and smiled at him as I narrowed the space between my thumb and index finger. "Maybe a little. He kept telling me I look pretty."

Dre nodded. "Ahhh, now I see why you were fishing for compliments. You out here with your daisy duke set on, the legs baby-oiled up, and the sky-high heels and he's complimenting you like you're wearing an Easter dress."

I burst into laughter. "You are so crazy!"

He laughed with me. "But I'm right, ain't I?"

When I finally stopped laughing, I responded, "You hit the nail on the head. I like a guy who's a little more..."

He cut me off with, "Verbal and confident?"

I nodded. "See, you understand. I tried to explain it to my sister, Melody, but she said I was being picky. Mel is impressed because he's a medical doctor and is retired from the Navy. I don't care about that if we can barely have a decent conversation."

"What kind of doctor is he?"

"He's into research."

Nodding, Dre added, "Medical research? He's a nerd."

"Basically."

He put the truck in drive and moved out of the space. "Let's go, security is checking doors. He was never going to find you in there anyway," he said.

I turned and stared at his side profile. "Why do you say that?"

"People like that aren't usually practical. He probably stood in the same spot waiting on you without realizing you had to be in a different spot. You wouldn't have been in there that long."

Frowning, I said, "But I waited too, and didn't move."

"He's the man, he told you to wait so you followed instructions like you were supposed to. He's supposed to find you. Not the other way around."

My eyes opened wide. "Okay, Dre, that had a slight chauvinistic back on it."

He grinned and licked his lips. If I were anything like my big sister, Lois, I would kiss him. But, I stayed in place and listened as he said, "Baby, I'm far from a chauvinist. I'm all for women doing whatever they want. But when it comes to a household and relationships the man needs to lead."

"I would agree, but it depends on your definition of leading," I quipped.

"I like you, you're smart. The average woman would have taken that statement and decided by lead I meant control. Lead means to guide, but at the same time understand that your woman is capable of providing good council."

Here I was again smiling because he said he liked me. Didn't take much for me to be impressed with him. "I agree with that, my parents had a good balance before my father passed. When my mother married Brock, I noticed the same thing with them. They just get along without all the drama."

Not only was Dre my secret high school crush, but my brother, Macon, was also married to his best friend, Dawn. That got ugly when they started dating. Dre was also a coworker of my stepfather, Brock, for over twenty years before his retirement a couple of years ago. I had no idea Brock knew him all those years.

"Same with my parents," he added.

"Why aren't you married with kids?" I asked.

He shrugged. "Honestly, I've enjoyed the variety."

My mouth opened wide. "Oh, so you're admitting you're a hoe?"

He smiled. "Depends on your definition. It's all about lexicography, baby."

"Why don't you indulge me? I'm curious to know your definition."

I rested my elbow on the console, waiting for him to explain.

"I assume that you think I run through women, or I have a bunch at once; that would be a hoe. I date, but I don't always get into a committed relationship. I enjoy a woman's company and when I'm no longer enjoying her or I'm interested in someone else, I exit left."

"Damn, ok, so you ghost, too?" I asked.

He laughed. "Come on, what man doesn't ghost or slide out wherever there's a crack? We ain't really equipped for the conversations and tears."

I shook my head. "Okay, Dre, so you loving them and leaving them. Mr. Fire and Desire in the flesh."

He laughed. "You hit me with a Rick James comparison? I'm not cold as ice as he would say, maybe a little chill, but not cold."

He dazzled me with a big smile, and I couldn't help but giggle.

"Isn't that tiring? You're getting up in age."

He pulled his head back in surprise. "Daaaamn, Tonya, you out here trying to pluck feelings tonight."

I waved my hands laughing. "No, no, no, what I meant was don't you get tired of the variety and want one flavor?"

His smile faded as if he were in thought. "Yep, you're right. When I said I enjoyed the variety, I was speaking past tense. Seems like everyone around me is married and I'm the last man standing. I wouldn't mind settling down with the right woman."

I nodded. "I'll keep that in mind."

"Uh oh, are you about to play matchmaker?" He laughed. "I'm particular about my women."

I wanted to hear this, but only because I was interested. I wouldn't dare pass him off to anyone!

"I want to hear this," I said and folded my arms.

"I'm just joking. I want a good woman without drama that can cook and give me sex whenever I want it. I got a healthy appetite." Smiling, he ran his hand across his beard.

"Food and sex?"

"And no drama."

"It doesn't matter what she looks like?"

He frowned. "That's a given, but I don't have a set type. Tall, short, curvy, thin—doesn't matter to me as long as I'm attracted to her. I do like a little meat though."

I guess that ruled me out. I was toned but I didn't have much extra meat. Melody and I weren't blessed with long legs and thick thighs like our big sister Lois. She would grab the attention of any man when she walked in the room swinging her hips and big butt.

"Ok got it, so someone my size is too small? Do you want thicker? Asking for a friend," I said. One would think I didn't have anyone knocking on my door, but my eye had been on him for years.

"Oh no," he said, and my heart sank. "That lil' tight body you got? I would have you locked up in the house for days. Girl, you trippin'." He laughed then paused. "You trying to shoot your shot?"

I sure was, but he didn't need to know it, so I laughed. I threw up my hand and said, "You can't handle me anyway."

"Is that a challenge? Because..." he stopped. "Hold up, where am I taking you? I don't know where you live. Hell, I'm heading to my house."

I was so caught up in the conversation I forgot.

"Oh, I'm sorry, I'm going to my parents' house, I parked there. You know where they live, right?"

I assumed he did because they lived on the street adjacent to Dawn and Macon.

"Yeah, I know where they live." He smiled and asked, "So you're a tease, too?"

I frowned. "What do you mean? Teasing who?"

"The nerd." I wrinkled my forehead in confusion. "You go out with him looking good enough to eat but you have him pick you up from the folks' house so he can't come in."

I covered my eyes with my hand in shame. "I wasn't quite thinking... okay maybe I did, but..." I threw my hands up. "You're right but what was I supposed to do, wear loose jogging clothes?"

He laughed. "Naw, but you ain't have to do him like that though. Even a nerd would have a hard time keeping his eyes off you all night in that outfit."

"It's not like I have body parts hanging out, I'm completely covered," I argued.

He looked at me and kind of rolled his eyes upward. "This is what we're doing, Tonya? I thought we were cool."

"We are, what do you mean?" I asked innocently.

"Yeah, you are covered but you know that thing is hugging everywhere. What do you even call it? Is it a jumpsuit? But then it's shorts."

I crossed my legs and sat up straight. "It's a romper."

"Sounds like something a baby wears," he said, and laughed out loud.

I laughed too and playfully pushed his arm.

He continued with, "But for real, you got on your little black romper and then you're mad because he said you looked pretty. That's a nerd's word for fire. Dude was trying."

I rolled my eyes playfully because he was right, but I just wasn't interested.

"And for your information, I wore my romper because I think I look nice in it."

"And you wanted him to notice you, but he used the wrong words. Tonya, I know how y'all women are, you wanted the compliments and the unapologetic looks throughout the night. The problem is, a nerd doesn't know the difference between a sensual stare and a perverted stare."

I laughed out loud. "You are so crazy, what are you talking about?"

"I'm telling you; the average man sees you come out in that and he's immediately thinking about the end of the night. If it's the second date, like you and the nerd, you let her know how good she looks, you keep her close, and maybe do some innocent touching throughout the date. Which is how you pursue the prize. A nerd isn't confident and usually doesn't know the art of the pursuit. All he knows is he wants the prize, but he feels bad about it and doesn't want to come off as a pervert, so he's awkward. That's the difference between a man with swag and a nerd; it's all about the art of the pursuit and confidence."

"I guess you would know, you've been working at this form of art for fifty years," I said casually.

"I'm forty-seven, not fifty," he corrected.

"Sorry," I said, and smiled.

"Ain't no thing, I'm knocking on it. But I look good and I'm in shape." He patted his flat stomach. I wondered what he looked like without clothes. He was about six feet, so he leaned over whenever he hugged me and I was never able to get a good feel.

"I think I see a roll or two," I said jokingly as I eyed his stomach.

"You're a tease and a hater? Damn, I thought you and I were going to get along."

I laughed as he turned on my parents' street. My smile dropped when I saw all the cars parked in the driveway and on the street.

"Something is wrong," I said. "Why is my whole family over here?"

"Yeah, something is up, they are all outside," Dre added.

My parents, my brother Macon and his wife, Dawn, my brother Donald and his wife, Tori, and both of my sisters, Melody and Lois. Even the next-door neighbors, Calvin and Janae, were outside.

Dre slowed down and parked in the street because they were parked all over the cul-de-sac.

Well, there wasn't an ambulance, and everyone looked intact, maybe it was one of my nieces or nephews.

Dre's windows were heavily tinted. They knew his truck, so all eyes were on us as we both got out at the same time.

Everyone screaming at once scared me.

"Where have you been?" Macon yelled.

"This child of mine is going to send me to an early grave!" my mother yelled.

"What's going on?" I finally asked as I walked toward them with Dre on my heels.

"D and I were on our way downtown to look for you is what's going on!" Macon yelled.

"Right!" Donald added.

"But why?" I asked, completely confused.

Macon turned away and made a phone call. His wife, Dawn, chimed in with a concerned look on her face. "Because your date called Macon and told him you went to the bathroom, and he never saw you again. He said he waited outside the bathroom forever and then finally went to security. They pulled the video of you leaving with a man. We didn't know what happened. Daniel has your phone so no one could call you."

I put my hand to my mouth. Dre was supposed to charge his phone, but we were so deep in conversation I forgot.

My sister Lois had tears running down her face. She walked to me and hugged me tightly. I felt so bad, her husband passed away about a year ago, and she had been an emotional wreck since.

"I'm so sorry, everyone. I didn't mean to worry you all. When I bumped into Dre, he offered to bring me home. We waited for Daniel at the entrance, but he never came out."

Macon came back in with, "I called him to let him know you're here. He should be here soon with your phone."

Everyone was visibly shaken, and I felt like a jerk because I had been batting my eyes at Dre while my family was worried.

My mother wrapped her arms around Lois and me, and said, "Come on in the house, it's late. You don't need to be on the street tonight, you stay here."

I wanted to sleep in my own bed tonight, but I wouldn't argue with her. Macon and Donald lived in the same subdivision as my parents. Melody and Lois lived within five minutes of them. I, on the other hand, lived about twenty minutes away.

Brock, my stepfather, raised his hands. "No, I want everyone to go where they pay the mortgage. I finally got a night without one of you or one of your offspring in my house. I want to keep it that way."

Everyone laughed except my mother. "Honey, I almost lost my baby. She needs to stay here."

He walked over and removed her hand from my shoulder. "You did not almost lose a baby." He whispered in her ear, and she smiled. "Now, I want all of you off our property. Macon and Donald, take your wives and go. Melody, you and Lois live next door to each other so go to one of those houses. Calvin and Janae, you two go on back inside. Lastly, Andre, would you please follow my daughter home so that she doesn't get lost again?"

I rolled my eyes but was kind of happy he said it.

"I sure will," Dre said.

"Why don't you let Daniel follow you, I'm sure he's worried," Melody said.

I wanted to kick her. She wasn't the biggest fan of Dre after all that happened with him, Dawn, and Macon. That was water under the bridge as far as I was concerned.

Bright headlights turned onto the street; it was most likely Daniel.

"I asked Andre to do it because clearly, this other fella can't keep up with her," Brock said.

Melody rolled her eyes but kept quiet.

Brock grabbed my mother's hand and guided her up the driveway. "Goodnight, children! And if any of you set foot in our house before noon tomorrow, you're going to see some things you won't be able to get out of your mind!"

Everyone groaned.

"We out!" Donald said.

We all hugged and kissed each other goodbye and I quickly walked over to Daniel, who was standing outside his car holding my phone.

"Hey, Tonya, I'm so sorry about all this, but I had to call Macon," he said.

"Oh, no please don't apologize, you did the right thing. I don't know how we were separated."

"When I watched the video, we were both outside the restroom, but you were on the opposite side. You left out of the wrong door, so you were in the other hallway."

Palming my forehead, I said, "I am so sorry, I guess I didn't notice there was more than one entrance."

"I'm glad you're okay. When I saw you getting into the car with a man I called Macon."

I can only imagine how that call went. Macon was my levelheaded brother unless it involved the women in his life.

"Yeah, he's a family friend I bumped into and he gave me a ride. Thanks again. I'll let you get home, it's late. Thanks for bringing my phone."

He hugged me awkwardly. "I will call you tomorrow, maybe we can finish our date. Have brunch or dinner?"

I couldn't do it again, so I politely said, "I have plans tomorrow, maybe another time."

"Ok, it's a date!" He smiled. "Can I have another hug?"

What grade were we in? Who asked for hugs? Nerd!

"Sure," I said and opened my arms. He held on a little longer and finally let me go.

I stepped back and waved as he turned around and drove up the street.

My family had dispersed, leaving Dre sitting in the blacked-out Rover.

Padding over to him in my socks he let the window down.

"You didn't tell me the nerd was short," he said with a smirk.

I laughed out loud. "He is not short, he's taller than me."

"That ain't hard to do," he quipped. "And what's up with the church hug? He was supposed to get in there." He made a grinding movement.

"You know you're silly, right?"

He laughed. "I know, I'm just messing around. Let's go, Sexy Mama. You lead the way. Oh, wait, give me your phone number just in case."

He handed me his phone and I quickly typed in my number.

I walked away hoping he was watching but I was too much of a chicken to look behind me. If I had Lois' hips and butt I would have walked away doing lunges. Instead, I swayed my slim thighs as much as I could without embarrassment.

As soon as I got in the car and moved out of the driveway my phone rang. It had to be Dre; I didn't recognize the number.

"Was that walk for me? Or is that normal?"

So he was checking. "Nope, just my regular walk."

"Mmmm, okay, Tonya. You're playing bait the hunter."

"Bait the hunter? What is that?" I laughed.

"I'll let you figure that out."

We chatted for the twenty minutes it took to get to my place. I lived in a condo with underground parking.

I swiped my fob to open the gate and Dre pulled in behind me.

"Where are you going?" I asked.

"I'm making sure you get inside as Brock asked me to do."

"I'm just checking. I don't want you thinking you're about to get some," I said jokingly and ended the call.

He parked next to me and got out of his truck with a smirk on his face. He stopped in front of me and said, "I'm not that type of dude, ok?"

"What type of dude is that?"

"The kind that pretends to walk a woman to her door hoping to end up sleeping with her. It's not me, and I've never had to hope for sex."

He smelled so good and he was staring me in the eyes. "Well excuse me."

His smile finally dropped. "I know I play around a lot, and I've gone out with my fair share of women. But I don't prey on women, I pursue who I want, and I make it known. Besides, you're my best friend's sister-in-law, I'm not trying to go there with you."

I had to do a quick recovery because that stung. *Like, was I not to be taken seriously? What did that mean?*

I didn't know what else to say other than, "Good, because I won't be going there with you either." I smiled. "Now, come on and walk me to my door."

He nodded and licked those lips. "Alright, Tonya. But I do need to use your bathroom if you don't mind."

"Of course," I said and moved toward the elevator. I was glad I cleaned my place this morning or else I would have been embarrassed for him to come inside.

We went up the elevator to my floor and walked down the hallway. My condo was at the far end.

"I didn't realize I would have to walk a mile to get to your bathroom."

Looking over my shoulder, I smiled. "I'm on the end, I like it down here. I can't hear my neighbors."

Once we were inside, I turned on a few lights and showed him to the powder room near the front door. My condo had two levels. The first level housed an open two-story foyer, a half bath, and an office/exercise room. Five steps up from the foyer was the main level, where my kitchen and great room combo, two bedrooms, and two bathrooms were located.

I quickly went upstairs to my bedroom while Dre was in the powder room. When I came down the hallway, he was standing in the foyer looking at my artwork.

"You see something you like?" I asked, as I made my way down the steps.

Without turning around, he said, "I like this painting, it reminds me of the one Tori has in her house."

Tori was my sister-in-law; she was married to my brother Donald. She was also a good friend of Dawn's.

"Same artist, Gavin Gray," I said.

He turned to me and grinned. "That's the porno artist, right? So, what am I looking at? I know his stuff is like an optical illusion, right?"

I laughed. "Yes, he does do erotic art but this is just his regular abstract work. I do have one from his erotic collection upstairs."

He shook his head. "I didn't know you were like that, Tonya. I thought you were a good girl."

"Good girls like a little fun too."

He smiled and looked around as if he were trying to see the great room and kitchen. It was partially visible from the foyer.

"Do you want a tour?" I asked.

"Oh, yeah, if you don't mind. It's nice in here. I thought these were all garden-style condos. I bought a few rental properties over the last five years, and I almost had one in this building but the association said no."

I nodded. "They don't allow rentals over here, it's the reason I purchased here. Only the condos on the top floor have two levels." We took the steps and walked into the kitchen area.

"This is nice, I like it. Did you put these floors in?" he asked, referring to my toffee-colored hardwood floor.

"I did. Well, Brock put them in," I corrected.

"He did a great job. You know I forget who's step and who's biological because you all don't use the term."

I leaned against the kitchen counter. "I know. Everyone says that it's hard to believe Mom and Brock were married when we were out of the house. I think Macon was the only one living at home when they married."

"Really? I assumed you all grew up in the house together."

I shook my head. "Nope, they dated when I was in high school but married when I was in college. So Lois, Melody, Macon, and I have the same parents. Our father passed and later my mom married Brock. Brock had Donald and Dale. We all kind of blended perfectly. They call my mom Lady B and we call their Pop, Brock. However, they call all of us their children. I couldn't have asked for a better second father."

He nodded. "That's what's up. That's real cool. I call your mom Lady B, too. She's a nice lady."

"She really is. Do you want to sit down?"

My feet were still hurting from the shoes.

"Are you sure you don't mind? I don't want to keep you up."

I waved him off. "I'm a night owl. Have a seat, I'll grab us something to drink. I have water, tea, and lemonade. Unless you want something stronger."

"I'll take a tea and lemonade mix," he said and went to the great room and sat on the sofa.

I made the drinks and carried them in on a tray. I added a bowl of potato chips as well.

"Thank you, and good looking out. I could use something to eat."

"You're welcome. I'll be back in a second. The remote to the tv is on the table."

I left the room and went to my bedroom. I could not believe after all these years, *the* Andre Brown was sitting on my sofa eating chips. I would have never thought this evening would end this way. Of course, nothing was going to happen tonight, but I wanted to know if his true personality matched up with his good looks. After crushing on someone since freshman year of high school, I think I deserved to know and put it to bed. Or would it be worse than I imagined?

Chapter 2 ~ Dre

Tonya walked from the back part of her condo wearing gray fitted stretch pants and a long gray t-shirt tied in a knot on her left thigh.

She had washed the makeup from her face. She was pretty with and without makeup and again her body didn't disappoint.

She had one of those bodies that was naturally toned, but she had to do some sort of exercise because her legs in that romper thing was how I noticed her at the comedy show.

I didn't know her in high school because she was a freshman during my senior year. But I will admit I most definitely noticed her a few years ago when we were introduced at Brock's retirement party. However, during that time I was trippin' out over Dawn, and I didn't focus on her. We'd been around each other a lot over the last few years, but nothing beyond casual talk. She was definitely my type of woman, but I needed to walk slow with her, or not at all. I didn't want any misunderstandings with that family or Dawn.

Tonya was short with brown skin, a small little thing with a perfect body. I was watching her, but she didn't know it. Her hair was cut short with a curly or wavy pattern to it. Like tapered in the back and on the sides, but longer on the top.

She walked in carrying a small plate filled with bite-sized sandwiches. She put them on the tray with the chips.

"I'll never leave if you keep feeding me," I joked.

She laughed and took a seat a few feet away from me on the couch. "That's all it takes are sandwiches and chips?"

"I'm a simple man." I popped one of the sandwiches in my mouth. "These are good, and that drink is good too, something different is in there."

She smiled and tucked her feet under her behind. That's when I noticed her big breasts. *Where had she been keeping those?* I had to look away, I was coming off like the Nerd. But damn, I swear I thought she was like an A-cup based on the clothes she wore. I was a leg and breast man, how did I miss those?

"I used my infused sugar when I made the lemonade and tea. The tea has hibiscus sugar and the lemonade has basil sugar."

"That's right! I forgot about the big grand opening of your new spice store. Dawn mentioned one of you did flavored sugars."

She nodded. "Yep, I do infused sugar. Melody does infused honey and Lois does all the spices. I'm glad you like it."

"That's real dope, we need something like that around here. You couldn't have picked a better location, right in the heart of Greenwood. And right next door to Tori's shop."

Tori owned a beauty and barber shop combo named Whip N' Fade. They had the best of the best in there and everybody patronized them.

"I am so excited about the grand opening. I've been testing out a few new flavors, especially for next Saturday. Are you coming?"

I frowned. "Of course, I'll be there. Three black sisters opening a store? I support my people. The whole city will be there."

"We have a lot planned for that day. Free tastings, food trucks, vendors, a DJ, and free cocktails made with our products! We are excited!"

"Hey, I'm happy for y'all. If there's anything I can do to help, let me know." And I meant it. I wanted them to succeed. "How did you all come up with the concept?"

"This was all Lois. You remember her husband passed a year ago?"

I nodded. "Yeah, I remember. I went to the funeral. He was a cool older cat."

"Oh, okay. I didn't know you were there. Anyway, after he passed Lois spent a lot of time in the DC area with my brother Dale and his wife, Di-Di. She wanted a change of scenery to get her mind off everything. Di-Di took her to this black woman-owned place called The Spice Suite and she fell in love with it and the concept. Mel and I weren't onboard at first, but when she put together the business model and presented it to us we were both in. She will be there full time, but Mel and I are part-time. We each own twenty-five percent with Lois owning the other fifty."

I took down the last of the tea and lemonade. "I can't wait to see the place, sounds like it's going to be a great success story."

"You want more to drink?" she asked.

"I hate to put you out. I already took down those sandwiches and chips while you were talking. But I could take another glass."

She waved me off. "No problem."

She stood and leaned over to grab my glass off the table. My last sandwich stopped midair because her perfect round ass poked through her long shirt. I had to focus. I knew Tonya was fine, but I had never been in her personal space.

I expected to see a pudgy stomach or at least a little cellulite from a woman in her forties, but she was tighter than I thought she was. I was going to work a little harder on keeping my eyes focused when she came back into the room.

A minute later, sure enough, she came walking back in with bouncing breasts. And I knew she was wearing a bra because a piece of the strap was visible when she adjusted herself on the couch. I closed my mouth and focused on my glass.

I wasn't trying to ogle her, but I thought I knew what she looked like, so I was staring more out of surprise. And a pleasant surprise.

We talked more about the grand opening until my eyes must have faded because the next thing I knew we were both knocked out on either side of the sofa.

I checked my watch; it was almost five. I grabbed a blanket and covered her up then went to the bathroom to relieve myself.

I thought about leaving, but I was sleepy and I also didn't want to wake her. I'd catch a few more zzz and then head out.

The bright sunlight peeking through small slivers of the closed blinds woke me up. Stretching, I looked to the end of the couch where I'd last seen Tonya, but she was gone. I checked my watch; it was almost nine. I rarely slept late but this couch was comfortable.

I went down to use the bathroom. She'd left a basket on the counter that wasn't there last night. The basket had toothpaste, a toothbrush, mouthwash, floss, soap, and towels. This was a nice touch because I did need to rinse a little of yesterday off.

After I finished in the bathroom, I went back upstairs. She was in the kitchen with her back to me mixing up something in about five or six different bowls. She had on earbuds, and she was dancing.

She must have been listening to upbeat music because she was moving pretty fast. Her clothes were similar to last night's stretch pants and shirt, except they were yellow.

She was putting on one hell of a show. Currently, she was doing a light twerk with one arm in the air. Or maybe she was doing the nae-nae? I didn't know, but she looked good doing it.

She finally made a slow turn and opened her eyes. She blushed and said, "Who's being a pervert now? Watching me like a nerd."

"I'm impressed, you got some decent moves." I laughed and moved closer to inspect the mixing bowls.

"Dancing was a big part of my childhood. My father always danced with my mother. Every Saturday morning we had breakfast and a dance-off."

"That's the one thing I miss about being an only child. I didn't get that connection that siblings have with each other."

She stared at me. "Is that why you and Dawn are so close?"

I nodded. "Probably so. When we met in fourth grade it was like she was always meant to be in my life."

She didn't respond, she just kept mixing in the bowl.

"What are you making?"

"Sugar for the grand opening," she said. She swung around on her heels. "Hey! Can you taste-test for me?"

"Sure but what are you putting the sugar on?"

"Do you like oatmeal? It's bland so you will get to engage with the sugars."

I laughed. "Engage with the sugars? You sound like a true salesperson."

She smiled and shrugged. She was so damn cute; I couldn't stop looking at her. She made me want to pick her up and sling her over my shoulder.

"Oh, do you need to go? I don't want to infringe on your day. I haven't cooked the oatmeal so it would be a while before it's done."

"The only plan I had for today was to go jogging. I'm good, I'll try your sugars. And thanks for the little hospitality kit."

She snickered. "That was for my benefit. The way you were calling hogs last night I should have a whole farm outside. With all that air you were taking in, no way you didn't need mouthwash this morning."

I laughed out loud and put my hands up. "I've been told I snore a little bit."

She stopped moving and stared at me with wide eyes. "A little bit? You mean a whole lot. At one time I had to make sure you were still human. There's like a loud noise with a whistle at the end."

I smiled and shook my head. "You're starting with the jokes early today."

"I'm just saying. How are you pulling all these women sounding like that when you sleep?" She laughed and mimicked my snoring noises.

"It's about what I do before we go to sleep, remember that. Once I knock you out, my snoring won't matter," I said proudly.

She countered with, "You must take a two-by-four on your dates because you would have to knock her in the head to not hear all that noise."

"Is it that bad?" She had me feeling a little self-conscious.

She laughed. "Let me stop playing with you. It was bad but it didn't last that long. It was a lot of noise for about five minutes and then you were quiet."

I wiped my forehead. "You had your boy worried for a minute."

She smiled hard. "That's the other thing about having siblings. It's nonstop joaning so you develop thick skin early or you become insecure. No in-between."

She was right about that one, my extended family held no punches at the family reunions.

I nodded. "So back to this sugar thing, do I get some bacon or sausage to go with this oatmeal?"

"Just say you want some breakfast, Dre," she said and moved to the refrigerator.

"I mean, you can't feed me oatmeal like I'm a kid." I rubbed my stomach. "I can help you. I know my way around the kitchen."

"Really?" She turned to look at me. "I would say yes, but you're still wearing your nice pants and shirt from last night. I don't want you to get food on them."

I guess I was still in my dress pants and shirt. I hated to be all up in her space, but hell I did spend the night, so I asked, "Do you mind if I take a shower? I have my gym bag in my truck."

"I'm sorry, I should have offered for you to use the guest bath up here. Of course, let me grab you some towels and stuff. Take my key and fob to get back inside and up the elevator."

"Ok, I'll be right back."

What was I doing? I thought as I walked to the garage. It wasn't like I was trying to sleep with her, I was just enjoying her company. She felt good to be around. She was funny, held great conversations, and she kept feeding me. Guess that was all I wanted outside of sex.

After I made it back inside, I stopped in the kitchen with my gym bag on my shoulder.

"Which door is the bathroom? I don't want to walk into a room I'm not supposed to see."

She looked up from the stove top and said casually, "My sex dungeon is at the far end of the hall, and I keep it locked anyway. The bathroom is the second door on the right."

She went back to stirring the pot while I stood there with my mouth open.

"And here I was about to tell you not to sneak in the bathroom and look at me while I was in the shower. I better hope you don't lock my ass in there and tie me up," I said.

"Next time," she quipped and went into the refrigerator.

I said nothing. When she closed the refrigerator, she burst into laughter.

"I wish you could see your face," she said. "Boy, go take your shower and come on and test my sugars."

I walked off slowly. "I'm kind of scared to taste that sugar now. You might put me under a spell."

"Too late now, you had some last night in that lemonade and tea. You mine now!" she yelled as I went into the bathroom.

I laughed out loud and closed the door. Tonya was cool as hell. Who would have thought a night out with my coworker would have ended with me hanging with her?

I showered and changed into my running shorts and t-shirt that read 'BEAST' across the chest. When I walked into the kitchen Tonya had six small bowls with oatmeal in each of them. Next to each bowl was a small shaker of what I assumed was infused sugar. A bite-sized piece of sausage was on a toothpick next to each shaker along with a glass of water.

"Where's your food?" I asked. Her back was turned; she was rinsing dishes in the sink.

"I'm not hungry. I'm going to take notes while you taste test." She had the biggest grin on her face.

"What's so funny?"

"Oh nothing, I'm just anxious to see what you think."

"Do you make everything sample sized?" I asked, referring to the small bowls and small pieces of sausage on a toothpick. Not to mention the bite-size sandwiches from last night.

She shrugged. "Sorry, it's a habit. I have this thing with hors d'oeuvres. I always prepare my food tapas style or like passed hors d'oeuvres."

I laughed and shook my head. Damn, she was so cute. "Ok, what do we have?"

She clapped her hands together. "Okay, the first bowl is lemon-blueberry sugar."

I took it down in one spoonful. "It's pretty good, but not something I would want on a regular basis."

"Noted; try the next one, it's strawberry. But eat the sausage to clean your pallet and drink some water after each one."

I followed her instructions and ate the next one.

"Oh yeah, that one is really good, it tastes like real strawberries."

"Perfect! This one is cardamom-cinnamon-nutmeg."

"This is fire! Tastes like it should be in a sweet potato pie."

The next two were orange-lemon and mango-pineapple. I liked both of them as well.

"Ok, this is the last one, this is one of my staples and will probably sell the most in the shoppe. Well, at least I think it will. It's brown sugar."

I frowned. "Like regular brown sugar?"

"Just taste it," she demanded.

I put it to my lips and my eyes opened up. I ate the rest. "I want a whole bowl of that one, quit playing. What's in there? Damn, girl! That's real good."

She threw her hands up and said, "Yes!"

I had to drink my water because the breasts were loose again. I swear this woman didn't have breasts in public. This shit was crazy.

"I knew you would like that one! It's my favorite too. I made the brown sugar using molasses but I added a fig reduction with it and a pinch of smoked sea salt."

I licked my spoon. "Give me some more of that one. Matter of fact, I want to preorder some for the grand opening. Give me three."

She laughed and moved to the cooktop. "You don't need that much; you just sprinkle it on whatever you want."

I shook my head. "Naw, that's going into my meat rub for the grill. I can taste that already on some ribs and chicken."

"Are you trying to outshine Brock on the grill?" she asked teasingly.

"Hell no, Brock makes classic 'que like my father. I put a spin on mine, make it a little more gourmet."

She handed me a larger bowl of oatmeal and I sprinkled the good brown sugar on it. After my first bite, I said, "You should name this after me."

She frowned. "And why would I do that?"

"Because my last name is Brown. I could be your poster man for advertising, all the women would want to try it."

She stopped moving and turned her head to the side. "Are you really this full of yourself all the time?"

I shrugged and creased my forehead. "I wouldn't say that, I just deal in facts. And the fact is women love me. Put me on a poster and you would have a line out the door."

"Yeah, a line of grandmas and aunties, with your old butt. I want to appeal to all ages."

I laughed and shook my head. "See that's where you're wrong. The pups love me too. I just don't mess with young girls, I like 'em seasoned." I winked at her and held up the brown sugar container.

She playfully rolled her eyes. "All I know is when I was twenty-five or thirty, a man with gray in his beard and hair was not appealing as advertising. So, no thank you."

I ate the last bite of my oatmeal. "I forgot you're a hater, and haters are gone always hate because that's what y'all do." I stood from the island. "Well I hate to eat and run but I have to. What are you doing today?"

I kind of wanted to hang out with her a little more, she was fun.

"I am going out jogging first, then I'm going to the farmer's market to get more figs for my brown sugar. You've convinced me I may need more on hand for the grand opening."

"You can go jogging with me, that's where I'm going now. Where do you usually go?"

"Oh, so you literally meant eat and run."

"Yep."

"I go to the park around the corner. I run around the lake."

"Same here. You know I don't live too far from here."

She frowned. "Why did I think you lived near my parents?"

"I used to; I moved out here a year ago. I broke my leg in a car accident and had to stay with my folks because all of my bedrooms were on the second floor. Decided I'd get a ranch-style house."

She smiled and nodded. "You're getting the geriatric home set up, that's nice and smart."

I laughed. "I'll show you who's geriatric when I run your lil' ass down on the lake. Are you trying to hang with the big dog today or what? I'll show you how to get an efficient run in before it gets too hot outside."

"I like to run alone or with my running group because I can keep my own pace."

"Ah, that's cool, I can slow down for you. I had all that oatmeal anyway."

She rolled her eyes. "You know what, let's go. Because you are just too cocky."

I had no idea what she was talking about, so I shrugged.

∞ ∞ ∞

No matter how much I willed my legs to move faster I could not keep up with Tonya around the lake. We were on our second loop, and she was ahead of me by about ten feet. She had ear buds in and had tuned me out. I had mine in as well, but I was barely paying attention because I was trying to keep up with her.

The only thing that kept me going was her little tight body. When she took off her t-shirt when we arrived, I was like, ok Tonya. She had a flat, toned stomach. Now the sculpted legs made sense. If she ran like this regularly, she had no choice but to have perfect legs.

Finally, we finished the loop. She started stretching right away. I was trying to pretend like I wasn't out of breath, so I didn't talk.

She pulled her ear bud out. "Nice run, we will have to see what you do when you aren't sluggish from the oatmeal."

I kept moving around and didn't respond because I couldn't, I was still out of breath.

She waved to get my attention, and I waved back as if I didn't know what she was doing.

She pointed to her ear, and I finally pulled my ear bud out and said, "You were talking to me?"

My breathing had finally normalized.

She laughed and put her hands on her hips. Widening her stance, she leaned over with the top of her head almost touching the ground.

Damn! That was impressive! Her hands were still on her waist.

She lifted up and down a few times then stretched from side to side.

I did a few stretches but to be honest my eyes were glued to her. We could definitely do some things together. But I needed to chill, this was Dawn's family, and I wasn't messing that up.

"You catch your breath, yet?" she asked.

Frowning as if I didn't know what she was talking about, I asked, "What do you mean?"

"Hey, if you want to preserve your ego, I won't talk about me running your ass down around the lake, Mr. Geriatric."

"Girl, you trippin'. I wanted you in front of me, I'm a gentleman. What would I look like if I left you?"

She stretched her arms. "You would look like you ran faster than me."

"Excuse me for looking out." I put my hands up and she laughed out loud.

"I didn't expect you to be able to keep up with me. I've been running since I was five. Royal Knights track then high school and college."

I lifted my shirt, showing off my abs. "You see this? I run too."

Yeah, that caught her off guard. She had to blink a few times.

I dropped my shirt down and asked, "You good over there?"

"Yeah, I was just confused by that patch of gray hair on your chest."

What the hell? I didn't have any chest hair. But I was at the age when weird shit started happening to my body. Quickly pulling down the neck of my shirt, I looked down at my chest.

"There's nothing on my chest," I said.

She grinned and said, "Made you look." She took off running toward the parking lot.

Damn! I had to chase her or else she would call me out on being tired.

I ran behind her yelling, "Wait until I catch you!"

She turned around and ran backward. "Come on wit' it, slow poke!"

I slowed down because I was laughing. "Oh, I got your slow poke!" I yelled back.

Taking my last bit of energy, I sprinted and passed her. I stopped, turned, and picked her up, throwing her over my shoulder.

"Ahhh!" she squealed.

"Yeah, you might run but you don't know nothing about them football moves."

She was in a fit of laughter as I carried her across the parking lot over my shoulder.

"You still calling me old?" I asked.

"We are both old," she said while laughing.

She was over my left shoulder, so when I turned my head, her ass was right there. It took everything in me not to bite it. But I did playfully slap it. I wasn't that strong.

She was laughing so hard she couldn't say anything.

When we finally made it to my truck, instead of bending to put her down, I made the mistake of sliding her down my chest.

Fuck! That was going to be on replay in my mind. It was time to go home before I got lost in the moment with her. I couldn't deny she felt good, too good in fact.

"You don't play fair, we were running. Not playing football," she said as I opened the door for her.

"I'm all about the switch-up," I said, and closed the door.

I resisted the urge to smack her on the butt again. I was turning into the Nerd. I kind of felt bad for him, because I now understood how he felt. Having someone like Tonya in front of you and not being able to stretch her out after all of this playing around was rare for me.

I jumped in the driver's seat. "You ready?" I asked.

"Yeah, because you need to take your rest. I know this is a lot of activity for you."

I started the truck and laughed. "What does this shirt say!?" I pointed to the word 'BEAST' on my shirt.

She squinted and read, "I snore like a beast."

"You are such a hater." I pulled the mirrored visor down and said, "It says..." I paused.

There was a small sticker right above the word 'BEAST'. I pulled it off my shirt, and it read, 'I snore like a...'. It was hand-written on one of her sugar labels.

Slowly turning to face her smiling face, I said, "Oh, you got jokes for real now."

Her eyes widened and I quickly reached over and started tickling her.

"Stop..." she laughed.

"Nope!" I said and continued tickling her as she moved around laughing.

She laughed so hard tears were running down her cheeks. I laughed too because I had not had this much fun with a woman in a long time.

I had my female friends, but that was different because I didn't want to kiss them.

"Stop!" she yelled, and I finally let her go.

"Good to know you're ticklish," I said.

29

She wiped her hair away from her face and put her seatbelt on. "I have not been tickled in years."

I backed out of the space. "That's because you go out with nerds."

"I do not! My last boyfriend wasn't a nerd, he had a lot of swag."

I nodded. "Yep, too much swag is worse than a nerd."

She turned to face me with her lips turned up. "You think you know everything about dating."

"I do! It's the same as me saying I want a polished sophisticated woman. If it's too much she's boring because she can't relax and have fun. Same thing with a dude that's too cool. Those jokers can't loosen up, won't dance because they are too cool."

She nodded. "Okay you got me on that one, he wouldn't dance. We went to my cousin's wedding one time and he barely moved on the dance floor."

"See, you need that middleman, like me. I'll tear the dance floor up. But I'm still cool with it."

She laughed. "Yeah, I ended up dancing with other people. We were up in Chicago so of course he was not trying to Step."

"Hold on, you know how to Step?"

"Yeah," she said and crossed her arms.

"Don't be lying, Tonya. Can you Step for real?"

"Yes," she said louder.

I turned into a parking lot at the intersection and stopped the truck.

"Let me see, let's go." I opened the door and connected my phone to the car system.

"What are you doing?" she asked with wide eyes.

"We are about to Step, come on."

"Dre, we are literally at an intersection with traffic. We are going to look crazy dancing."

I jumped out. "Let's go! I don't care about these people. I want to see you Step. And I'm turning on a faster pace song so you better know what you're doing."

"I am not about to dance at this intersection." She crossed her arms.

I walked around to her side and opened the door.

"I've picked you up once today, I'll do it again. If I have to pick you up, I'm break dancing instead of stepping." I rolled my arm in a break-dancing move.

Her mouth opened. "Alright! Please stop that!"

I took her hand and led her back to my side. I reached in and started the music.

Her eyes lit up when D'Angelo's 'When We Get By' started playing.

"This used to be my jam!" she said.

As soon as the beat kicked in we started moving. She was good and we were in sync. When we were side by side she shimmied her shoulders.

"I see you," I said, and she smiled.

A few people started blowing their horns as we flowed around to the beat of the music.

After a while, the traffic noise and horns faded. It was as if we were in our own personal dance room. Her skin had a little sheen to it that glistened as the sun beamed down on us. She was beautiful and so carefree with me. She had the biggest smile on her face and I would be lying if I said mine didn't match hers.

When the song ended, people at the stop light clapped, honked horns, and yelled out the windows.

We waved at them and I said, "Are you going to take a bow?"

"Absolutely," she said.

We held hands and bowed like we'd performed a Broadway play.

Once we were back in the truck, she said, "I have enjoyed hanging out with you. I didn't know you were so much fun."

"I do it for the people, I gotta give' em what they want." I ran my hand over my beard.

She laughed. "I'm serious."

"I can say the same about you. I thought you were the shy sister. Lois is loud and Melody is mean as hell."

I didn't care much for Melody because she tripped with Dawn sometimes. I knew she hated me but I didn't like her messing with my girl.

"Lois is loud, and Mel is a little abrasive. But I'm far from shy. My sisters are just louder than me so I don't need to say much when they are around.

Especially at family stuff, you've seen them. Donald and I are the quiet two that say the least because the rest of them won't shut up."

I laughed. She was right about that, I did notice it when I was around them.

When we made it back to her place, I drove around to the front of the building to drop her off.

"Thanks again for the ride home yesterday," she said.

"Ain't no thing. Thank you for the brown sugar, I'm using that immediately."

She gave me a bag of the brown sugar instead of making me wait until next Saturday at the grand opening.

"You're welcome, I'll see you next week," she said and reached to hug me.

I held her tight and then kissed her cheek. When she pulled back her lips brushed against mine and she stopped; we both stopped. Her eyes slowly lifted to meet mine.

"I'm sorry, that was an accident," she whispered.

We were face to face with about an inch of space between us.

"Don't apologize," I whispered back. I couldn't break the eye contact or move away.

"Can I do it again, but on purpose this time?" she asked.

Instead of answering and against my better judgment, I closed the tiny gap between our lips and kissed her.

It was innocent until her warm tongue darted between my lips. I let loose on her and sucked her tongue in my mouth and pulled her closer.

As soon as my hand slid down her back I pulled back. I couldn't do this with her, not like this.

After a few moments of silence, she said, "Ok, now that we got that out of the way, are we cool? You've been trying not to kiss me since last night."

Damn, ok, I was glad she cracked a joke because it got a little too heavy in here for me.

I laughed. "I think that was you wanting to kiss, not me. You know I told you I can't keep the ladies off me."

"Whatever! Bye! I'll see you next Saturday at the opening."

"Alright."

She opened the door but stopped. "You aren't going to start acting like a nerd because I kissed you, are you?"

I pulled her back by her arm. "Let's get something straightened out. Your lips touched mine on accident. I'm the one that kissed you on purpose."

"Because I asked you first!" she said.

"So that makes you the nerd, you asked for a kiss instead of doing it."

She opened her mouth and then closed it. "You're right, I am the nerd in this scenario. My date from last night asked for a hug and I thought the same thing about him."

I shook my head laughing, she was crazy as hell. "Go on. I'll see you later, Nerd."

She jumped out of the truck and smirked.

As she walked to the main door, she took off the t-shirt she was wearing over her biking pants and cropped sports top she ran in.

She did a cartwheel and went down into a split. She got up and started twirling her hips.

What in the hell is she doing? Whatever it is, I am a fan!

I let the window down and stared before yelling, "What are you doing?"

"I had to do an urban ho-down for you to counteract that last nerd move!" She blew a kiss. "And take that too!"

I threw my head back laughing. "Get over here!" I got out and met her on the sidewalk.

"So you can do a ho-down outside but you were shy about dancing decently in the parking lot?"

She shrugged. "I couldn't let you go out on top."

I grabbed her around the waist and kissed her then backed away. "I stay on top, baby!"

I jumped back in the truck and waited as she slowly walked to the door.

I drove away laughing once she was inside.

A minute later my phone pinged. I had several text messages that I hadn't read. Of course, I went to the newest one from Tonya.

Tonya: Expect a lap dance in the future.

I laughed out loud. This girl was crazy!

Me: BET!!!

Tonya: LOL! See you Saturday. I had fun.

Me: I know you did, you were with me.
Tonya: Keep talking and that will be your last bag of brown sugar.
Me: I'll get some, all I have to do is kiss you.
Tonya: I went from a nerd to slinging brown sugar for kisses. So sad.
Me: LOL

The car behind me blew the horn. The light had turned green, and I was deep in texting.

This had been a pleasant turn of events. I had to get my head on straight and think about this one. Tonya was cool and fun but if I wasn't trying to pursue her exclusively, I couldn't do it at all.

I was tired of dating different women but I hadn't quite cut off my squad. I'd had hella calls and texts while I was with Tonya. I had to mute my phone.

When I made it home, I looked at the text messages from the two main people I had been seeing.

One I had only been out with a few times, but the other was my kickstand, Michelle.

We went back and forth for a long time. The sex was great but that was about as far as it went with her.

Chelle was about five ten and stacked up perfectly. She wanted more, but she was one of those women that had to have everything with a name-brand label on it. I didn't mind it, but just do you, there was no need to talk about people who didn't do it. Basically, she had an elitist attitude. She had called last night but I sent her to voicemail.

I dialed her number and she answered on the first ring.

"I know why you sent me to voicemail last night," she said when she answered.

"Chelle, quit trippin', since when did we start questioning each other?"

"Since you were dancing on the corner with that pocket-sized chic. You were just in my ass three weeks ago and now you're flaunting Pre-School around."

I ran my hand down my face.

"But you and I are not exclusive. I know you see other people."

"I am not sleeping with other people, Andre! My sister saw you and sent me a video."

"Now this makes sense, you're mad because your sister saw me? And you are the only person I've been with since we started back up a couple of months ago."

"Get the fuck out of here! I saw how the two of you looked. You're having sex with her. I'm not stupid! You could have said something, but instead, you embarrass me!"

"I don't have to lie to you, she's a friend and nothing happened between us. But for real, Chelle, I'm not about to be explaining myself to you. You know how things are between us and if you ain't cool with it, we can wrap it up."

"That's alright! Go ahead and be with Pre-School! I'm done with you for real this time. And when you come back talking sweet when you get tired of her, I won't be around. I hope you enjoyed it three weeks ago because that was your last time with me!"

She hung up.

I tossed the phone down and went to take a shower. I wasn't paying attention to Chelle. This was why the sex was so good because she always tried to win me over with it. If I wanted, I could go to her place right now and stretch her out any way I wanted.

But for real, this was getting old. I wanted to have fun with a woman and laugh. Chelle came with bomb sex, no jokes, and an elitist attitude. That Pre-School nickname was probably the funniest thing she'd ever said.

I chuckled to myself, and my mind went to my little pocket-sized Tonya with her cute self. I had to clean house, and thin out my squad, if I was trying to go there. I'd let it ride for now, I didn't have to figure it out today.

Chapter 3 ~ Tonya

The last couple of days were busy for me. I'd been working at my regular job, but I'd also been at the commercial kitchen prepping for the grand opening this upcoming weekend.

Lois, Melody, and I rented a commercial kitchen to prep our products for the shop. We always tried to plan to go together to cut expenses. We used our home kitchens for testing and the commercial kitchen to make the master batches and bottle.

The saving grace was that we did find a local company that supplied our containers and labels. We mixed and filled the containers ourselves.

The three of us had invested quite a bit of money in the business so I hoped it worked out. I had finally made it home when I got a text from Lois.

LoLo: You been holding out and Sis gone be mad at you.

There was a video attached to the text. I assumed she meant Melody would be mad at me but I had no idea why.

I hit play.

The video...

"With all the violence and sadness in the world, and especially in our city, we like to end our news segments with feel-good stories. Start the video, please...Our camera men caught this couple enjoying their Saturday morning by dancing in a parking lot at an intersection! The couple is having a fantastic time executing what's known as Chicago-style stepping."

"Wow! They look great! And they seem to be having a great time! Look at the smiles on their faces."

"Oh yeah! Seems as though the mood hit them, and they pulled over and danced. By the way they're dressed, it appears like they were either leaving or on their way to a morning workout."

"What a way to start your day with your significant other! Do we know who they are? What's their story?"

"Well, after a little digging, we learned the woman is Tonya James. She's a native of St. Louis and is one of the proprietors of the SHE-iS spice shoppe scheduled to open this weekend in the Greenwood District. She has some moves, doesn't she? Look at that shoulder shimmy!"

"What about the guy?"

"His name is Andre Brown and he's been featured in the top one hundred most eligible bachelors in St. Louis for the past three years. I have to tell you, ladies, from the looks of this video, he's no longer eligible."

"Oh yeah, this guy is going to have my wife questioning me when I get home. Look at how he's looking at her. There is love all over this video. Look at them! If dance like no one is watching was a person, this would be it!"

"Can't deny something special isn't brewing here. I tell you what, I'm going to the grand opening. Maybe they will give out a dance lesson. I could sure spice up my marriage by doing this with my hubby. Look at how in love they look!"

"I wonder if they practiced or if this was made up on the spot. Do we know what's happening here? I wouldn't know how to do this with my wife, and we've been married twenty years."

"Well, maybe you and our viewers can pick up some spicy lessons at the grand opening. Our team will be covering the ribbon cutting with the proprietors and the municipality founder of Greenwood, Samuel Valentine."

"I'm sure my wife will definitely have us there after seeing this video."

"We posted the full video on our site and the viewers have named them Chi-Louie since they are doing Chicago stepping in St. Louis. If you would like to see it, go to our website and Facebook page."

"What a great video! And with that, we bid you good night!"

"Goodnight, St. Louis. Hey, dance like no one's watching."

I had no words for the video of Dre and me dancing broadcasted on the news. I wondered if he saw it. It was only a little after eight and the video was shown on the news at five.

I called Lois immediately and waited for her to answer.

"Hey now! My munchkin looks like she should be on tv. Oh wait, she was." She laughed out loud.

Lois had been calling Melody and me her munchkins since we were kids.

"Lo-Lo, stop it," I said.

I didn't know how I felt about my personal time with Dre being shown to the whole city. I wasn't embarrassed because we looked good dancing. It was more...I don't know how I felt.

"Start talking because I don't know how this got past me. Are you messing around with Dre? Ok, sis, he is fine, but you know he keeps a lot of women."

I rolled my eyes. "We went jogging together and we were talking about Stepping, that's it."

"So he followed you home on Friday night and the lady on tv said that video was Saturday morning, so ummm, you're skipping part of the story."

Lois was the reporter in the family, as she said, nothing got past her.

"He came in and we talked. We fell asleep on the sofa and went for a jog on Saturday. And he taste-tested my new sugars."

"Mmmm. What else did he taste?" She laughed out loud. "You can tell me; I won't tell Mel. You know she can't stand him."

"We slept upright fully dressed on the sofa and he only tasted the sugar." She didn't need to know about the kissing. "Mel don't run me. I don't care who she hates for no reason."

"I know that's right! But for real, Tonya, why didn't you get some? I know you haven't been seeing anyone since Brad. And I know you ain't trying to sleep with that short, weird guy who lost you at the comedy show."

I laughed. "Daniel is not short! And I haven't talked to Brad in months."

"Uh-huh, and again, why didn't we have sex with Dre as opposed to sitting upright on the sofa?"

"It wasn't like that; we are just cool. Besides we didn't even have each other's phone numbers before Friday."

"But y'all was dancing in the street, yeah ok. As fine as Dre is? I would have laid him out as soon as we walked in the door." She laughed.

My other line rang, it was Dre. I guess he saw the video.

"Lo, I gotta go, I'll call you back."

"Don't call me, call Dre. Bye!"

I ended the call and answered Dre's call with, "Hey, dance partner."

He chuckled. "I guess you've seen the news too?"

He didn't sound like himself. "Lois sent it to me; I've been at the commercial kitchen making my sugars since I left work. Are you okay?"

"Yeah, baby, I'm good. I had a long day at work and then I came home and put some meat on the grill. My folks called me about the video. Moms was mad because I didn't tell her in advance, she thought I knew about it."

I laughed. "So what did you think about the video? I didn't realize how good I looked on camera," I joked.

"Aye, we both looked good, they got my good side." He perked up a bit.

I wasn't sure how he would feel because I didn't know how I felt. Honestly, I didn't want the inquisition from my family. I enjoyed having what I thought was a private moment with just him.

"You looked alright," I said.

"Girl, don't play. Anybody that looks that good after a run needs to be on the news."

I laughed. "Too bad they didn't get me smoking you around the lake on film."

"Just for that, I'm not telling you what I did with that brown sugar you gave me."

My eyes widened. If it was one thing I like to know, it was anything regarding my products. "Come on, tell me, pretty please with my brown sugar on top."

"Nope."

"I'll let you win a run."

He laughed out loud. "You're not going to let that go, are you?"

"Ohhh, no! I'm like a dog with a bone with that one. The way you were saying you would slow down so I could keep up with you? And then you were out there running like Fred Sanford."

When he finally stopped laughing, he asked, "What is it going to take for you to forget about that lake run? Or give me a do-over?"

I smiled. "We can't erase history, but I will give you a do-over if you tell me what you did with the sugar."

"I rubbed it on my meat…" He paused, and my mouth opened wide. "That didn't sound right, did it?"

"I mean, hey, it's out of my hands once I gave it to you, so umm, if that's what you do in your free time."

He laughed. "I gotta stay on my toes around you."

"You better."

"Remember I said I would add it to my ribs and chicken? Well, I did it last night and I put it on the grill today. It was fire."

I clapped my hands. "I bet it was good. What part of the chicken?"

"I'm a breast man in every sense of the word."

I blushed and said, "Stop being a pervert."

"Baby, I like what I like. I need to ask you something that's a little personal."

I already knew what he was going to ask because I caught him staring at my breasts several times. He wasn't ogling so I knew the deal, every man I've dated has asked the same thing.

"I wear a double D bra cup. They appear smaller in clothes because I wear a minimizer bra. My frame is small, and I prefer to look proportioned in my clothes."

"Oh, that's nice, but I was just going to ask what kind of detergent you use. I like the way your clothes smell."

That was embarrassing. I covered my mouth and said, "Oh, umm, sorry. I thought since you mentioned breasts that's where you were going."

He chuckled. "Who's the pervert now?"

"Shut up!" I said playfully.

"I'm messing with you, that is what I was going to ask."

I laughed. "You make me sick; I knew your little nosy butt was going to ask that because I saw you looking."

"Damn, you did?"

"Yep."

"It was more because I was curious. Usually, breasts get smaller on women when they get in the house not the other way around."

My phone had been ringing nonstop, but I ignored all of them. I'd talk to everyone later about the news clip.

"I don't have time for it, I need them out of the way when I'm moving around."

"Never heard that before." He chuckled. "Have you eaten?"

"Nope, why? You offering up chicken and ribs?"

"I am. You did provide the sugar."

I smiled wide. "Sounds good to me. I can come and get them."

"I'm a gentleman, I'll bring them to you."

"What are you waiting on?"

"Let me hop in the shower and I'm on my way."

"Okay, see you in a minute."

"Ok, bye." I ended the call and smiled to myself. I was excited to see him again.

I needed to jump in the shower as well. Before I tossed my phone down I scrolled the missed calls from Macon, Donald, Melody, Tori, Janae, and even my brother, Dale, that lived in the DC area.

I scrolled through the text messages.

Mel: I've been with you 3 days and you didn't tell me about Andre? I should come over there!

Don-Don: You in the streets like that, sis? LOL

Mac: Are you for real?

Dale: I see you, sis! That was lit!

Brad: Missing on you, see you Saturday

Daniel: Tonya, I hope you are well. I tried to call. I will come to your grand opening Saturday. I would like to take you out.

Wow! Even Brad saw the news. Whatever. I tossed the phone down and went to take my shower.

About an hour later, I buzzed Dre up. I had no idea why I was so excited to see him, but I was. And this silly smile needed to be gone before he got up here.

I couldn't figure out what to wear so I opted for an orange strapless sundress that came to my knees. It was loose and only fitted from the waist up.

I walked down the few steps after the knocks.

"Hey," I said, as I opened the door.

I had to stop myself from jumping on him. He looked good in his black t-shirt and grey sweatpants.

"What's up with you?" he said, as he walked in carrying a brown paper bag with handles. He seemed to be trying not to smile as well. He drug his teeth over his bottom lip.

I closed the door and turned to walk away. I made it up two steps before I noticed he wasn't behind me.

"Are you coming up?" I asked.

"You didn't greet me. No hug or anything."

"Oh, are we exchanging hugs for chicken, or are you asking me for a hug like a nerd?"

He finally smiled wide and slowly walked to me.

We were eye to eye with me on the step, so I wrapped my arms around his neck and hugged him. He wrapped his free arm around my waist and held me.

"You smell good," he said.

I loosened the hug and pulled back until we were eye to eye again and said, "Thank you, so do you."

He kissed me with two long pecks.

"You are not going to be kissing all on me every time I see you," I said, and grinned.

"I didn't kiss all on you. If I had I would have done this." He kissed my exposed collar bone, my neck, my cheek, and my lips again. "But that's not what I did."

I had to stop playing around before I ended up taking Lois' advice and laying him out.

His smiled faded and he backed up. "Hey, I'm sorry. I'm overstepping."

"What do you mean?" I was confused.

"Your facial expression. You stopped smiling."

Ohh, he mistook my 'I want to have sex right now' face for the 'get away from me' face. I couldn't tell him that, so I said, "I was looking at your eyes, I thought they were jealous."

"What are you talking about?" He rubbed his eyes.

"You know, cross-eyed. If one keeps looking at the other, it's called jealous eyes."

He smiled wide and then laughed. "I don't know why I subject myself to you. Get up the steps!"

I turned and jogged up the steps. "You know you like me."

He turned his lips up but didn't reply, instead, he handed me the bag of food.

"I hope you ate because it's about to go down." I danced around the kitchen gathering utensils and a plate.

I opened the container and was hit with a wonderful smokey barbecue smell. "This smells good." I cut a small piece of the chicken and popped it into my mouth. "Dre, this is delicious! Oh my goodness, this tastes better than Brock's. And if you tell him I said it, I will have no problem lying."

He smiled. "I know it's good. You don't have to tell me what I already know."

I sat at the island and began eating as he watched me. "You want some more tea and lemonade?"

"Yep, but you eat. I can get it."

I nodded and watched as he moved around my kitchen. His toned back muscles poked through his shirt as he raised his arm to get the lemonade and tea from the refrigerator. I didn't know what I liked better, the food or him.

After he sat back down, he asked, "So what kind of feedback have you been getting from your people about the video?"

I nodded. "I've only talked to Lois, everyone else I'm ignoring until tomorrow."

"What did my girl say?"

I shrugged and said, "She doesn't understand why we haven't had sex."

He choked on his drink and laughed. "See that's why I've always liked Lois. She's my kind of girl."

"Were you wondering the same thing?"

He stared at me. "Tonya, you know it wasn't like that. I don't want to sleep with you."

Oh wow, he's hurting feelings. "Pardon me."

He shook his head. "I didn't mean it like that. You're beautiful, and of course, I'm attracted to you, but for real I like being around you. It's not about the sex with you. Ok well, I mean I won't say that, but shit, I don't know, it's hard to explain. I'm just trying to be around you."

"You been thinking about me?"

"Real talk?" I nodded. "I've been trying to figure out how to get back over here since I left on Saturday."

I smiled. "Why didn't you just call?"

"Because I wasn't trying to seem pressed. I don't even know why I told you that."

I shrugged. "Be yourself with me. If you want to hang, you call—simple as that. You want to talk, you call."

"You're right. Well, I'm trying to hang out and talk tonight. You down?"

I was exhausted but I was down. "Yep, but I thought you were tired."

He grinned. "I'm good. Are you going to eat all of that food?"

Lifting my head from my plate, I asked, "Did you or did you not bring this for me? And who made these baked beans?"

"I made everything. I used your brown sugar in the beans, too. I'm telling you, you need to rename it Brown's sugar. With me in the video and my name on the sugar you will sell out in no time."

He stood and did a little dance.

"Let's go in the living room," I said as I danced alongside him.

Once we danced our way to the sofa, he asked, "So how much damage has the video caused with the Nerd?"

We were seated in the exact spots from Friday night, although I wanted to be a little closer.

"My stock went up; I got a former ghoster texting."

His eyes open wide. "Oh yeah?" I smiled proudly and nodded. "That wasn't my goal but how are you feeling about that?"

I shrugged. "I don't really care. What was your goal?"

"I wanted to see your stepping moves, didn't think it would land us on the news."

I knew he had to have a few calls from the ladies. If it was me watching him dance with someone else, I would be sooo jealous.

"What about your harem?"

Oops, I must have hit a nerve. He stared at me with a frown.

I raised my hand in defense. "Don't even try it, Dre. I'm sure you are seeing more than one woman which qualifies as a harem. I'm not judging, I'm dealing in facts."

"Tonya, I'm not exclusive with anyone I do date. I'm not out here misleading women."

I shook my head. "Hence me saying harem, they know they aren't the only ones."

"Well the harem as you call it, is gone after that video. I got a 'this ain't gone work for me' text and hung up on."

Hmmmm, only two? I expected more. I guess he is a little mature to have too many. I'm sure he had plenty back in his twenties and thirties.

"That's funny, the women leave, and the men step it up. So, I guess my lemonade and tea serum worked on you last week? You mine now."

I tried to break the ice because homeboy had the sad face.

Finally cracking a smile, he said, "You still want me, fresh out of leading a harem?"

I shrugged. "I don't mind, gigolos get lonely too."

He threw his head back and laughed. I laughed along with him.

"You are a trip!" he said.

Touching his arm, I said, "Seriously, Dre, I'm only joking around. I don't judge about you dating, I'm kind of jealous I can't find a plethora of good men. I would have them lined up too."

"Naw, I don't think I would like sharing you."

"And it's okay for me to share you?"

"My lineup is empty, that won't be a problem."

I smirked and shook my head. "Naw, Playa, I don't want you by default."

He moved on me and started tickling me. I laughed but held my hand to my chest to keep my dress up.

"Stop," I yelled.

"Default?"

"Okay, I didn't mean it!" I yelled as I laughed.

He finally stopped when we were face to face and said, "You are not a default type of woman, you're a woman a man would choose."

"And you know this after a few days?" I asked seriously.

I liked Dre a lot and I didn't have time to get my feelings hurt because I was the shiny new toy.

He sat back on the sofa and looked at me. "Hey, listen, I'm not saying I'm in love with you or anything like that, but I'll admit I'm feeling you. And I don't care if it's only been a few days. As you said, I'm not new to dating and I've never wanted to be around any woman this much."

I hated to say it, but I had no choice, so I asked, "What about Dawn?"

"I was wondering if you were going to bring her up."

"All I know is that you were trying to break her and my brother up. I don't want to start liking you if you're still pining over my new sister."

He nodded. "That's fair. I'll be honest with you. I did try to break them up because I didn't like that I was losing her."

I frowned. "Losing her?"

"That girl has been my ride-or-die since we were ten. I was always the one who took care of her, no matter what was going on. When Big Baby came along, I..."

I laughed out loud. "Is my brother Big Baby?" He nodded. "Oh, he left that out. Does he know you call him that?"

"Damn, I don't even know."

"Ok, so did you love her more than a friend?"

He nodded. "At the time I thought I did but I couldn't give Dawn what she needed. My hat goes off to Macon, he's a good dude. Took me a while to admit it."

"Did you tell her you wanted more than friendship?"

He nodded. "Best and worst mistake of my life."

I frowned. "Explain that one."

"It was good that I told her for myself because it gave me a chance later to understand that I loved her, but not like a man should love his wife. Had I not told her, I would have always wondered. She was the one that helped me figure it out. She said, and I quote, "Dre, you love me, but you don't look at me the way Macon does, you don't desire me, and you never have. You just wanted our friendship to stay the same and you equated that to being in love with me.". She was right, and it would have been a disaster if we tried to be romantic. I would have ruined our friendship."

I nodded because it made a lot of sense. I did remember in high school how the two of them always hung out together.

"Ok, so I understand why it was the best decision, but why was it also the worst?"

"Because I hurt my best friend and I never want to hurt her, we've been through too much together. When she met Macon that should have been the best thing going on in her life. Instead, I tried to come between them; shit wasn't right. But I've been told I can be selfish, so I was thinking of me, and not her."

Okay, this conversation was a load off my mind. I really thought they had dated or slept together at least once over the years. But I guess since I was the one lusting over him for the past thirty years, I couldn't imagine someone not wanting him as I did.

"But telling her, in the end, seems like it was best because it put your new relationship with her into a better place once she was with Big Baby. And it cut out you wondering 'what if' for the rest of your life."

He nodded. "Exactly! Sometimes bad shit has to happen for the good stuff to happen."

"Have you ever told anyone in the harem this story?"

He frowned. "Why would I? That ain't something you put on blast. It was a big adjustment for me when they got married."

"I'm sure it was a big deal for her as well."

He shook his head. "Not really. See, Dawn has always been in tune with herself, and apparently me too. She was in love before Macon. I haven't been in love, and I only confided in Dawn, she was like a crutch. Of course, when they got together, I couldn't have her at my disposal anymore."

"So she spoiled you rotten?"

He smiled and shrugged. "Basically."

"Wait! You've never been in love?"

He rolled his eyes. "Nope, and nothing is wrong with me."

Folding my arm and nodding, I said, "You mine for real now, go ahead and drink up that lemonade."

He laughed out loud. "Is this a love potion or something?"

"We will find out soon."

We continued talking about everything under the sun until my eyes were shut.

"Dre?" I asked sleepily.

"Yeah, baby?"

Even in my sleepy state, it turned me on when he called me baby. Plenty of people called me that in the past, but coming from him it was different.

"You can't drive home this sleepy," I said.

"Yeah, I know. I think something is in that lemonade for real."

I was too tired to sleep on the sofa and I wanted him with me.

"You can sleep in my room or the guest room," I said. I at least had to give the man a choice.

His head popped up with a sleepy grin on his face. "Girl, you already know where I'm going, stop playing."

I stood and held out my hand to help him off the sofa.

As we made our way down the hall, I pointed to the hall bathroom.

I went into my room and dug out some decent pajamas before going into my bathroom to change.

Once I quickly changed and went into the bedroom, he was walking in taking his shirt off. Maybe this wasn't a good idea, his chest was a lot more muscular than I thought.

I quickly turned before he saw me watching and got into bed. When he pulled the gray sweats down revealing black boxer briefs, I had to cross my legs.

I hope he was sleepy because if not it was going down tonight.

He hopped into bed on his back and put an arm behind his head. "Why are you all the way over there?" he asked. "Your bedroom is nice, I'm glad you have a king bed."

I slid over closer so that our arms were touching. "Better?" I asked.

"Nope." He turned on his side and tucked me up under him so that we were spooning. "Now, that's better." He kissed my cheek a couple of times.

"I thought you said you were glad I had a king?"

He chuckled and it vibrated from his chest through my back. "You thought that meant we were spreading out?"

I laughed. "I might have thought that's what you meant."

"Naw, baby, I need you close. Physical touch is my love language."

"Says the man who's never been in love," I quipped.

"Aye, I know how I liked to be loved."

"Of course, you do, selfish."

He chuckled again. "Take your ass to sleep." He slapped my thigh and slid his arm right under my breasts. He wasn't touching them but if I sneezed, he would get a good feel.

"Goodnight," I said.

"I need my goodnight greeting," he said.

"There's no such thing."

He tickled me until I turned over facing him.

I wrapped my arms around his neck and kissed his cheek. He grabbed my face and kissed my lips a few times then squeezed my butt.

"Now, I can go to sleep."

A thought came to mind, and I sat up in the bed, and asked, "Where in the hell do you live? You might live on the street for all I know."

He laughed out loud. "Bring your ass over here and go to sleep. I'll pick you up tomorrow after work and take you to my place. Don't bring whatever this bullshit is you're sleeping in either. I can't feel any skin."

I smiled and settled back in our spooning position. This time he slid his hand under my shirt and rubbed my stomach. This was going to be a long night.

∞ ∞ ∞

The next morning, I woke up stretched out on top of Dre with both of his hands down the back of my pants. He had one butt cheek in each hand.

He was knocked out but gently squeezed my cheeks. *Wow, he was lusty in his sleep.*

"Good morning," I said.

He stirred a little and squeezed me tighter. I had to get off of him because something extremely long was growing between my legs.

"Mmmm, good morning," he finally said, sleepily.

"Good morning, Pervert. You want to take your hands out of my underwear and off my ass?"

His eyes widened and he snatched his hands out of my pants. "Shit, I'm sorry. I told you I like to touch skin."

"Yeah, okay. It's awfully dark outside I guess it's still early."

Rain was hitting my skylight.

I moved off his chest and reached for my phone. "SHIT! It's after ten!" I jumped out of the bed.

"WHAT?!" He scrambled out of the bed and grabbed his joggers. He disappeared down the hall.

I ran into the bathroom to brush my teeth. As I brushed at top speed, I realized I hadn't had a day off from work in a long time. And today, I was taking off. I was tired and I wanted to get a few more things done for the grand opening.

I washed my face and walked back into the bedroom slowly.

"What are you doing back in the bed?" Dre had his t-shirt and joggers on, laid out on his back.

"I'm taking a personal day, I'm tired. By the time I go home and change then get to work it would be after lunch. I'll walk you out and go home when you are heading out."

I put my hands on my hips. "I'm not going in either."

He smiled. "We Netflix and chilling today?"

I grinned. "I guess so. But I do have to go to the spice shop today."

"Ok, let's watch a movie then we'll go over to the spice shop. You can show me around. Then we can go to my place."

"How do you know I don't have plans today?" I asked as I sat on the side of the bed.

"You better tell him it's Dre Day and your plans changed."

I grinned. "Naw, he has more time in than you. You just came on the scene last week."

He grabbed me from behind and pulled me on his lap so that I was facing him. He kissed me and I kissed him back, wrapping my arms around him.

His tongue slipped in my mouth, and I savored every moment of it. His kisses were gentle yet demanding. His lips were larger than mine, so he sucked them in his mouth and swirled his tongue around mine. He ended it with a few pecks and then asked, "What's today?"

I smiled and said, "Dre Day."

Chapter 4 ~ Dre

I was so far out of character I didn't recognize myself. It was the day of the grand opening and I had just walked Tonya to her car.

She spent the night at my house the last two nights, and we still hadn't had sex. The strange thing about it was that I didn't care. I just wanted her with me. It was crazy, it was like she was a best friend, the homey, and someone I wanted to most definitely be my lover, all wrapped into one cute package.

I could not keep my hands off her. I had always been touchy-feely, but this shit was creeping me out.

We ended up taking off two days and organizing her section of the store.

I had to call Dawn and my boy Rob, both of them had been calling me since the video aired on the news.

Tonya had not talked to her people either, except Lois and Lady B. Melody caught us in the shop last night and she asked Tonya to come to the back office.

I had no idea what was said, but Melody came out and apologized for not speaking. She even hugged me.

I had to call Dawn before I saw her at the grand opening, and she stared me down. I couldn't take that from her, never could, not even when we were kids.

I waited a few rings and she answered with, "Well, well, well, you finally decided to call your former best friend. And I say former because you wouldn't do me like this if we were still good."

I chuckled. "Quit playing, girl. So what's up with you?"

"Dre, I swear I will kick you in the shin if you don't start talking. I got a slight story from Lois along with the news clip of you dancing in the street with Tonya. How did all that happen?"

I rubbed my face. "I don't know what happened. I followed her home, we talked, and we both fell asleep on her couch. We went jogging and danced in the street. Shit, we took the last two days off together. We've been getting the shop together, watching movies and shit. D, you there?"

"Umm-hmm, I'm here, I'm listening."

"But here's the biggest thing. I've spent four nights with her, and we have not had sex. And I don't even care! I'm texting her when she leaves, this is crazy. And it's been a week."

Dawn laughed out loud. "I've been waiting on this for years! My little baby has fallen for someone. And it's going to get worse. I can't wait to see this. But first and foremost, I know you better cut those other women loose. Don't do Tonya dirty, I will have to kill you first so that my husband doesn't torture you."

"Yeah, when I hung out with her on Saturday, I decided to chill because you know I always keep a squad going and I didn't want her involved. So I was thinking I would clean house because I kept thinking about her after I left, you know? Couldn't really get her off my mind. But shit, everybody jumped ship when the video came out. I thought I would start ghosting my squad and then take her out. Shit! Damn D! I haven't taken my girl out on a proper date! I'm trippin'. I gotta do something big for her today though, I'm proud of what she's doing. We were in there until midnight last night setting up. Dawn, you there?"

"Oh, I'm listening with my mouth hanging open. I've never seen this before. Listen, Dre, I know you steamroll everything. Take it slow and make sure it's right. I think Tonya is perfect for you, but don't bulldoze her. You know how you are with stuff."

I nodded. "But I just can't get enough of her. She's like you, Rob, and a fine ass woman in one package."

"Umm, first of all, to hell with you for not classifying me as a fine-ass woman. But I get what you mean."

I laughed. "You know what I'm saying. I ain't trying to touch you the way I touch her."

"Well let me give you a heads up, my husband is going to say something to you. Before you get to posturing, let me explain."

Yeah, I needed to hear this because Macon may be bigger, but I would fight his ass if he stepped to me wrong.

"Go ahead," I said.

"Dre, he knows you show up with different women to everything. He needs to know you aren't trying to put his sister in that rotation. I assured him you weren't, because I know you wouldn't play with the family like that. But you know how you men are; I've talked to him already and now I'm telling you. Take that shit in the chin, the same way he took it from you when you were looking out for me, ok?"

Damn! She had me on that one, I was a complete asshole to Macon when he and Dawn first started dating. Dude kept his cool no matter what I did, out of respect for Dawn.

"You're right. I'll hear what Big Baby has to say."

"Thank you, and just to be clear. Big booty Chelle is gone, right?"

"You wrong for that, D." I chuckled. "Chelle's sister saw us out Saturday, she called and cursed me out. She called Tonya pocket-sized and said don't call her when I was done with the Pre-Schooler."

Dawn kept laughing and she finally said, "You know Chelle will not have you embarrass her. She might let you get away with it if she was the only one who saw, but you all were on the news. She's way too important for that."

"Yeah, she's stuck-up. Pretty much why things couldn't work with us, she would have never danced with me like that. Chelle wasn't good but for one thing for me."

"Okay, you are getting me mixed up with Rob, I don't want to hear anything about you and Chelle's sex."

I laughed. "I gotta go get ready for the grand opening. I got a few things in my truck I need to take to Tonya."

"Day-yum! And you're running errands? That's what I'm talking about."

"Be quiet, bye. Love you."

She laughed. "Love you too, bestie brother-in-law."

I shook my head and ended the call.

I heard what Dawn was saying about me bulldozing, but that's who I was. No need to change this late in the game. If Tonya was who I wanted, she was going to be mine, simple as that.

∞ ∞ ∞

The grand opening was on and popping, it was packed. I had been there most of the day and helped replenish the shelves a few times. Tonya was exhausted and asked if I would pick up her favorite coffee from Kahawa Coffee across the street.

As I moved through the crowd, I almost dropped the coffee because some cat was all up in Tonya's face. And she was no longer wearing the little sparkle sneakers. Instead, she was wearing another pair of those sky-high heels.

The sparkling shorts and t-shirt with sparkling letters that read, 'SHE-iS...sugar' didn't help this dude's eyes stay where they needed to be.

"Aye, Dre! Let me holla at you for a minute."

Damn, I did not have time to talk to Macon right now, but he was in front of me.

We slapped hands. "What's good, Macon?"

"Aye, apparently you got it. You want to step outside for a minute?"

When dude ran a finger down Tonya's thigh, that was it. I knew I couldn't make a scene, but this shit wasn't going down in front of me.

"Yeah, man. I'll meet you outside after I take this coffee to your sister."

He must have been watching me watch her because he said, "That's the ex, Brad. She got a lil' crew up in here today. But yeah, I'll see you in a minute." He patted my shoulder and walked off.

A crew? Who else was here?

That didn't matter right now, I had to get Brad out of her face.

I walked right up to her like dude wasn't standing there and said, "Baby, here's your coffee."

Her eyes opened wide. "Ummm, thanks. Oh, Dre, this is Brad. Brad, Dre."

I held out my hand and he reluctantly grabbed it. This had to be the cool dude she mentioned that couldn't dance. He was stiff as a board with a hat cocked to the side.

"What's up?" I said as I shook his hand.

He squinted his eyes. Oh yeah, he probably recognized me from the news clip.

"Yeah, yeah, what's up? So umm, T..."

A lady interrupted him and asked, "Ohh, you're the guy she was dancing with on the news? I thought that was you, I was hoping you would be here. Can I get a picture of you two, please? Y'all were so cute."

"Thank you, sure you can get a picture," I said. "Come on, baby, you want to take a picture for the nice lady?"

I made a full show of wrapping her up in my arms and smiling for the picture.

"Y'all are too cute! Aren't they?" she asked Brad and he ignored her. "Let me get one more."

"Anything for the customers here supporting her business," I said, holding her around the waist. I kissed her cheek for the picture and the lady squealed.

"I wish my man looked at me like this. Girl, you are lucky."

Tonya smiled and said, "Thank you, and thanks for coming out today."

Once the lady walked away, I said, "Baby, I'm going to holla at Macon for a minute. Did you want me to get your other shoes? I know those hurt your feet."

"No, I'm fine." Her arms were crossed with a smirk on her face.

Brad mumbled, "Fuckin' butler or something?"

I had to ignore that one or else we would end up tearing the store up, so I said, "I'll let you finish talking to your friend. I'll be back."

Before I walked off, I whispered in her ear, "He ain't smooth enough to dance like me."

She tried not to giggle. I kissed her ear, threw my head up at Brad, and walked outside. My work was done.

"I saw what you did over there," Macon said with a huge grin. "I never liked him anyway. He's only here because he saw her with you on tv. He's simple."

"How do you know all of that?"

"The girls stay talking. Whatever my mother knows, I know."

Ohhh, so Brad was one of the clowns that contacted her earlier this week.

"Look, Dre, you and I ain't the best of friends, but we are cool because of my wife. But this is my sister. I've been watching and hearing what you've done over the last week and I'm asking that you keep it a buck with her. I know you and my wife are friends, but if you fuck over my sis, the shit ain't flying with me. And this is man-to-man right here, I know you feel me on this one. Wasn't too long ago you were saying this same thing to me about my wife."

I held my hand out and he shook it. "Your sister is in good hands, man. All I ask is that y'all give us some space to see where it's going."

He laughed. "You are getting about as much space as you gave Dawn and me."

I had this coming so I just laughed with him. Karma leveled my ass up real good today.

"Look at my two favorite guys over here choppin' it up," Dawn said, as she put her arm around Macon.

"Two favorites?" Macon frowned.

"You are always my number one," she said smiling up at him.

"Let me go talk to Brock and Lady B, they've been watching me all day."

Macon laughed. "Aye, baby sis is the one you need to watch out for, she's mean."

"She hugged me yesterday, it's all good."

Macon shook his head and laughed. "He's got a lot to learn, doesn't he, Sweetheart?"

"Yep," Dawn replied.

"I'll catch up with y'all later. And, I want Tonya, not Melody. She'll be okay."

Dawn and Macon shook their heads as I walked away.

Tonya walked up to me as soon as I was a few feet away.

"So you're just tinkling all around my shop today, huh?" She had her hands on her hips and a smirk on her face.

"Tinkling?"

"Peeing; marking territory."

I laughed. "I gotta let the people know. What do you tell me every time I have some of your sugar?"

She frowned. "Wh..." She paused and covered her face.

"Yeah, uh-huh, you mine now," I said, and we both laughed. "The nerd has been waiting to talk to you, too. I ain't gone mess with him. I feel sorry for him."

"We went out on one and a half dates. He is not worried about me. Any of your harem up in here?"

"I've seen a couple, but my focus has been on my brown sugar. I like this outfit, by the way."

I had to stay clear of that conversation. I spoke to the two ladies I dealt with in the past and that was it.

"Thank you, you look pretty fly today yourself."

Brushing my shoulder off, I said, "You deserve to be with somebody as fly as you," referring to 'Fly as Me' by Silk Sonic.

She laughed. "You are so full of yourself."

"You like it though." I shrugged and winked at her.

I wanted to hug and kiss her so bad, but this was business, so I kept my hands to myself.

"I'm having a hard time not touching you right now. That punk ass Brad touched your thigh."

She rolled her eyes. "He's being extra, he was not worried about me until he saw the news. We've done a little back and forth over the years, so he thinks he can just roll back up in my life."

"You mine now, you better tell him," I said jokingly.

"Dre, stop gassing me up, we've been hanging a week."

I frowned. "Gassing you up? Naw, baby, I'm serious about this. I want us to see where this goes."

"We will talk about it later," she said.

As far as I was concerned there was nothing to talk about, but I kept my mouth shut. Today was about her and her sisters.

I slowly looked her up and down. "You just let me know where I need to be tonight. My place or yours."

"Oh, I won't be home tonight, I'm going to Lois' house so we can discuss the event. Then I'm back here tomorrow morning."

"I have to sleep by myself tonight?"

She shook her head. "You'll survive, just pretend this is last Thursday before you saw me at the comedy show."

"I'll let you skate on this one, but Sunday night, that ass better be in my bed."

"We will see. I have to go, it's time for the intro and pictures."

She reached up and hugged me. "Alright, baby, go do your thing. Let me know if there's anything I can do."

I watched as her slim and toned legs walked away from me. She looked over her shoulder and caught me watching. She winked and slipped into the crowd.

"Man, it's like you are on drugs," my boy Rob said as he smacked my shoulder. "You're in here working and watching."

"Shut up, Rob," I said jokingly and took his hand off my shoulder.

He laughed. "Come on! You're in here like a little soldier. Serena has been laughing at you since we got here."

Serena and Rob met while we were in college and had been married for years.

"I'm not paying attention to either one of you. This business is important and I'm doing whatever she needs me to do."

He held his hands up. "All I'm saying is this isn't what you usually do. She's got your nose open. You sure y'all ain't had sex?"

"I told you when I talked to you earlier it's not about that with Tonya. I like her outside of sex. She's good people."

"Well, my friend, when you do get the goods, it's going to be a wrap for you. You'll finally be married. Does she want kids?"

I frowned. "Man, damn we ain't that far along. And just so you know I've had plenty of goods in the past, that doesn't move me."

"That's where you're wrong. You put sex together with a woman you're vibing with and that's all you'll ever want. Remember when I told you back in college that I was going to marry Serena? And you didn't get it?"

"I thought you were too young, but I was wrong. Y'all are still together after all these years."

"Exactly! Nothing to do with age or time. It's a feeling and you are about to find out real soon."

I had a feeling he was right. Tonya had been on my mind constantly since that night I gave her a ride home. She was the type of woman I wanted to be around. I didn't know what it was—energy, vibes, etc.

"Yeah, time will tell. They are about to talk now."

Tonya, Melody, and Lois, along with a few political people stood at the front of the store once the music stopped.

The girls all had on their matching shirts. Melody's read, 'SHE iS...honey' and Lois' read 'SHE iS...spice'. And of course, my girl's was about the sugar. I was so proud watching her stand with her sisters on this new venture.

Samuel Valentine, the municipality founder of the Greenwood District took the microphone.

"Good afternoon, my fellow Greenwood residents and visitors! I want to first thank everyone for the support you've shown from Greenwood's inception. We continue to strive to make this area the best African American community in the nation!" The people clapped.

He continued with, "This is why today is so important. We need viable retail stores in our area and the SHE-iS spice shoppe will be a pillar in this community. I've already tasted and purchased quite a bit today. My instincts are never wrong about business so I know we are looking at longevity. And possibly a second location, isn't that right, ladies?" He turned to the girls and they smiled.

"I want to end by again thanking you for your support and officially welcoming the SHE-iS spice shoppe to Greenwood! Let's welcome the proprietors, Delores James-Norris, Tonya James, and Melody James."

The crowd went wild as Samuel hugged each of them and Lois took the microphone.

"Thank you, Greenwood, for your support! My sisters and I are overwhelmed by the turnout today. We are restocking the shelves as fast as we can to accommodate everyone. The concept of our shop is to ultimately give you the tools to make gourmet meals at home. The name SHE-iS is an acronym for Sugar, Honey, and Everything Spice. As you can see by our shirts, each of us specializes in different items. Tonya makes the infused sugars you've been enjoying today. Melody makes the infused honey. And I, the spicy sister, make the different spices." Everyone laughed. "This dream came out of sadness after I lost my husband a year ago today. And again, I want to thank my sisters for joining me with this idea and working tirelessly to get the shop up and running in honor of my late husband. I want to also thank our family and friends for their support. This was one hundred percent a group effort. In keeping with this black woman-owned venture I want to mention four important women who worked with us. I want to bring my bonus sisters up here now. Dawn James, Diane Brock, and Tori Brock. By the way, Tori owns the salon and barbershop next door, Whip-N-Fade. As they make their way up here, I want to thank my brothers for bringing such amazing women into our family. Last, but certainly not least, the matriarch and queen of our family, our mother, Lila James-Brock. She's the one that keeps us in line."

Once everyone made it to the front and the crowd cheered, she continued with, "I want all of our children up here as well, the kids helped out quite a bit. And I see my brothers mean mugging me. You know I would not leave you out. We have the best brothers in the world. Dale Brock, Donald Brock, and Macon James, please make your way up here. And thank you all for giving us so much of your time and your wives' time over the last year. Again, lastly, and certainly not least, I want to bring the patriarch of this crew up here, our king, our leader, and the other person that keeps this bunch in check, our father, Dexter Brock!"

The crowd cheered while the media outlets and everyone took pictures. I snapped a few of them as well.

Later in the day as we were approaching the closing time of the shop, Brock and Lady B finally caught up with me.

"Well, hello there, Andre. I was beginning to think you were avoiding me," Lady B said.

I smiled and held my arms out to hug her. "Never that, Lady B, I've been busy helping out today."

I shook Brock's hand but he didn't say anything.

She smiled. "I've heard about all the helping you've been doing. You know my Tonya is a good girl, she would make a good catch for you."

I tried not to laugh because Tonya would die if she heard this conversation.

"Tonya's a special woman," I added.

I'd known Brock since I graduated college and started working at the local aerospace company with him. He took me under his wing back then and showed me the ropes. I didn't find out he was related to Macon, Lois, and the rest of them until I went to his retirement party with Dawn a few years ago.

"And she deserves a good husband. I hear you're still single," she said.

Brock cut in with, "Alright, Honey, I want to talk to my former coworker for a minute. We don't want to sell our daughter off either, without her permission."

"But Lois told me that..."

Brock took her hand and whispered in her ear. She smiled, then nodded.

"I'll see you later, Andre. Bye, Sweetie." She kissed Brock and walked away.

"What do you whisper in her ear? I've seen you do that on multiple occasions."

Brock stuck his chest out. "First rule of being married, is internal affairs. What goes on in our house is between us, and us alone. You'll figure it out when you finally jump the broom. Speaking of which, I like you for my daughter. I've been waiting on this for a while now."

I frowned and asked. "Waiting on Tonya and me?"

"Yep." He nodded.

"Why did you think something would happen between us?"

"Because I listen and I observe. I was around when you first met her and I saw it then. That's why I was a little confused when I found out about you liking Dawn. But when we got to the bottom of that, I knew you were just being your normal territorial self so I brushed it off. Over the last few years you've been at a lot of family functions and I've noticed you noticing her. Why do you think I suggested you follow her home last week?"

Stretching my forehead, I said, "I thought it was odd that you asked me and didn't let her date follow her home."

He nodded. "Same reason I said she had to go home. You know I don't mind my girls staying at our house. But if she had, then you would have left and none of this would be happening, would it?"

I stared at him in disbelief. "Okay, well I definitely owe you a thank you. You're still looking out for me after all these years."

He waved me off. "No thanks needed, you just do right by my daughter."

I held my hand up. "Brock, I wouldn't dare try to play Tonya. She's special and she's you and Dawn's family."

"Look, Andre, I know the rest of them give you a hard time about the women you keep. They talk about it because they have done the same thing, but not as respectfully as you. As far as I know, you don't have a bunch of kids running around. And not one unruly woman showed up at the job in the twenty-plus years I worked with you. Not even a phone call from a scorned woman. So that tells me, whatever you did, it was respectful. You have no problem with me, Son."

Brock was always dropping gems.

"I appreciate you saying that, Brock. It means a lot. To be honest, things are moving a little fast, we will see where it goes."

"Nonsense, no such thing as moving too fast when it comes to who you want. I knew I would marry Lila as soon as we went on our first date after her husband passed. She didn't know because she was still mourning, but I knew and I waited until the time was right. I was a little younger than you are right now and I knew it. And so do you." He patted my arm.

Tonya was walking fast in our direction without a smile on her face, she seemed upset.

"What's wrong?" I asked as soon as she was in front of us.

"I have to make more of the brown sugar tonight. I'm almost out. I can't believe this, I'm exhausted."

Brock raised an eyebrow and looked at me. "What about the sugar I brought over with me? That batch was for tomorrow."

She threw her hands up. "That batch is almost gone too. I thought I made more than enough."

I wrapped an arm around her. "Hey, this is a good problem. Don't worry about it, is there enough for today?"

"Yes, barely."

"Okay, after you close up, we'll go to the kitchen and make more for tomorrow. Even if we have to stay up all night, ok?"

She nodded, but she was on the verge of crying. "I'm tired. There's no way we can get it all bagged up tonight. This weekend was supposed to be perfect for us, especially Lois."

"Come with me." I grabbed her hand. "Excuse us, Brock, but this is an internal affair."

Brock smiled and nodded slowly. "You go on and let Andre fix you up." He patted her on the back and she nodded.

I took her to the parking lot to my truck. It was the only private space around.

Once we were inside, I turned on the air conditioner and the music. The song we danced to by D'Angelo started playing and she smiled.

She took my hand and closed her eyes until the song ended.

"Thank you, I needed a little time to get my thoughts together. Running a business is hard work."

"Baby, you got this. All those customers were here for you and your sisters. It will get better once your demand stabilizes."

"It's very overwhelming. Thank you for offering to help me with the sugar but I'll do it."

"I'm helping you and I'm driving you, ok?"

She smiled and nodded. "I am tired and you're only driving me because you don't want to sleep alone tonight."

I laughed. "Even if you're right, it's happening so it doesn't matter." I leaned over and waited for her to kiss me. "Now slide over here so I can feel you up before you have to go back inside."

She slowly scooted over to me with a smirk on her face and said, "Thank you for helping tonight. Lois and Mel are tapped out."

"Let them rest and we can knock it out in a few hours, ok?"

A knock on the passenger window scared both of us. It was Melody. She had her hands cupped on the window. My windows were tinted so she couldn't see inside.

"Should I let the window down? Or leave her out there?" I asked.

Tonya giggled and leaned over to let the window down.

Melody directed her attention to Tonya and said, "Lois said you needed one of us to help you tonight with the sugar. It's time to close in a few minutes. I can run home, shower, and then go on over."

"Go on home and rest, Dre is going to help me."

Tonya's back was to me, but she must have been giving Melody the evil eye because she gave me a forced partial smile.

"Thanks for helping my sister, Andre."

Other than the older folks, she was the only one that insisted on calling me by my full name.

I smiled and said, "No problem, Melody, whatever she needs, I got her." When she sort of rolled her eyes, I added, "If you or Lois need help let me know, I don't mind."

"Yep, sure will. See you inside, Sis." She walked away.

Tonya let up the window and we both laughed.

"Why does she hate me?" I asked.

Tonya stopped laughing and said, "My sister hasn't been happy for a long time. She does a good job of covering it up most times."

Damn, now I felt sorry for her mean ass.

"Come on, let's get you back inside before the warden comes back out."

"I need a kiss first," she said and leaned over.

Gently cradling her face, I kissed her softly. Never in my life had a woman's kiss soothed me the way hers did. I knew physical touch was my thing, but it seemed to be Tonya's touch was really my thing.

Chapter 5 ~ Tonya

The last couple of weeks after the grand opening had been a whirlwind. The customers loved our store so much that we were in the process of hiring a company to pack our products.

We were only open Friday, Saturday, and Sunday, but the demand far exceeded our expectations. If things continued on this path we would also need to open an online store.

My phone rang, it was Dre.

"Are you on your way?" I asked.

"I am, are you sure you feel like going?"

"I'm fine. I'm off tomorrow anyway until I go to the shop."

"Okay, Baby, I'll be there in a few minutes."

"Okay, bye." I ended the call.

Dre and I were having a double date with his friends, Rob and Serena. I met them at the grand opening, they seemed like a very nice couple.

We were still going strong, and he made it clear the night of the grand opening that he was officially pursuing me. And that he was making me his. Of course, I was elated about his announcement. However, we had not seen much of each other since the shop opened. We went out for dinner a couple of times, but other than that, we were both working.

He was on a new project at work that kept him working until after six or seven in the evening. After I finished working, I would be in the commercial kitchen or having a meeting with Mel and Lois. Although Lois was the majority owner, each of us kept track of the financials. It was a lot of work but the money was flowing in. At the rate we were going, our initial investment would be returned within six months. Once we figured out the online store, we would really be taking in the money.

I buzzed Dre up and waited for him to come up. He refused to have me meet him outside.

"Hey, come here," he said as soon as he stepped inside.

I held out my arms and hugged him. "Hello, to you too," I returned.

He held on, rocking me back and forth. "Mmmm, you feel good. Damn, I missed you." He let me go and kissed me.

Smiling like a school girl, I said, "Dre, we talk several times a day and you were at the shop with me two days ago."

"But that ain't the same, you haven't spent the night with me but a couple of times in the last two weeks."

He was right, we hadn't done many overnights because of our schedules.

"I know. I'm free tomorrow until I go to the shop. Can you stay over tonight? We will have to set the alarm, I know you have to be up early for work."

He blew out a breath. "Yeah, this new project is kicking my ass. I have to work this weekend too. But tomorrow I told them I wasn't coming in. I can't work seven days and not have one day off. So, go get a bag, you're staying with me tonight."

I put my hands on my hips. "What if I wanted us to stay here?"

"You don't have the breakfast food that I have at my house, especially those mini croissants I'm making tomorrow."

I ran up the steps. "Say less, I'm packing a bag."

He laughed as I skipped down the hallway.

Dre cooking for me was my favorite thing. During our last two busy weeks, he somehow managed to bring me dinner to the kitchen. He brought all of us food. Melody tried to hate on it but she ate it.

Last Week...

"Y'all hungry? Dre is going to bring dinner by," I said as I came back into the commercial kitchen.

"Where is he going?" Lois asked.

"He cooked, he's packing it up now. I just need to know if you want something. He made grilled chicken breast, potatoes, broccolini, and corn. He cooked it all on the grill. He cooks very well."

"I want all of it!" Lois said.

"No thanks," Melody added.

Her back was to us. Lois looked at me and rolled her eyes.

"Mel, are you sure you don't want anything? We are going to be here late," I said.

"I don't have a taste for that, I'll have one of the kids drop something off for me."

I didn't say anything. I sent Dre a text message.

Me: Lois wants everything, Mel said no.

Dre Bae: I'll bring her lil' mean ass some anyway. LOL! See you soon, Baby.

I smiled wide because I just loved when he called me baby.

"Why are you over there smiling, he's only bringing you food," Mel said.

"Shut the hell up, Mel!" Lois yelled.

"I'm just saying, it doesn't take all that for some guy to bring you food."

"He's not just some guy. We are dating," I quipped.

"You and everybody in St. Louis," she said.

"Mel!" Lois yelled.

I was pissed. "He's seeing me and only me for your information. And even if he isn't, guess what? It's none of your damn business, is it?"

The three of us had three separate areas in the kitchen so we were yelling back and forth.

"So, you'll take a piece of a man just to have one?" Mel asked.

"Your ass did it!"

She threw her gloves on the table and turned to face me. "He was my husband! Not some dude that used to like my sister-in-law, and sleeps around the city."

"What's the difference? You didn't do anything when you found out! You still had a piece of a man while the streets had the rest of him!" I returned.

The door opened; Mama and Brock entered the kitchen.

"What's going on in here!" she yelled.

"She started it!" Mel and I twinned.

"Both of you be quiet! Lois, you're the oldest, why are you allowing this?"

Brock closed the door and left. He never got in the middle of us.

"Why am I being blamed? Those are your children."

"I won't have my girls not getting along. I'm old and I won't spend my last days refereeing like I did when you were teens. This makes no sense at all! Tonya, you leave your sister alone about her marriage. You don't know the first thing about it because you've never been there!" I opened my mouth and she raised her hand.

Mel had a smug look on her face. "That's right, Mama!" Mel added.

Mama swung her head to Mel. "And you need to mind your own business when it comes to Andre! That man is way better than the one you used to call husband, you have no room for judgment."

Melody's face crumbled and I felt bad. Her ex-husband was a piece of shit in the end.

I took off my gloves and walked to her with my arms open. A tear fell from her eye just as she embraced me.

"I'm sorry, I just don't want you to go through what I went through with him," she sobbed.

"I know, Mel. And I love you for trying to protect me, but Dre is a good guy."

"That's how they all start off."

I didn't respond, I just held her and let her cry. My poor sister.

"Come give me a hug, I'm going now. Brock and I stopped by to see how it was going on our way home." We hugged Mama and she left.

For the next thirty minutes, we worked without talking to each other.

Dre walked in and stood by the door. "Hey, ladies, I have your dinner."

"Thanks, Dre! I'm starving!" Lois said.

"Hello, Andre," Mel said.

I took off my gloves and apron. "Hey," I said, when I was in front of him.

"Hey, Baby, you sure you don't need me to stay and help." He leaned down and pecked my lips.

"No, you have been working all day, get some rest. I can handle it. Come on, I'll walk you out."

He grabbed my hand and placed the bag of food on the table.

"I'll see you, ladies, later. Melody, there's a plate for you too in case you change your mind."

She looked over her shoulder and said, "Thank you, Andre."

When I returned from walking Dre out, guess who had a mouth full of food?

"Thought you didn't have a taste for that?" I asked.

"I mean since he brought it, I may as well eat it." She shrugged and continued stuffing her face.

"The food smells good and tastes good too, that's why her greedy butt is eating it!" Lois yelled.

The three of us looked at each other and laughed. One thing about our sisterhood, we didn't stay mad long.

Dre was stretched out on the sofa when I returned with my overnight bag. I dropped it at the top of the stairs and sat beside him on the sofa. He was so handsome, even with the snoring he was doing. It had been three weeks since the comedy show and we moved like a full-blown couple. I was completely blown away by him.

My biggest worry had been his personality matching up with my fascination with his good looks and demeanor. That was quickly put to bed. He treated me like a Queen. Always there to help and listen when I needed him. Even after working long hours.

"How long are you going to stare at me?" he asked, with his eyes closed.

I jumped. "I thought you were sleeping, you were snoring when I walked in. Are you sure you're up to going?"

Kissing the back of my hand, he said, "I'm good, I want to treat you to dinner. And I want you to get to know my friends."

"Let's go, I'm ready."

"You look nice," he said and laughed.

He stood from the sofa and I rolled my eyes at him for mimicking Daniel.

"Come here." He grabbed my hand and said, "Baby, you know I'm playing. Bring your sexy ass over here."

I smiled wide as he kissed my cheek. "Much better," I said.

"Let's go, Sexy Mama."

∞ ∞ ∞

"How do you put up with him?" Serena asked.

We were at a restaurant not too far from Dre's house.

I shrugged. "He is fine, I can't argue the truth."

Rob and Serena laughed out loud and groaned.

Dre put his arm around me and kissed my cheek. "See why I like her so much?"

"Sis, you can't stroke his ego like that, he's bad enough as is," Serena said.

I laughed. "He's not that bad, is he?"

"No, I'm not. Serena's a hater."

We all laughed and I asked, "Serena, do you do any local fitness classes?" She was a fitness choreographer and she was ripped.

She nodded. "I do, I offer classes a few times a week when I'm in town. I can give you my info. I would love to have you come out to a class."

"Baby, your body is perfect, you don't need a class," Dre said, and I blushed.

"So y'all just compliment each other to death? That's what y'all do?" Rob asked and I giggled.

Dre frowned. "Her body is perfect, it's a fact."

Rob shook his head. "Never thought I would see the day this dude found his equal."

We all laughed and enjoyed our meal. They were a nice couple.

As we were finishing up dinner, Rob's phone rang.

"Why is your child calling?" he asked, referring to their college-aged son.

He answered but didn't say much. He ended the call and said, "Welp, we have to go, this boy had an accident."

"WHAT!" Serena yelled. "Why didn't he call me too?"

"Because of what you're doing right now. Rena, he's fine. He hit the mailbox in front of the house."

"We got one kid! Just one! And he can't help but find trouble," she said, as they got up.

Rob was looking for the waiter.

Dre chuckled. "Rob, I got y'all. Go ahead and take care of my nephew. My boy stays in y'all pockets."

Rob shrugged. "I think we would be millionaires if we didn't have him. I just gave the boy the car this summer and look at him."

"Tonya, it was so nice having dinner with you, we have to do it again when the kid goes back to school."

I laughed and stood to hug her. "No problem, and I look forward to your fitness class."

"Let me get your number, I don't trust Dre."

"Serena I'm not playing with you. Don't have my baby in there doing shit that's going to have her looking weird," Dre said, and we all laughed.

I exchanged information with Serena and we waved them off to see about their son.

"Are you ready?" I asked Dre.

"Nope, I'm still eating and I want to stay out late with you," he said and smiled.

I had a different idea, and it didn't involve us sitting in this restaurant.

"I'm going to the restroom," I said.

He stood and helped me from my chair.

When I approached the table on the way back, his fork hit his plate.

I sat down, and he stared at me with his mouth wide open.

"What's the matter?" I asked innocently.

Leaning over to whisper in my ear, he asked, "Did you take your bra off in there? Why do your breasts look like the ones from at home?"

I tried not to laugh, so instead I yawned and my braless breasts lifted even further.

"So, are you ready to leave or are you still eating?" I did a slight shimmy to make the girls vibrate.

Finally lifting his eyes to meet mine, he said, "That ass is mine tonight."

I replied, "I'm ready when you are."

I wasn't ready for Dre! I wasn't ready!

"Please! Please!" I yelled.

I scooted so far across the bed my head was hanging off the other side.

His mouth, tongue, teeth, and probably his uvula were nestled between my legs, suctioning, tugging, kissing, and licking while I screamed.

I was on my back in a frog position trying with all my might to close his head up between my legs, but his broad shoulders and big hands had me locked in place.

"Dre, baby, I can't take anymore, please!" I yelled.

Tears ran down my face as I sobbed and shivered from the stimulation. My orgasm came down hard as he finally eased up and pulled me back on the bed.

"I know miss stripping in the public bathroom ain't crying," he said, as he kissed his way up my stomach.

I couldn't talk, I just lay there whimpering.

He chuckled. "Baby, you'll be okay in a few minutes." He slowly massaged my over stimulated clit with his thumb until the throbbing stopped.

When I was finally able to talk, I croaked out hoarsely, "You didn't have to do me like that."

He laughed out loud. "You thought you were going to seduce me in the restaurant, and then come here and put it on me, too?"

I nodded. "Maybe."

"I'll let you do it next time." He chuckled.

I smiled because he was mocking me about our run around the lake.

"You know what they say about payback?" I asked.

"I do, and I welcome anything you got."

Turning over on his back, he pulled me on his chest and grabbed each of my butt cheeks. I was exhausted, and I hadn't done anything but scream and cry.

"Are you okay?" he asked quietly.

"I'm fine." I lifted my head to meet his eyes.

"Good, because this night is just getting started. And I'm not stopping until every inch of you is satisfied, ok?"

I couldn't look away from him or speak, so I nodded.

"You with me, Baby?"

"I'm with you," I said quietly.

He pulled me further up his chest until my breasts were at his mouth. He massaged them while he stared into my eyes. Finally, lapping up my right nipple, he gently swirled the tip of his tongue around it until it pebbled. He switched to the left nipple and repeated the same movement.

Gently guiding my face to his, he kissed me. Our tongues danced around each other until I felt him poking to get inside me.

"Baby, let me get a condom." I slid off his chest while he dug around in his night stand.

Once we were lined up perfectly with him on top, I lifted my legs and wrapped them around his waist. He slid inside me and began to slowly move, as I adjusted to his size.

He felt amazing as he glided in and out of me at an unhurried pace. Kissing me gently, I held on and enjoyed him inside me for the very first time. After dreaming about him over the years, it was wonderful to finally experience him.

His slow and methodical strokes felt so good, I couldn't do anything except quietly call out, "Dre... Dre... Dre."

"I got you, Baby," he whispered and slowly rimmed my ear lobe with his tongue.

And with that confirmation, a tear fell from my eye. I relaxed into another orgasm while he pushed and then stirred inside me.

His chest vibrated as we held on to each other and descended from our climax.

∞ ∞ ∞

The next morning, I had no idea why I was embarrassed about all the crying. Maybe it was more of the emotions as opposed to the tears. I wouldn't say I was in love with him, but I would say I felt connected to him. Love wasn't new to me, I'd been there and done it several times. But this connection I felt with Dre was very new. Almost like I was now tied to him. It was an odd feeling, but also comforting.

He was in the kitchen cooking when I walked in.

"Good morning!" I sang.

He lifted his head and smiled. "Here comes my crybaby."

I stopped walking and frowned. "What are you talking about?"

"You don't remember crying last night and again this morning?"

I put my hand to my chest. "Who me? Not at all."

He turned a few nobs on the cooktop and walked over to me. He kissed me quickly and said, "Good morning."

Before I could respond, he lifted me over his shoulder and carried me to the kitchen table, and said, "I will have you for a breakfast appetizer right on this table if you don't tell the truth."

I was giggling by now and squirming to get down. "Okay, okay, I cried!"

He put me down. "That's what I thought," he said, and moved toward the cooktop. "I made those eggs you like, are you hungry?"

"I'm starving." I rubbed my hands together.

He prepped our plates with eggs, bacon, mini croissants, and fresh fruit.

After he blessed the food, he asked, "What time do you have to be at the shop today? I'll drop you off."

"Around four. I can drive myself. I don't want to tie your day up."

He shook his head. "You don't think I saw you limping when you came in here? I'm driving you."

My mouth opened. "You saw me!?"

He smiled wide. "Yep!"

So maybe along with the tears, I caught a Charlie horse in my upper thigh while I was sleeping. He was never going to let me live this down.

"You know I took that long run yesterday and didn't drink my electrolyte water. And then you and I were active last night, so I caught a Charlie horse," I explained.

He had his chin resting on his fist. "When was the last time you caught one?"

"I mean, it's been a while but..."

He cut me off with, "Last time?"

I shrugged slowly and he smiled wide.

"After we finish eating, Dr. Dre will massage your legs." He proceeded to eat.

That was it! Hopefully, Serena offered a yoga or pilates class I could get in by next week. No way I was going out like this! Tears? And a cramp? I would pull a Cirque Du Soleil move on him next time.

"Are you over there plotting sex revenge in your head?" he asked without looking up from his plate.

I tried not to laugh, but I couldn't help it. "You get on my nerves!" I said, playfully.

"Baby, listen, I'll concede to the lake run if you concede that I'm the...best you ever had," he sang, mimicking John Legend's song *Tonight*.

Game on!

I ate the last of my food and took my plate to the sink. Marching across the great room toward his bedroom, I dropped my robe on the floor, revealing my freshly washed naked body. His eyes widened. "Ton..."

He stopped talking when I lowered into a split. And I didn't care that my already throbbing leg pained even more. I got up, looked over my shoulder at his open mouth, and said, "Are you ready to go or are you still eating?"

Turning to face him, I backed out of the room shimmying, with the girls on full display.

∞ ∞ ∞

Dre parked in front of the spice shop and yawned. I yawned right along with him.

"Are you going to make it today?" he asked.

I nodded. "Yeah, it's only four hours."

Lois worked the shop during the day on Fridays from noon to four. Mel and I came in from four to eight to help with the evening rush.

"You need me to do anything before I go?" he asked.

"I got it covered. I have enough sugars to get us through the entire weekend."

"Ok, good. Call me if you need anything."

"You're going to take a nap, aren't you?"

He smiled and said, "Hell yeah. I'm tired."

After my naked split, things got real unorthodox in the bedroom and in the tub. My leg was better, but I still had a slight limp. I didn't care because I redeemed myself by working him completely over.

"I'll see you later." I leaned over to kiss him and he grunted. "Your back hurts, doesn't it?"

"Just a little," he admitted and smiled.

I laughed. "You know we are too old for this, right?"

"Damn right. We are cuddling tonight."

We both laughed.

I reached for the door handle and he touched my shoulder. I turned to look at him.

"I'm serious about us, ok?"

"I know, I felt it last night, you were so tender with me," I said and grabbed his hand.

He kissed the back of my hand. "You mine now," he said, staring into my eyes the same way he did last night.

I rubbed the side of his beard. "I know," I said, and pulled his face to mine for a few kisses.

"I'll pick you up at eight."

"Ok." I got out of the truck and walked toward the door.

"Where's my sexy walk?" he yelled from the window.

"I lost that at about two this morning!" I yelled back.

He laughed and drove off after I went into the shop.

Lois and Mel were staring at me when I walked in laughing.

"Hello, sisters," I said, as I made my way to the back to put my things away.

"I'm glad we have a small break without customers because I want to know what you lost at two this morning," Lois said, as soon as I came back to the front of the shop.

"It's an inside joke with Dre," I said.

"Uhh-huh, girl, tell me! Would you deprive your sad widowed sister?"

Mel and I looked at each other in shock. Lois never mentioned her late husband in jest.

"You two can stop staring at each other. My grief counselor told me I should talk about him however I wanted."

"Umm, I don't think she meant that way," Mel said.

"I was married to that man for twenty years. He had the best sense of humor, he would get a kick out of me using him to get info." She smiled.

Mel shrugged and I said, "I'm not telling you anything, forget it."

"I knew it! I told you, Mel! I'm just trying to see if he can back up all that talk in the bedroom."

Mel walked to the back and closed the office door.

Lois said, "She ain't had none in a while. Well, if that's what you call that medicine-based sex with that sad ass ex, then maybe so."

"What!?" I whispered and walked over to Lois. "What do you mean sex with her ex?"

Lois and Mel lived next door to each other. Mel kept the house after she divorced the sad-ass ex. Lois purchased the house next door to her after her husband passed. She didn't want to continue to live in the house they formerly shared.

"She swore me to secrecy, but I caught him coming out one morning. He was parked in the garage."

Lois couldn't hold water. "Why is she messing with him after what he did?"

"She's lonely, and he's familiar."

I blew out a breath. "No wonder she's been so angry lately. She can't heal if she's still seeing him. Do the brothers know?"

"I doubt it, Dale would have told me."

Lois and Dale were thick as thieves, they told each other everything. He knew more than me and he didn't even live here. It was only a matter of time before she told him about it.

"I'll go check on her," I said, and walked toward the back.

"So you're not going to tell me about Dre?"

I stopped walking. "I cried and got a cramp, ok?"

"Hell naw! I'm jealous! But I'm so happy for you, Sis. You deserve him, I don't care what Mel says." She gave me the biggest hug.

"Thanks, Lo."

I had one sister that was healing from losing a great husband, and another that was on the opposite end; healing after losing a shitty husband.

Knocking on the office door, I poked my head inside. "Hey, Baby Sis, you okay?"

"She told you, didn't she?"

I feigned innocence. "Huh?"

"When the two of you got quiet after I left, I realized I should have stayed in there to keep Big Mouth from spilling the beans."

"At least she didn't tell Dale, yet." I shrugged.

She smirked. "Now that you know I'm messing around with that bastard, what do you have to say? I've already heard it from Lois."

The smirk was to keep her from crying. I didn't want to go in too hard on her.

"If he makes you feel good right now, then I'll support you. I don't have to like him. But I have a feeling the sex is only a temporary good feeling. I can't imagine how you feel when he leaves."

"I hate that you're always so reasonable, why can't you be mean sometimes?" She smiled and wiped the lone tear that escaped.

"Because you're my baby sister and I love you. I want you to be happy." I hugged her tightly.

"I know, I'm working on it," she said.

"Good," I said. "So let's work on getting you some sex with someone that doesn't need a pill to get it up."

Her eyes widened. "It still works the same!"

"But isn't there like a waiting period?" I asked, with my face scrunched up.

She laughed out loud. "Let's go, I don't even want to think about him. When I'm done with him, I'm replacing those pills with a laxative or some anti-diarrheal pills."

"Yeah, back that ass up," I said, and we both fell into laughter.

Lois met us in the short hallway as we approached the front of the store.

"Umm, you got company," she announced.

"Who?" I asked.

"Dre's mother and Brad."

You have to be kidding me. Dre's mother had been on him since the news clip aired about bringing me to dinner. I'd met her once or twice in the past, and then again at the grand opening for a quick minute.

I walked into the shop and moved past Brad. "Hi, Mrs. Barbara, how are you?" I held my arms out to hug her.

She smiled. "Oh, there's my daughter-in-law. How are you doing? My son couldn't have picked a more beautiful woman. Look at that beautiful hair and this little petite body. You look like me when I was your age."

I smiled awkwardly. I didn't want to hear that I looked like his mother after sleeping with him. Maybe frame-wise and skin color, but other than that, I didn't think we favored.

"What brings you in today?" I asked her.

Brad was in my peripheral vision soaking up the entire conversation.

"Well, I've been baking with that special brown sugar and I'm all out. I put some in my sweet potato pie and my Larry loves it." Leaning in to whisper, she said, "Have to keep the men satisfied no matter how old you get." She bumped my elbow and smiled.

"Yeah well, we better get you some more. We want Mr. Larry happy."

I looped my arm with hers and walked her to the sugar section as Brad and Lois flanked us. If Lois wasn't being nosey she could have kept him from ear hustling.

Mrs. Barbara and I picked out a few more sugars, a bottle of mango honey, and a salt-free garlic and herb blend.

I rang her up and bagged her products. I gave her our family discount and she smiled wide. "Oh, I can't wait to brag about my discount. Thank you. I've been telling my sisters and my friends all about you. They love this store, they'll be so jealous I get a discount."

I smiled. "You're welcome, Mrs. Barbara."

"You can call me Mom if you want."

Dre would be so embarrassed, I giggled to myself.

"Also, I'm not sure if Andre mentioned it to you, but I want to have you over for dinner soon. Put your number in my phone and we will set it up. That son of mine is always dragging his feet." She handed me her cell phone.

As I typed my number in, I said, "You know he's on a new project, he's been busy lately."

Pursing her lips, and tossing her long gray and black hair over her small shoulder, she replied, "He still has to eat. And what better way than to have a meal with his elderly parents and his girlfriend."

Mrs. Barbara was in her late sixties, but she was far from what you would describe as elderly. Serena told me she took her Zumba class regularly.

She was wearing a slightly fitted green maxi dress with silver sandals. Freshly painted toes and nails and plenty of trendy jewelry completed her outfit. And her hair was bountiful with large curls.

"I will let him know we should come for dinner soon," I said, as I walked her to the door.

She hugged me. "Thank you, I can't wait. I'll make a dessert with your brown sugar when you come. Oh, this is so exciting, your best sugar is named after us. You'll be a Brown soon too, I just know it."

And on that note, I said, "Your hair is beautiful, did you just come from next door?"

I was referring to my sister-in-law, Tori's, barber and beauty shop, Whip N Fade.

She shook her head from side to side to bounce her hair. "Yes! Isn't it gorgeous? You know I miss Tweet but Macy does a great job too. Look at how bouncy it is, it makes me look so much younger, don't you think?"

No denying where Dre got his confidence. "Yeah, you look my age. I miss Tweet too," I added. Tweet was the former manager of Whip N Fade and Tori's younger sister. Our little Tweet was married with a baby and living in the DC area.

"Honey, don't you let my Larry hear you saying I look like I'm in my forties. He would never want me to leave the house." She giggled and tossed her head back making her hair bounce even more.

"My lips are sealed." I smiled and held the door open for her.

"I'll call you in a couple of days about dinner. I know you're working here this weekend." She waved and got into her car.

I nodded and waved back with a huge smile.

One visitor down, one to go.

When I turned around, Lois and Mel watched as Brad walked toward me with his arms outstretched.

I moved to the side and asked, "Brad, why are you here? You don't cook and you don't live anywhere near here."

He smiled. "I can't come by and support my lady?"

Brad was very handsome and his slick talking would have had me swooning in the past. He was a little under six feet with light brown skin. He was bald with a full beard that he thought was his signature. Brad's eyes were gray and of course, he thought he could pull any woman he came across.

"Sure, what are you here to buy?" I asked, because I knew he didn't plan on buying a thing.

He moved closer and whispered, "Whatever I need to buy if you'll come by a little later. I miss you."

I rolled my eyes. "Goodbye, Brad." I walked away and he gently grabbed my arm.

"Tonya, come on, it's me. I know you ain't worried about that lil' dancing dude."

The bell chimed on the door, and Dre walked in.

Chapter 6 ~ Dre

I stopped in my tracks when I saw What's His Name with his hand on Tonya's arm. This shit right here was new to me, and I didn't know what to do. *Should I knock his ass out?* Naw, this was her place of business. *Should I call her name and make her come over to me?* Naw, she already mentioned me peeing on her last time.

I didn't know what to do that wouldn't land me in jail or at home alone tonight, so I stood in place and stared at her.

Yeah, that was the right move. I would act like I didn't see him; he didn't matter anyway. I was the reason she was limping today. It was my name coming from her mouth a couple of hours ago. And I was the reason she was currently snatching her arm away from him. *That's right, Baby, come to your man.*

She walked over to me smiling.

I returned the smile and held her phone up.

Her eyes widened. "I didn't realize I didn't have my phone with me," she said as soon as she was standing in front of me.

"You know I got you, I take care of my woman," I said.

What's his name was standing in the middle of the store watching us. He could have been one of the shelves as far as I was concerned, I wasn't paying him any attention.

She took the phone and smiled. "Thank you."

I wasn't worried about this dude because it didn't take a microscope to see that I was the better catch in this scenario. But apparently, he didn't understand Tonya was no longer available.

I took her hand and opened the door. "Hey, ladies, Tonya will be back."

When we were outside, she giggled. "You know I like you, right?"

Opening the passenger door, I frowned. "You think I'm worried about his generic ass? I'm messing with him because he's being disrespectful. You mine now." I closed the door.

Once I was inside, she said, "Brad thinks he can walk in and out of my life. I allowed him to do it because I was bored and lonely, not because he was all that great."

"Whatever it was, is over and he needs to stop coming around uninvited."

She crossed her arms. "I hope you keep this same energy when your harem comes around."

My harem as she called it put me down as soon as that news clip aired. Either way, I wasn't interested.

I leaned over and kissed her. "You have nothing to worry about my Brown Sugar."

She smiled wide. "I think I like that name."

"Good, because it matches what you taste like."

Her eyes widened. "Don't get me started in here."

I laughed. "Your cripple butt can't do a thing right now anyway."

She laughed along with me. "Before I forget, your mom came by and wants us over for dinner."

Damn! That woman would not chill! I didn't mind taking her over there for dinner, but it was too soon. Moms would be all over her about marriage and a baby. She needed to like me a little more before Moms got to her.

"I'll talk to her. We don't have to go anytime soon."

"Unless you don't want me to go, I have to, she has my phone number now."

I groaned. "Naw, Baby, it's not that. She just does a lot. She wants a grandkid... bad."

Tonya threw her hand at me. "Aw, that's cool. We can get her one of those by next year."

I said nothing. I stared at her.

She continued with, "You just told me I was yours, right? And you don't want Brad around, right?"

I had no comeback or response, so I scratched my head. Finally, I asked, "So, you want a kid?"

A smile crept across her face, and she laughed. "You should see your face!"

I smiled because she had me for a second. I leaned over and tickled her side and said, "You're going to stop playing with me."

"It's too easy," she said.

Rob did ask me if she wanted children and I said it was too soon to talk about it. I guess it was something we needed to discuss. It wasn't like we were twenty or thirty and had plenty of time. This was crazy, I had never asked anyone about kids. It was usually them asking me.

"But do you want a kid?" I asked seriously.

She stopped laughing. "Dre, I said I was joking. I wasn't dropping hints."

"I know, but I'm asking for real."

She let out a long breath. "I wanted a baby when I was around thirty, but I wanted marriage first. That didn't happen so then I thought about having a child with the guy I was dating about four years ago. We broke up and now I'm forty-three. I kind of let it go. What about you?"

"I don't know," I said honestly. "It seems like the juice ain't worth the squeeze on the kids."

She smiled. "I wouldn't say I have to have a child or that I don't want one. I'm like whatever life brings me."

I nodded because I could go along with that motto. I couldn't figure life out anyway, no need in trying now. Definitely didn't see myself with Tonya this time last month. This came out of nowhere.

What's His Name walked out the door and went to his car. We both watched him. He looked back at my truck, but he couldn't see inside because of the tint.

"I should let the window down and slob you down," I said.

After he drove off, she said, "Listen, Dre, I like you and all but based on your reaction about kids I feel like I need to let you know what I'm thinking."

"Okay, what's up?"

"You made it clear you are pursuing me. I get that, but as what in the end?"

"I…"

She cut me off with, "Let me finish. I don't expect you to know right now because it's been less than a month since we started seeing each other. My point is you aren't certain about me because it's too new, right?"

I nodded. "Yeah, I'm sure you feel the same way."

"I do, which is why you don't get to knock the other players off the board."

I frowned. "Say what?"

"Until we both figure out whether we are both here for a good time or a long time, I don't think it's fair to run off other people. I let you slide at the grand opening, but now you're figure skating all over the place."

I blinked a few times because I was a little shocked.

"So you're trying to see that glass-eye dude and me at the same time?"

"That's not what I said. But if I want to, I will, because we haven't drawn any lines in the sand."

Was this some type of reverse psychology?

"Are you serious right now?"

She cocked her head to the side with a smirk. "Okay, I see what's going on. You usually dictate terms with your actions and the women fall in line, right?"

"I wouldn't say fall in line."

"You know what I mean. I don't get down like that. I'm in my forties and I learned a long time ago that I have to be clear on my path. Until we both decide if what we're doing is for a long time, I won't be running any women off and you won't be running any men off." She shrugged.

Shit, I understood what she was saying but no one ever said it to me. And honestly, I didn't like it.

"Are we good?" she asked and reached for the door.

"Wait, so I can go out with other women, and you're cool with it?"

"If that's what you desire to do, I would never try to stop you. Do you want to go out with other women?"

"No! I thought we were seeing each other."

"We are seeing each other because that's what we each want, not because the other person has demanded we don't see someone else. We will see where it goes."

All I wanted to know was if that glass-eye punk was coming back after I left, and if he was, that shit wasn't sitting right with me.

"I have to go back in, I see a few customers coming."

"Okay, I'll see you later." My mind was running crazy. *What in the hell just happened? We were fine fifteen minutes ago.*

"Are you coming back to get me when we close?"

"Yeah, yeah, I got you," I said, trying to play off the confusion in my head.

Leaning over, she kissed me and said, "Thanks, see you later. We can talk more tonight."

I held on to her and kissed her a little longer. "Now you can go," I said and smiled.

She giggled. "I'm glad to see that handsome smile, I thought you were getting weird on me."

"Never that, Baby."

I watched as she got out and closed the door.

I let the window down and yelled, "Can I get my walk or a ho-down?"

She turned and laughed and then threw her small curvy hip at me as she disappeared inside.

I sat there a minute before I drove off because I wasn't cool with what she said. I had to call Dawn, she knew her, and she could make me understand what was happening.

I called her up and she answered with, "Why aren't you at work?"

"How do you know I'm not at work?"

"Because I hear *We Want Easy* in the background."

I turned the music down. "I took off today because I have to work this weekend."

"They working you on that project, huh?"

"Yep. What are you doing? I need to talk. Tonya said some stuff today that has me tripping."

She laughed. "Trouble in paradise already? I'm at home cooking dinner. Macon isn't here yet; he should be home in a couple of hours. You want to come by?"

"I'm on the way."

I tossed the conversation with Tonya around in my head until I pulled into Dawn's driveway. I made sure to park in the right spot so I wouldn't block Big Baby from getting into the garage. One thing Dawn didn't play about was him.

I respected it because he made her happy, and as far as I could see he was good to her. Pretty much worshipped the ground she walked on.

The front door opened. Dawn was standing there with a big smile on her face wearing her uniform, as she called it; yoga pants and a t-shirt with "Macon's Wifey" written across the front.

"Come on in here and tell me what you did," she said.

I stepped in and kissed her cheek. "Do you ever wear that shirt in public?"

"Shut up and stop hating." She laughed and continued with, "I love my husband and I have no problem broadcasting it."

"Whatever. It smells good in here, what did you cook?" I took a seat on the couch in the family room. The room had a wall of windows with a view of the subdivision lake.

"Not much, it's taco night. Macon is picking up the tequila on the way home." She sat on the opposite end of the couch and tucked her feet underneath her. "What happened?"

I told her what happened at the spice store and waited for her response.

"Dre, you have to fall back a bit. Tonya's right. You can't tell her what to do or treat her like a fire hydrant. It's not time for you to mark territory."

"This dude keeps coming around, it's disrespectful," I said.

"She's not your wife. And you have not even decided to be exclusive, have you?"

I shook my head. "But I'm not seeing anyone but her. I'm not trying to see anybody else."

"Then tell her that and ask her if she's okay with doing the same thing until you two decide if it's going to be long-term. And you let her handle Brad; if she needs you to step in, she will ask you."

I heard her but I wasn't built to sit back and wait. I took what I wanted.

"D, I'm straight trippin', this ain't even me. I'm coming over to talk about a woman."

She smiled wide. "That's because you like her and she's not chasing you like the others. As she said, you're used to women making you the only one. You don't usually have to ask."

I shook my head. "Chelle saw other people."

Dawn rolled her eyes. "You know good and well you didn't like nothing on Chelle but that big ass. And she wasn't seeing anybody else. I'm sure she was just trying to make you jealous."

She did have a point. I knew Chelle wanted me for more than what I offered. And even if she was seeing someone else, she always put me first whenever I called.

"Dre, she wants you to not see other women because you choose to only see her. And you should want the same thing from her. You choose each other. Do you know why Macon never said anything about the time I spent with you when we dated?"

"I assumed because he knew we had been friends since the fourth grade."

She smiled. "Yes, that's one reason. But the other reason was that he only wanted me if I chose him. Not because he made a demand or had a pissing contest with you. It's always been about the two of us, no one else. Let Tonya choose you because she wants you."

I knew she was right, but my ass didn't have a lot of patience.

"I'll work on it. I guess I better talk to her after work."

"Just enjoy her and it will work out. Don't worry about the outside people. As long as you choose each other, at the end of the day, it will work out."

I stood up. "Alright I've had enough of this kind of talking, I know what to do. I guess I'll go since you didn't offer your boy tacos."

She laughed. "You can stay and eat; Macon will be here soon. He asked if you were staying for dinner."

"How did he know I was here?"

She frowned. "You'll learn how things go in a relationship when you get to that point with Tonya. He's my husband, Dre. We share this home, and he needs to know he's the King here at all times. I don't let my husband come home and there's another man here without him knowing about it, even if it is my best friend from fourth grade. And here's the thing, it's not because he demanded it. I do it because I choose to respect him, and he deserves it. He chooses to do the same for me. When he walks through that door he'll have fresh flowers for me. Not because I asked, but because he chooses to bring me flowers every Friday."

I wiped my face. "It's enough of this talk, you trying to have me out here all tender."

She laughed out loud.

∞ ∞ ∞

After I had dinner with Dawn and Macon, I felt a lot better. I'd watched them interact plenty of times in the past, but this time was different because of Tonya. I could see myself living like them.

I had to admit the shit was impressive. As she said, he came in with flowers and a few groceries. When he sat down to eat, she served him, but he served her too. It was almost like they were competing to see who could do the most for the other.

"You've been quiet this evening, are you alright?" Tonya asked, as she walked into my bedroom from the bathroom.

She'd taken a shower and was walking toward me with the house breasts on the loose, underneath her night clothes.

"I'm good," I said, as she climbed into bed and settled in next to me.

"You want to continue our conversation from earlier today?"

"What's on your mind?" I asked, and pulled her entire body on top of me so that we were face-to-face.

"I feel like you were bothered by what I said."

I nodded. "I was because I'm used to getting what I want. And I was told that I needed to allow you to choose me and not force the little glass-eye dude out."

She laughed. "Two points for my sis, Dawn."

"How do you know I talked to Dawn, and not Rob?"

"Because he's a man and he would never have suggested that. And you did bring me tacos from Dawn."

"Oh, I forgot that part."

"Listen, let's just enjoy what we're doing and see where it leads. You don't need to come around throwing me over your shoulder if you see a man around. And I won't be having any Barbara-Shirley conversations if I see you talking to a woman."

"Barbara-Shirley conversations?"

She nodded. "You know the old song the women used to live by back in the day, *Woman to Woman* by Shirley Brown. I ain't with that, because you'll choose who you want in the end anyway so why do it."

Once I finally recalled the song, I laughed out loud. "You are crazy! But my aunts did have that joint blasting back in the day."

"So did mine! I knew as a kid back then it wasn't right, I just didn't fully understand."

This was the thing I liked about her; she was reasonable and calm with me. She felt good, and not just physically but she felt good mentally. She relaxed my ass like no one had in the past. I understood what she was saying, but she was mine now as far as I was concerned.

"You plotting something?" she asked.

I locked eyes with her. "Yeah, I am."

"Do I even want to know?"

"Naw, Shirley, you'll find out later."

She laughed out loud. "How do you know I ain't Barbara?"

Pulling her shorts down, I said, "Because I would never sneak around with you. We've been on tv, remember?" I kissed her.

"Mmm, you might have more fun with Barbara, plus she didn't pay his bills. That's who I want to be," she said in between kisses.

I flipped us over and pulled her shirt over her head leaving her perfect little body completely exposed. *Damn, she was perfect.*

"In that case, you're my Barbara and my Shirley because I want you in public and private. And you'll never pay a bill with me, Baby. Dre don't get down like that. No more talking, open them legs up so I can taste my brown sugar."

Her eyebrows stretched as she said, "Say less."

Two weeks later we walked into the folks' house. Moms called Tonya and that was all it took. I held off as long as I could, but Moms always got what she wanted.

"Andre, is that you?" she called out.

"Yep! It's me!"

I walked into the kitchen with Tonya behind me.

"Where is she?" Moms asked as soon as I walked in. "What did..."

Tonya came in and stood by my side. "Hi, Mrs. Barbara."

Moms smiled wide and held her arms out. "Hello, Tonya! You call me Mom if you want."

She hugged Tonya, then me.

"Can you chill today? For real?" I asked.

Pop walked into the kitchen smiling. "Hey, Tonya. Good seeing you again." He hugged her and said, "Hey, Son."

"Hi, Mr. Larry, nice seeing you again as well. I want to thank both of you for supporting our store. I brought you some goodies." She held up the signature SHE-iS shopping bag.

Moms clapped her hands together. "Oh, you didn't have to do that. But I'm glad you did! Let me see what's inside."

She rummaged through the bag and smiled.

"Lois added infused olive oils to the inventory. She infused them with some of her best-selling spices. I hope you like them."

"She's going to love them," Pop added. "She stays in that shop. I love it because she's cooking all these fancy meals now."

Tonya nodded. "I will make sure I tell Lois. That was her purpose for opening the shop."

She was the most humble person I'd ever met. Even when she should be taking credit she didn't. I knew the shop idea was all Lois, but Tonya acted as if she was an employee and not part owner. Her sugar section was just as successful as the other stuff, but she always downplayed it and pushed Melody or Lois into the spotlight. Lois because the shop was her idea, and she was the majority owner. Melody because her ass was mean and going through a rough patch.

I tried my best to make sure she got her props, but she didn't care. Another thing that had me into her. And secretly claiming her as mine.

I hadn't seen Glass Eye around, but I made sure she was with me every night. I couldn't sleep without her little ass tucked up under me.

"Dre?"

I shook my head. "I'm sorry, Baby. What's up?"

Tonya touched my chest with her brows wrinkled. "Are you ok?"

"Yeah, I'm fine. I'm going to go in the dining room with Pop." I kissed her on the cheek, and she smiled.

"Tonya and I will bring the food in, you go on," Moms said, as she ushered me out of the kitchen.

Pop was sitting at the head of the dining room table when I walked in.

"I like her, Son. I'm claiming her, that's my daughter!"

I chuckled. "Come on, it ain't been long enough for all that."

"I'm sorry but how old are you? You don't have time to be playing around. You should be all played out by now."

I frowned. "I still got some good years in me."

"I jog with you once a month and I see how much slower you are now. You better settle it on down now, Son. It's time out for dating at this age. And when you find a woman like her." He pointed toward the kitchen. "You lock her down."

"We are still getting to know each other."

Pop threw his hand at me. "Your generation is dumb, you know that?"

I laughed. "My generation likes to enjoy each other. With all the economical freedoms men and women have these days it's too easy to walk away when it gets rough. We have to make sure we get along for the long haul."

"Like I said, y'all are dumb. It doesn't take all that. You meet a woman and if she cooks, cleans, and has her head on right you marry her. End of story."

"You just marry her? Don't worry about what she wants, right?"

"You're the man, you tell her what she wants by showing what you can do. All a man needs to do is pay bills and listen. You do that and your wife is happy. If she's happy you get a clean house, food, and sex. Look how happy your mama is, couldn't knock that smile off her face if you tried."

Moms and Tonya walked in carrying the food, so our conversation ended. We helped them bring in the last bit and then sat down and waited for Pop to bless the food.

Once our plates were filled Moms started right in.

"So how long has it been since you two have been together, seems like forever."

Smiling politely, Tonya answered, "Almost six weeks, not long."

"Oh, honey, at this age you count that in dog years, so it's like a year."

"Tonya, I know you have the shop, and you work at that chemical company out there where you and Andre live. But what do you do there?" Pop asked.

"I'm the head of Human Resources. It's a lot of work but I've been there a long time. It's one of the reasons we aren't open during the week. My days at work don't leave much evening time to run the shop."

"That's lovely, you're a smart woman," Moms added. "Tonya, I meant to ask when we were in the kitchen. Are you still getting your monthly?"

My head swung in her direction and Tonya laughed out loud.

"She will not be answering that question!" I said. "Pop, can you do something with your wife?"

"Alright now, Barbara, leave them alone."

Moms rolled her eyes. "I'm just trying to figure out if I can get a grandbaby. No pressure. If not, that's fine, I was just wondering."

"I told Dre we could get you one by next year, but he's not ready," Tonya said casually, and picked up her glass of wine.

I looked at her and she winked. Two sets of eyes were on me, waiting for me to answer.

"Andre, is this true? You're still denying me a grandbaby after all these years? All of my friends are about to have great grands and I can't have one grandbaby. Larry, I told you we should have had another child!"

Tonya was enjoying her food while I was in the hot seat. "Moms, Tonya is joking. We haven't discussed kids in-depth and like we said, it's been six weeks, so we have time."

I pinched her thigh under the table.

"Stop pinching me," she said loudly.

Pop looked at me and frowned.

"Andre, keep your hands to yourself," Moms scolded.

Pop moved on to another subject and I put my arm around Tonya. I leaned in and whispered, "Plan on limping to the office tomorrow."

The rest of the dinner went well. We couldn't stay long because I promised Rob's younger brother I would stop by his restaurant.

Rodney owned a high-end soul food restaurant named *Solstice*. The restaurant doubled as the location for a pop-up club from time to time. Tonight was his third time having the event and I hadn't been. I had to make an appearance, or I would never hear the end of it.

"We will see you two later, be safe," Moms said, as she let us out of the front door.

"Have a good time at *Solstice*," Pop said.

As soon as the door closed, I picked Tonya up and slung her across my shoulder.

She squealed. "Dre, I have on a dress! My butt is showing."

I smacked her butt and said, "You've been showing it all night, what's the difference? Now what were you saying in the house?"

She laughed and squirmed. "I'm sorry. I won't do it again."

When we made it to my truck, I put her down and said, "You're lucky we have another stop to make."

She smiled wide. "Are you trying to threaten me with a good time? I'm looking forward to limping tomorrow. Bring it, Baby. Just know if I'm limping, your back will be hurting."

"Get your little ass in the truck," I said jokingly.

Once we were in motion I asked, "Baby, you sure you feel like going? I know you have to work in both places tomorrow. I can drop you off at home and then go."

She pulled out a pair of high heel shoes from a bag. "I've been looking forward to this, I'm ready."

I shook my head. "Now I have to massage your feet when we get home? You know those kinds of shoes hurt your feet."

She continued putting them on. "These have a three-hour window for standing and dancing. I'll be fine."

"Why not keep the ones on that don't hurt?"

Holding her foot in my direction, she said, "Because I look good dancing in these shoes. I feel sexy. You'll see. You won't be able to keep your eyes off of me when you see me dancing in these."

I laughed. "The fact that you said that out loud has my mind blown. I thought you ladies kept that kind of stuff in your arsenal and used it for evil."

She shrugged. "Nope, ain't no shame in my game."

She did look good in the shoes. Her short dress was dark orange and looked good next to her brown skin. The shoes wrapped around her ankles. They were purple with orange butterflies on them.

"Whose place is this again?" she asked. "I've eaten there a couple of times, but never met the owner."

"It's Rob's younger brother. I can't believe he's grown with a wife and a restaurant. He was in first grade when Rob and I were in college."

"Y'all old," she said.

I parked and said, "Let's go in here and hit the dance floor, I'll show you who's old. You better hope those three-hour shoes can keep up. Your boy can get loose on the dance floor."

"Keep talking," she said.

Once we were inside, I spotted Rodney right away. He noticed me and walked to meet me. Rodney no longer wore locs like Rob. He was faded up with a sponged 'fro.

"Dre, what's up? I'm glad you came through!"

We slapped hands. Tonya turned to face us and his mouth opened wide. "Tonya!"

"Rodney!" she squealed and hugged him. "Where is Haven?"

Haven was Rodney's wife. I wondered how she knew them.

"She's in the back sitting down, she's pregnant. She's going to be so happy to see you."

"I can't believe it, you own *Solstice*?"

He nodded proudly. "Yep! Hey, you gotta dance with me. Please, you have to."

I interrupted. "Dance?"

Rodney frowned. "Man, you got to know you got the baddest salsa instructor in the city. Haven and I took one of her classes when we first got married. Are you still teaching?"

I watched Tonya as she blushed and shook her head. "I don't have the time anymore. I stopped shortly after you guys took the class. You were pretty good."

"I know, and Haven was terrible. I haven't been salsa dancing since you have to dance with me."

"Of course, I will, but I want to see Haven first."

"Wait, was that you on the news with Dre dancing?"

She smiled and nodded.

"I should have known with those moves. Y'all looked good. I'll go get Haven from the back. You all grab a seat and I'll come find you." He walked away.

"Salsa instructor? What else don't I know?" I asked, as I led us to a small table.

Once we were seated, she said, "I used to teach salsa as a continuing education course at the community college."

"Can you teach me?" I asked with a smirk on my face.

"Nope, your hips are too stiff."

I laughed. "You don't want me to be better than you, do you?"

Damn, Chelle was here. She wouldn't start anything but she would try to throw her ass in my face if she got the chance.

"Are you ok?"

"I'm good, Baby."

Rodney and Haven came to our table.

"Hi, Tonya, it's so good to see you. You see I have this big belly now."

"Congratulations, I'm so happy for you two!" Tonya said.

"Are you going to put my husband out of his misery and dance with him?"

Tonya nodded. "Of course, I told him I would."

She rolled her eyes. "He's so excited. You know I was awful at salsa so he's been wanting to go again. Oh hi, Dre."

Standing I wrapped her up into a hug and said, "About time you noticed me."

"Oh stop it, I haven't seen Tonya in a few years. I'll bring her back in a few minutes."

"Ok," I said as they walked away talking.

Chelle waited until Tonya was gone about five minutes before she made it to our table.

"I see you're still with Preschool," she said as soon as she was in front of me.

"How are you doing, Chelle?" I ignored her statement.

"I'm better than ever, I just came over to say hello."

"Good to hear."

And just as I suspected, she turned to the side and put her ass near my face. I blew out a breath because I wasn't interested.

In the past, I would have said something slick to her and told her I would come through later to stretch her out. But not this time. I was with the woman I was taking home with me.

A flash of orange caught my eye. It was Tonya on the dance floor with Rodney swinging her hips from side to side.

I stood from my seat. Chelle must have assumed I was going to talk to her but my attention was on the orange dress tearing up the dance floor.

Without taking my eyes off Tonya, I said, "Chelle, it was good seeing you. Take care. Excuse me." I stepped around her and her ass and walked to the edge of the dance floor.

There were plenty of couples dancing, but my baby in that orange dress and the three-hour heels moving perfectly to the rhythm of D'Angelo's *Spanish Joint* was hypnotic.

Rodney was doing okay, but it was clear that she was leading this dance. He stepped to the side and twirled her around. She caught my eye and winked the second time around.

And here I was standing on the side like a spellbound groupie. She looked amazing with her brown skin sparkling under the lights as she moved.

"She's good, isn't she?"

It was Haven talking, not that I could tear my eyes away from Tonya to look, but it was her voice.

"Yeah, she's perfect. And she's mine."

"I heard that, Dre!" Haven said and laughed.

That slipped, but I meant it.

Chapter 7 ~ Tonya

$\mathcal{N}$ow that's how you drop the mic on a woman-to-woman conversation without words. I finished my dance with Rodney and strutted off the dance floor to Dre.

I saw that heifer put her big ass in his face. Her ass might be ten times bigger than mine, but I knew once I hit that dance floor in these shoes and short dress, his eyes would be on me.

And like I told him a couple of weeks ago, I didn't do the Barbara-Shirley thing. I'd let him deal with her and choose who he wanted. In this case, I was his obvious choice and not Big Ass.

"Hey," I said with a big smile when I was standing in front of him.

He looked me in the eye without smiling and said, "Baby, I'm so turned on right now I don't know what to do with myself. You were amazing."

My smile faded. "Thank you. That dance was for you."

He briefly closed his eyes and touched his chest. "What are you trying to do to me?"

"Same thing you're trying to do to me," I responded.

Nothing Even Matters by Lauryn Hill featuring D'Angelo began flowing through the speakers while our eyes were locked.

"Will you dance with me?" he asked.

I nodded and stepped on to the dance floor. He wrapped me up tight and we moved to the music. My arms were around his neck and my eyes were still trained on his.

We stayed quiet, moving from side to side, taking in one another. He was mine. I was not giving him back.

"Tonya, I want you. I don't want anyone else."

I nodded and looked away. I was absorbing a lot at the moment.

Using his thumb and index finger, he gently grabbed my chin and turned my face to him. "I'm serious, no one else."

I nodded again because I'd been pining over Dre since I was about fourteen. He was always the guy I didn't think was interested in me and now here I was in his arms. I didn't care if I got hurt in the end, there was no point in living if you didn't take chances.

"I don't want anyone else either," I said. And I meant it; I wanted him.

He smiled a little. "Are you mine now?"

"I'm yours. Are you mine?"

"Without a doubt. You want me to announce it on the mic?"

I giggled. "Nope, because this is between you and me."

"Another Shirley Brown song?"

I nodded, referring to Shirley Brown's song *Between You and Me*, and said, "Yep."

He gently pecked my lips. "You're right because nothing even matters," he sang, mimicking D'Angelo.

We danced to a couple more songs and then took our seats at our table.

Solstice was a sleek restaurant and even better at night as a dance venue. The regular tables and booths had black linens instead of the dining white linens. The tables were candlelit and the house lights were down low. It was nice and I was elated to learn that my former dance students were the owners.

Rodney came by the table to check on us. "You two doing ok? I saw y'all on the dance floor all cozy."

Dre smiled and pulled me closer. "This is my lady right here, we stay cozy."

"That's what's up. It's a good look on both of you. How are y'all enjoying the D'Angelo tribute tonight?"

Dre and I both nodded. Dre responded, "I was wondering why all the music was by him. He has some good music, I'm liking it."

Rodney smiled wide. "I started doing tributes for the old school music to get y'all old heads in here."

Dre laughed. "Man, D'Angelo ain't old school."

"He ain't to you but he is for me. I was probably in kindergarten when he came out. I'll check on y'all later." He walked away.

I laughed. "Baby, we are old."

"Damn, I guess he's right, he did come out in the 90's."

"I have to go to the restroom," I said and stood.

"Ok, you want another drink?"

"Yeah, I'll take another white wine." I walked away throwing my hips from side to side because I knew my man was watching me. I didn't even glance back.

"Hey, Tonya," someone said.

I looked to the side and Daniel was standing with a drink in his hand smiling.

"Hi, Daniel." I smiled wide. He was such a nice man, just not for me.

"How have you been? I've called you a couple of times. I guess you've been busy. I still owe you a makeup date and dinner."

Now, I know he saw me on the dance floor with Dre. The place was good sized but it wasn't overly crowded, no way he missed us.

"Aww, thanks, Daniel. I appreciate it, but you don't have to do that."

"But I want to," he said and grabbed my hand.

I tugged it away and smiled. "Daniel, you're a nice guy but I'm with someone else now."

He nodded and took a sip from his drink. "Can't blame me for trying. I'm going to check back with you in a month or so. Maybe you'll be free. You look nice, by the way."

I internally rolled my eyes and said, "Thanks, I'll be seeing you around. It was good seeing you."

I walked off and went to the ladies' room.

After checking my makeup and hair on the way out, I walked out and Brad was standing near the door.

"Look at your fine ass," he said.

I was not about to play with Brad because he always tried to touch me without warning.

"Hey, Brad, good seeing you." I tried to keep walking but he grabbed my arm.

"You can't give me a minute?"

I pulled my arm away. "No, I can't because I'm here with my man."

That felt good to say.

"I know you aren't talking about the dancing dude, he's with a different woman every night."

"Well, guess what? He's mine tonight." I turned on my heels and walked off before he could respond.

As I approached the table a woman was talking with Dre. He was standing next to her.

"Hey, Baby, I was about to come look for you," he said and I smiled. He held his hand out to me and pulled me into his side.

The woman tried not to frown but she did. She was cute; brown skin, shapely, with long hair.

"Stacy, this is Tonya. Tonya, Stacy."

"Hi, how are you?" I asked.

"I'm fine, nice to meet you. Well, I'll let you get back to your date. Good seeing you, Dre. We miss you in the old neighborhood. The new people don't keep their yard as nice as you did."

Dre laughed. "Nobody can beat me in the yard. It was good seeing you too, take care," he said and she walked away.

We took our seats and he slid my glass of wine to me.

"You finish up that wine, I need some brown sugar before I go to sleep tonight. Plus, I'm at my limit." I wrinkled my nose because I was confused. "I saw The Nerd and Glass Eye. If a third one comes around, you're getting tossed on my shoulder."

I smiled and I laughed. "No, sir, we are two for two, don't play."

He frowned. "Who are you talking about?"

"Just like you saw my two, I saw Big Ass in your face earlier."

"Ohhhh, you saw that?"

"I did, and what about Stacy? She tried to cover but oh I know something went on there."

He put his arm around me. "So, Baby, how is your wine?"

I giggled and kissed him on the cheek.

"Dre?" He turned to look at me. "What did we say on the dance floor?"

"Nothing even matters," he said.

"And you're mine now and I'm yours," I added.

"You're right, Baby. Are you ready to go? I need to get you home."

I was thinking the same thing. Between our interlude on the dance floor and the wine, I was ready to have my man alone. But first, we needed to do one more thing.

"Can we have one more dance before we go?"

"Anything you want," he said.

I chugged the rest of my wine. He led us to the dance floor, and I made a quick stop to the DJ area.

He smiled when the song we danced to in the parking lot kicked in.

"You trying to hurt 'em tonight," he said.

I nodded. "We gotta give the people a little something," I countered.

When We Get By by D'Angelo blasted as we stepped perfectly in true Chicago form. We danced like it was just the two of us and I loved every minute of it.

By the end of the song, we had a small audience watching us. We took a bow the same way we did in the parking lot and made our way to the back area to find Rodney and Haven.

"We saw you two dancing," Haven said, as she walked toward us with her hand on her protruding belly.

"I'm just letting y'all know I recorded you and I'm using it as a promo. Is that cool?" Rodney asked.

"Aye, this is what we do," Dre said. "We make appearances."

I laughed. "Of course, you can use it," I said.

We hugged them and finally got to Dre's truck. My feet were hurting.

Dre handed me a pair of socks as soon as we started driving.

"Thought you had a three-hour window?"

I laughed. "I did! But that didn't include salsa and stepping."

"You have a good time tonight?"

I nodded my head enthusiastically because I had the best time with him. "I love dancing!"

"Why aren't you teaching anymore? You're really good."

I shrugged. "I got busy and now with the shop I don't know where I would find the time."

I wanted this shop to be successful for my sisters. Both of them had been through a lot in the last year. They deserved to have something good in their lives.

"If you ever need help, you know I'm here, right?"

"I do, and I appreciate it. But you have enough going on with work."

Dre was still on his project and working late.

"I can handle work and take care of you, ok?"

I nodded and blushed.

"I meant to tell you that you look nice tonight," he said, and fell out laughing.

"You know that's exactly what he said!" He was referring to Daniel.

"I know, I saw The Nerd salivating over you."

"Aww, but he's a sweet guy, though. He's really nice."

Dre frowned. "There was nothing sweet about the way he was looking at you."

We finally made it back to Dre's and my feet were on fire.

He opened my door and then turned around. "Come on and get on my back, your feet hurt."

I laughed, but I got on his back and wrapped my legs around his waist.

He walked the short distance from inside the garage to the door leading into the mud room.

Once we were inside the kitchen, I asked, "Are you going to put me down?"

"Nope, your feet won't touch the floor until tomorrow morning. I'm going to bathe you and massage your feet."

I grinned and hugged him as I held on, and he moved through the house. "Anything else you plan to do?"

"Some passionate lovin' is taking place tonight. I'm bringing you to tears again."

"I am so mad for crying that one time. Now you won't let me live it down."

"You should be happy your man can make you feel that good. That's rare."

He bent down and sat me on the bathroom counter. I watched as he started the bath water. I loved his infinity tub that filled from the ceiling.

I giggled.

"What's funny?" he asked.

"Thinking about you saying this tub was the reason you bought the house."

"Hell yeah, this is some exclusive shit. I walked in and saw it and had to have it even though I'm usually in the shower. But since my girl loves it, I would say it's money well spent."

I smiled as he removed my socks.

This had been the best evening and it was only getting better.

"Hey, y'all, the last customer is gone. I'm locking up," I yelled to my sisters.

We'd been busy all day and I was happy to finally get the store closed.

There was a knock at the door. I turned to see it was my hair stylist from next door, Nuri. She specialized in natural hair and she kept my coils poppin'.

I unlocked the door. "Girl, what's up?" I asked.

"I know it's late but let me get a bag of that brown sugar."

"Only for you," I said and walked to the shelf to grab a bag. "We have some samples I'm going to put in here too."

"Thanks!"

I rang her up and walked her to the door as Dre pulled up.

I hugged Nuri and yelled out to Dre, "Let me grab my stuff and I'll be right out."

I went to the back with Mel and Lois.

"Dre is here. I'll see y'all at eight," I said, as I grabbed my phone and purse.

"I guess you don't drive anymore," Mel said.

"Shut up!" Lois quipped.

Mel had been on one all day, and I was tired of hearing her mouth. I wouldn't tell her that he was also going to be at our family meeting tonight.

She'd find out soon enough. I loved my sister and I empathized with her situation. I knew it was bad, so I never talked to her about how happy I was with Dre. I didn't want to make her feel worse so I kept quiet.

I hugged Lois. "See you in a minute." I then whispered, "Thank you for taking up for me."

"She doesn't scare me," she whispered back, and I giggled.

"I know y'all talking about me! I'm right here."

I walked to Mel and hugged her tightly. "Love you, Sis. Even when you're in bitch mode."

I turned and left the office.

When I made it outside to Dre's truck, he asked, "What did she say this time?"

"It's nothing," I said, and put my seatbelt on.

"It is something when you're smiling one minute and then you don't kiss me the next."

"I'm sorry." I leaned over and kissed him a couple of times. Dre and I always kissed when we saw each other, and whenever one of us left the other.

"That's better, now tell me what she said."

"I feel torn. I can't tell you about her because I don't want you to hate her. And I can't tell her about you because she hates you."

He grabbed my hand. "I'm never going to hate her because she's your sister, ok?"

I nodded. I was tired. My main job was going through a transition that required a few extra hours in the week. And the spice shop was going strong. We found a packer that would be starting our production next week. No more bottling and packaging products. I would only use the commercial kitchen for small-batch products moving forward.

Working with my sisters was supposed to be fun but it wasn't, because Melody was miserable most of the time. Every once in a while she would laugh with us but most often she snapped at me.

Last Friday...
"What do you all think of the stations? I moved some stuff around."
"It looks good, Lo! I love the stations," I said.

Lois changed some shelves around in the shop during the week while we were closed.

The shop was still broken up into sections based on the product type. She added sample stations for each of us, instead of having one area in the middle. The stations were counter-height tables with tops made from epoxy. Each tabletop represented each of our specialties. My tabletop was black epoxy with sand and copper glitter splattered across the top, which represented my now famous brown sugar. Melody's tabletop was black epoxy with a waterfall of gold running through the middle, representing honey. Lois' table was like mine, but the sand and glitter were rust-colored, representing her spices.

"I'm glad you like them!" she said proudly. "Mel, do you like yours?"

"They are all beautiful, Lois!" Melody said.

I took a few pictures and sent them to Dre.

Me: Look at my new sample station!

Dre Bae: That's dope, it looks like the real Brown's sugar

I snickered because he personalized my brown sugar to his last name.

Me: That would be Tonya's sugar ;)

Dre Bae: And who does Tonya's sugar belong to?

Me: Me!

Dre Bae: Who else?

I could not stop the big smile on my face.

Me: ???

Dre Bae: Did you say you wanted some of those mini croissants?

He did not play fair; he knew I loved those things.

Me: I'm Brown's Sugar!

Dre Bae: FACTS!

"It doesn't take all that kee-keeing and smiling to send a text message," Melody said.

"If you're happy and you know it." I clapped my hands twice.

Lois snickered and clapped her hands twice too.

"When he's out with one of his other women let's see if you're clapping then. I'm telling you, I know Andre's type. They chase you and then toss you to the side when they find something else to chase. I'm saying something to him the next time I see him."

"*You aren't saying anything to him! You're going to mind your business!*" I yelled.

She smirked. "*Ohhhh, so your nose is so wide open he has you breaking sister code? I can't say anything to him? But you and Lois were both in my husband's face.*"

"*You're the one violating code,*" I said. "*I only said something to that piece of shit because you were in bed crying! I'm walking around smiling and you think you're steppin' to my man? Naw, Sis, we are not doing that.*"

"*Preach!*" Lois shouted.

"*Whatever! I'm going to the back!*" she said, and walked off.

We pulled up to my garage at my condo and Dre finally said, "Are you sure you want me to go to the family meeting? You can tell me about the vacation when you get home."

I shook my head. "Of course, you're coming, you're going on the family trip. I'm not worried about Melody."

"But you are worried about it. You've been staring out the window since I picked you up. If it's going to have you upset then I'll chill here until you get back."

I got out of the truck, and he followed behind me. Maybe he was right, I didn't feel like feeling all of the tension in the house with her tonight.

We rode the elevator and walked the hall in silence.

Once we were inside I walked up the steps and he stood by the door.

Looking over my shoulder, I asked, "Why are you standing there?"

He moved to the steps. "Come down here please."

I walked down and stood in front of him.

"This is not what you and I do," he said. "I understand you and Melody are beefing or whatever sisters do, but you're allowing her in our space. You even got out of the truck; since when do you open doors around me?"

I lowered my head. "She's a pain in the ass right now. And I hate that she doesn't see you the way I do."

"I get that and trust me if I had a sister or brother that didn't like you that shit would probably bother me too. She'll come around, because I'm not going anywhere, ok?"

I put my arms around his neck and pecked his lips. "I'm sorry."

"Ain't no problem. You want me to drop you off or do you want to drive yourself?"

"You can drive us," I said proudly and pecked his lips again.

"Baby, look, I'm trying to have some lazy sex tonight, get some sleep, and wake up with a full erection with your naked ass on top of me. If me going over there is going to stop any of that, I'm not trying to go."

I stared at him with a smirk.

"I'm serious. I've been at work six days in a row this week. I'm tired and I need you happy; not the dazed-looking you after being around Melody."

"You're right, but I'll be fine. Please come with me, unless you're too tired. Either way, I promise you some lazy sex tonight, ok?"

He smiled. "Okay, I'll go. But go upstairs and strip. I'm going to need something to get my mind right before we go."

My eyes widened. "Ohh, good thinking, I do need to knock the edge off. Let's hit the armless chair in my room and save the bed for tonight."

I turned and began taking my clothes off as I walked up the steps.

∞ ∞ ∞

"We don't have enough chairs; this one is for Mel." I looked around the room. "I'll grab a dining room chair."

"Come sit on Big Daddy's lap," Dre said. I shrugged and giggled before plopping down on his lap like a little kid.

I saw a few of them eyeing each other and smiling, specifically, Tori and Dawn, then Mom and Brock.

We were all crammed into Dawn and Macon's family room about to have our family reunion and family vacation meeting. Usually, this would take place at Mom and Brock's house, but they were getting their kitchen remodeled.

Everyone was present except Melody. She was running a few minutes late according to Lois.

"I guess you two are dancing around the city for coins now?" my brother, Donald, teased. He was sitting to the right of Dre and me.

"You know me," I said and shimmied my shoulders.

Aside from my sisters, Donald and I were the closest among the boys. When my nephew, Elijah, was little, I would stay with Donald the entire time he was in town to help. Elijah and his mother lived in the DC area and she and D had joint custody. Elijah was my baby and D and I grew close during that time.

I loved all three of my brothers, but when I needed to talk to one of them, he was my go-to. Now that he was married to Tori, I didn't bother him with the drop-ins and overnight visits we used to do back in the day.

"How did we look?" Dre asked.

"You are always looking for compliments," Tori teased from the other side of Donald.

Dawn and Macon were sitting next to them. Mom and Brock were sitting in a pair of chairs while Lois sat in a chair next to Dre and me.

"How far away is Mel?" Mom asked.

"She's a few minutes away," Lois answered.

"Can you all get the new video of Andre and Tonya dancing on the tv?"

Rodney and Haven did a social media ad to boost interest in the pop-up club. They used the video of Dre and me dancing at *Solstice* last month in the ad.

"I got it!" Dawn announced and fired up the tv. "I have the one from the news too."

"Play both of them," Brock said.

Our video from the news came on first, followed by the second one. We looked good in that one because we were dressed up.

"Those shoes though," Dre whispered in my ear.

"I told you," I said proudly.

"Look at my baby!" Mama yelled. "Your father would have been thrilled to see you doing what he loved to do."

I caught Mama's eyes and nodded slowly, holding my hand to my chest.

Our father passed away in a car accident when I was in high school. Daddy and Mama used to go out dancing all the time. I danced with him the most, he was the one who taught me to Step. Daddy was originally from Chicago and taught all of us.

After he passed, Macon would dance in the living room with Mama to cheer her up.

"You okay, Baby?"

I nodded. I was okay but the thought never crossed my mind until now. Dre was so much like my father. The same gregarious, over-the-top personality who didn't mind hitting the dance floor at any time. Daddy was always the life of the party. And Mama would always sit on his lap.

I looked at Mama again and she nodded. She was thinking the same thing I was thinking.

Macon went to the door while the video was playing and came back with Melody.

"Hey, everybody," she said and glanced at the tv while the video was ending. "Glad I missed all of that."

No one said anything about her comment, we all kept talking about the video.

"Y'all are too cute!" Tori said.

"Aren't they?" Dawn added. "Macon, we have to go there the next time they have it."

"Most definitely," he said.

"We should go when they go," Tori said to Donald.

"Let's make it a party, we are all going. Dre and Tonya, let us know about the next one and we will go," Donald said.

"That's going to be fun!" I added.

"No one asked us. I can Step better than all of you," Mama said. I looked at her and she said, "Well maybe not Tonya but I can take Tori and Dawn."

We all laughed.

"Lady B, you come with us," Tori said.

"We'll be there," Brock added. "I can't dance as good as your mama, but I can keep up with her."

"I want to go too," Lois said. "Dawn, I need to borrow my brother on a few songs."

"You got it, Sis," Dawn quipped.

"Y'all are passing me around like a piece of meat," Macon said, and we all laughed.

I glanced at Melody and her face was in a scowl. I hated this and I wasn't used to everyone not participating. I'd lived in the same city with my sister my entire life, except for our college days, and I'd never seen her this miserable. Instead of asking her if she was okay, I decided to do what everyone else was doing and ignore her mean ass.

"Can we get to why we are stuffed in here like sardines?" Melody asked.

Donald glanced at me, and I rolled my eyes.

"Okay," Brock said. "Our family is hosting the reunion this year and I want to add on something at you girls' shop. Maybe the meet and greet, I don't know. But it needs to be big because I want to show my girls off. Get those balloons and stuff you all did for the grand opening."

"I have an idea," Tori said. "Since my shop is next door, we can have both places open. We can decorate the vestibule at my place and then combine the parking lots. We can have food trucks and a DJ outside and inside."

Brock clapped his hands and pointed at Tori. "Sho' you right! I like it! My daughters are smart! Can you girls get together and organize it? And there won't be any free shopping for spices. Y'all know how Mervis is about not paying for stuff."

Uncle Mervis and Brock were always in competition. But Uncle was cheap.

We all laughed and agreed to oversee the meet and greet.

"Everything else for the reunion will be the same unless you can figure out some more things to add. The big thing I wanted to talk about is the family cruise."

Mama cut in with, "And before you ask, this is mandatory. I won't be around forever, and I want all my kids and grands to take a cruise with me while I'm still able to walk."

We looked around at each other because she was using her wild card. No one would miss it after she said all of that.

Brock continued. "We are getting dates together so let me know if there are days you can't make it. It won't be but a few days because we know some of the grands are in school. The ones that work can't take off like that so it will be more of an extended weekend. So get your calendars out and let me know by next week." He paused and asked Mama, "Did you talk to Calvin and Janae, already?"

Calvin and Janae lived next door to Mama and Brock. They adopted them as extra kids. Janae was also best friends with Tori and Dawn.

"They know, they are trying to decide if they should leave the baby or bring him. I told them I didn't care either way."

"Is this a family trip? Or a family, friends, neighbors, and Dawn's entourage trip?" Melody asked.

The room went silent, and everyone stared at Melody.

"Mel, you are taking it too far," Macon warned.

"Oh sorry, we don't want to upset the new queen of the family," she said sarcastically. She picked up her purse and phone.

"What's that supposed to mean?" Dawn asked.

"Melody, I won't have this with you today!" Mama said.

All eyes were on Melody as she stood. "And what are you looking at!" she yelled at Dre.

I jumped off his lap. "You leave him out of this!" I yelled.

"Not surprised you're taking up for him, you've been in love with him since ninth grade! I'm gone!" She moved to walk to the door. "All I was saying was this was supposed to be a family meeting and we got extra people in here that ain't family." She looked at Dre. "And now we're bringing neighbors too. Or like I said, Dawn's entourage! And why are we even having the meeting here?"

"Because she's my wife, Mel!" Macon yelled.

Melody put her hands up and turned around. She walked out the front door and slammed it behind her.

Dawn hopped up from the sofa and followed behind her.

Brock stood and stopped Macon from following Dawn. "This is long overdue, let them get what they need to say off their chest. Dawn can handle herself, and Melody."

"That's my wife!" Macon yelled.

Calmly, Brock replied, "I know she is, but Mel is your sister. You don't want to get in the middle, you won't win. Let them handle it."

"I'm going out there!" I said.

"You go ahead, Tonya," Brock ordered.

Macon paced around as I slipped out and closed the door behind me.

They were standing in the driveway.

"I've been ignoring your comments for the last year because of your situation! But you will not come in my house and talk shit to me, or about me!"

Melody's face was in a scowl as she yelled, "I finally get my baby brother back after twenty years of being in the Navy and here your wide hip ass comes taking him away again! Then your little minions, Tori and Janae, take my other brother and even the next-door neighbor! Now your little former boyfriend, boy-toy, bestie, or whatever you call him is with my sister. Who's next? You got an uncle or cousin for Lois waiting around!"

Now, Melody didn't have to say that, and it was uncalled for, and I was going to stop her. I started to speak but Dawn came right back.

"Basically, you're jealous because nobody wants you! Not even your husband!"

I covered my mouth.

Melody looked at me. I was standing on the porch. "You see how she is? But y'all have let her and her whole crew infiltrate our family. Got my baby brother so far up your ass he can't think straight!"

"First of all, MY husband is up my ass because he's comfortable there. Second, I have done nothing but support and love this family and you; including your spice shop. Third, you know nothing went on between Dre and me! Don't do that to Tonya. Let her and Dre be happy together. And lastly, don't you ever slam shit in my house again, or that's your ass! Now, are we finished, or are we done?"

Melody's eyes were watery but her stubborn behind refused to drop a tear. She didn't say anything, so Dawn walked up the driveway.

She stopped and hugged me. "Sis, I'm sorry. I know she's your sister, but she can't come for me in my house." I nodded because she was right. "And don't you listen to anything she says about Dre. He's crazy about you. I've never seen him like this."

I smiled. "Thanks for saying that. Let me check on her. Send Lois out."

She nodded and went into the house.

Melody was standing at the edge of the driveway shivering. She'd done that since we were kids when she was mad.

I walked to the edge of the driveway and wrapped my pinky finger around hers. I didn't say anything or look at her. A few minutes later, Lois came outside and got into position. She stood on the opposite side of Melody and took the pinky finger of her other hand.

This was our sister bond, whoever was hurting was in the middle because she needed both of her sisters. Mama did it with her sisters and she taught us how to support each other when we were kids. That was the only reason she hadn't been out here, because there was no way she hadn't looked out the window. If she didn't see us in formation, that meant tempers were still flaring.

Lois started with, "Mel, you're going to need to talk to somebody, smoke a joint, or have an edible before you come around. You can't be blowing up the spot like that."

"And you owe Dawn an apology. You've been picking at her for the longest. She's been nothing but nice to you. Macon is pissed, you should talk to him too," I said.

"Can you all be quiet! Damn! Stop telling me what I need to do!"

Lois and I looked at each other and did as she asked.

"I'm not coming to the shop tomorrow. My honey is stocked. Can you all cover for me?"

"Sure, Mel. But why don't you just come back in and squash all of this?" I asked.

She kissed both of us and wiped her tears away. "I love both of you, but I need to go."

She walked to her car and slowly drove away without looking at us.

"What are we going to do with her?" Lois asked.

"I don't know, but she better leave Dre alone. He didn't even want to come because of her."

I hated this! I felt bad for my sister and at the same time I had to protect Dre.

Chapter 8 ~ Dre

Melody showed her ass last night at the family meeting. I kind of felt sorry for her because I had been around her a lot the last few years and she didn't always act like this.

She used to be cool, but after that husband tripped, she hadn't been right, according to Tonya.

My baby was going through it too. She felt like she was caught in the middle. She wasn't because I didn't have a problem ignoring Melody. The meaner she was to me, the nicer I was to her. I could do this shit all day long, I was built for it. Did it daily at work.

Tonya was jogging alongside me around the six-mile trail in Forest Park. I knew she wanted to run faster because it's what she did to clear her mind. I was a jogger, not a runner. But I couldn't let her come to this park alone. It was early and too many knuckleheads were around so I came with her.

She stopped and sat on a bench.

"Thanks for coming with me, I know you were tired."

I leaned over with my hands on my knees trying to catch my breath. "I'm fine," I finally said.

"You sound like you're about to lose a lung, sit down."

I sat on the bench next to her. We had about two miles left. I wasn't sure I could make it, I was out of steam from going four miles without a break.

"I'm glad you stopped."

"I'm sorry, we could have taken a break earlier," she said.

I shook my head. "You needed to clear your head. Do you want to talk about the family meeting?"

After we got home last night, she didn't want to talk about Melody. Instead, she cooked dinner and catered to me the whole night. I enjoyed every second of it, but I didn't want her trying to compensate for her sister's rude ass.

"I'm sorry," she said. "It's embarrassing. She's nuts! No one can say anything to her without her going off or crying. She needs to save that energy for her ex, but she gives him sex instead." She covered her mouth.

"Daaaamn! Straight up?"

"Dre, you cannot say anything. I know she doesn't want anyone to know."

I frowned. "Baby, come on. What you and I talk about is between us."

"You can't tell Dawn either, she'll tell Macon."

That irritated me. "Why would I tell Dawn?"

"You tell her everything."

"I used to tell her everything before she was married to Big Baby. Do you trust me, Tonya?"

"Yes, I do."

"Good, then know what we do and talk about is between us, no one else."

She nodded.

Something that Melody mentioned had been on my mind since last night, so I asked, "Is it true you've been liking me since high school?"

She looked to the sky. "I should kick Melody's ass for saying that, it was so embarrassing."

"So is it true?"

"Yeah," she finally said.

I couldn't hold back my smile. "You been feeling your boy the whole time?"

"I cannot with you! Do not start! I'll run off and leave you!"

I laughed and pushed her leg. "Don't be like that, I like that you've been wanting me for almost thirty years. Did you put hearts around my picture in your yearbook?" She cut her eyes at me and I laughed. "You did, didn't you?"

"Dre, I swear I will take off running," she said jokingly.

"I got the keys, you ain't going too far. I'm guessing when I walked up to you at the comedy show you were like a groupie?"

She tried to get up and I put both of my arms around her.

"Let me go!" she said while laughing.

"You gotta give me this one, Baby. That was the best thing Melody said last night."

She finally stopped squirming and said, "I do owe you for last night, especially after you said you didn't want to go."

"Tonya, look at me." She turned to face me without smiling. "You don't owe me anything. Melody hates me; so what. She'll come around. I have thick skin, it doesn't bother me."

She nodded. "I know you say that, but it has to get on your nerves."

"Yeah, it does. But when you look the way I do, it comes with the territory. People are always hating on me."

"I can't with you," she said and laughed.

I wanted her to know it didn't matter what happened. I wasn't going anywhere.

"Can I tell you something?" I asked.

"Okay."

"I was checking you out at Brock's retirement party. That was the first time I met you."

"I know because you didn't notice me in high school," she said and rolled her eyes.

"You were a freshman my senior year, I didn't know any underclassmen. At Brock's retirement party, you were wearing a tight black jumpsuit. And a pair of black shoes with a tall gold heel. Your hair was longer back then. It was pinned up at the top of your head. You had on this lipstick that made your lips look larger, it was two shades of pink."

Her mouth opened wide. "That was like three or four years ago. Why didn't you say anything?"

I shook my head. "I wasn't any good for you back then. I was confused and thought I was in love with Dawn. But I did notice you."

"I was there with my ex anyway."

"I know, I remember thinking you were too fine to be with him."

She smiled. "I really was."

"See, I was checking you out too. I mean, it wasn't thirty years though."

She laughed and pushed my arm. "Be quiet."

"It wasn't our time," I said honestly. "But now, it's all about us, no matter who's against us. Melody included, ok?"

She nodded and kissed me. "You're right."

She pulled her phone out and answered, "What's up, Lo?"

She was silent for a moment.

"Ok, I'll be there a little before noon. Can you call Dawn and Tori? Ok, bye."

She blew out a long breath and then looked at me.

"What's wrong?" I asked.

"A bus load of the Kinloch ladies are visiting the shop today at one, and Melody didn't tell us. And she's not coming in today. Lois has been calling her and she isn't answering the phone. She's not home either."

"I'll help, what do you need me to do?"

"It's your day off, you stay home and relax."

I shook my head because she needed my help today. "Let's head back to the truck. We will go home and change then head to the shop. I'm going with you, end of discussion."

I stood and held my hand out to help her up. "Okay," she said. "I appreciate it. Maybe you could do the cash register because the ladies will have a lot of questions about the products."

"Whatever you need me to do. You want me to call my mother? She knows most of the Kinloch ladies."

Her face lit up. "Yes! My mom is coming with Lois, the two of them can do the samples."

I chuckled. "If you give her one of those SHE iS shirts she will probably be in there every weekend working."

She smiled and took my hand as we started walking on the trail. I was so glad she didn't want to run the last two miles back.

"Thought I would give you a break," she said.

"I appreciate it."

"Tell me what happened in the house while we were outside yesterday."

Tonya told me about the big blow-up between Melody and Dawn on the way home but we didn't get around to what went on in the house.

Last Night...

Melody was trippin' tonight. Tonya ran out behind her and Dawn while Macon walked back and forth in the foyer. He was mad.

"Macon, come sit down," Lady B said.

"Naw, Mama, Melody doesn't get to talk to my wife like that for no reason! You know how many nights she was at that shop stocking shelves and decorating with them?"

"I know, I know. Your sister is hurting," she replied. "I'll talk to her."

"Yeah, I get that, but this is too much!"

Big Baby was really mad. It wasn't right, but I'd never seen him this mad.

"Alright, Lois, get to talking," Lady B said. "I know your sister is upset but this is a lot from her."

"She still talks to him," Lois said.

Everyone's heads swung to Lois.

"What!" Lady B yelled. "Since when!"

"I'm not in her business like that."

"Lois, you stay in everybody's business, what's so different now?"

"That's all I know."

Brock cut in with, "It's more to the story than her talking to him. Andre, are you okay?"

I nodded. "I'm all good. You know nothing rattles my cage."

"Macon, come have a seat. I want to talk to all of you," Brock said.

"Melody is the one that needs a talk," Lois quipped.

Macon sat on the edge of the couch next to Donald and Tori.

"Melody isn't ready to listen so no need in talking to her, I'll let your mama deal with her. But I want the rest of you, Macon and Donald, to listen up."

"What did we do?" Donald asked.

"It's not what you did, it's how I expect you to proceed. This family was not put together by blood, we bonded by love and respect. Macon is just as much my son as the two that came from my loins. And from what I suspect, I'm going to have another son soon. Isn't that right, Andre?"

Everyone looked at me but I didn't say anything.

Brock continued. "I'm saying that to say, everyone needs to support Tonya and Andre. I've never seen that girl this smitten. The past is the past and that's where we are going to leave it unless you want me to start bringing up what you all have done.

Moving forward, Andre, my boys here are going to invite you when we men get together. Isn't that right?"

He looked to Donald, then Macon.

"I mean that's cool," Macon said.

"Fine with me," Donald added.

I didn't know if that was good or bad. I knew they all hung out on a regular basis because Dawn mentioned it in the past.

"Now that we have that settled. Macon, you take it easy on your sister when you do talk to her. And when those girls are arguing, you men stay out of it. I don't care if it is your wife. That's a fight you don't need. They will make up, they always do."

"Maybe you can counsel her, Macon," Lady B added. Macon worked as a therapist or counselor for the VA hospital.

"Ma, I can't counsel her, I do grief counseling, for loss."

"She's lost her mind," Lady B countered.

Everyone stared at her and then laughed.

"I know that's right!" Lois said.

Dawn walked in the door and Macon went to her immediately.

"Lois, Tonya wants you outside," Dawn said.

"That bad?" Lois asked, and Dawn nodded.

We watched and waited for her to tell us what happened. Instead, she and Macon went upstairs while the rest of us waited to see who would come in next. Lady B went to the window and watched them.

Tonya smiled. "You get to hang out with the fellas?"

I nodded. "I guess I do, since you're all smitten with your boy, according to Brock. And you've been feeling me since freshman year."

She laughed. "My family talks too much."

"My mother asked about your cycle and told you to call her Mom. I think we are even."

"True!"

We finished our walk and went home to prepare for the day at the shop.

There were a lot of people in the shop today. The bus load of Kinloch ladies were all over the place sampling and asking questions.

I was doubling as a cashier and stocker with Macon, Brock, and Donald.

Tonya, Lois, Dawn, and Tori were helping the ladies shop and answer questions, while Lady B and my mom worked the sample stations.

Moms was in heaven working in here. Tonya gave her one of the SHE iS shirts with their logo to wear. Their logo was dope, it was a circle with images of three women with big hair in the center. Their hair color and lip color matched their specialty. The bottom portion of the logo spelled out the meaning of the acronym and shop name SHE iS; Sugar, Honey, and Everything Spice.

"Hello, there," a lady said when she approached the counter. "I'm ready to check out. Your mother told me you could help."

"Yes, Ma'am, let me take your things," I said with a smile.

"You're handsome, are you single? I have a daughter."

Macon was next to me. He turned to face me.

"I'm sure your daughter is beautiful, just like you." She blushed. "But I have a girlfriend."

She turned to Macon. "What about you? You're handsome, too."

Macon held his chest. "Aw, that hurts. You come to me after him?"

She smiled wide. "I couldn't choose! I'm sorry! I haven't been around this many good-looking men in years. I saw another one around here too with real pretty eyes. She's not picky she will like any one of you."

Macon chuckled and held up his left hand. "I'm married."

"Oh shoot, what about Pretty Eyes?"

Macon shook his head. "That's my brother, Donald, he's married too."

"Estelle! Leave those boys alone!" one of the other ladies yelled from behind her. "You're holding up the line!"

After the lines went down, Macon and I went to the back to restock a few items.

"So umm, we are getting together to help Brock test out some new stuff on the grill for the reunion. You know your way around a pit?" Macon asked.

I assumed this was him asking me to hang out with them. Although, I was pretty sure they would iron me out a bit when Brock wasn't around. I did it to him when he dated Dawn.

"Yep," I answered.

"Gas or charcoal?"

I stopped moving and stared at him. "I'm from the Lou, what other way do you que?"

He chuckled. "I'm just asking. Some people don't like to get dirty with the charcoal."

"Come on, man, I que, grill, smoke, and whatever else you can do with food and an open flame over charcoal."

"Alright, I hear you. Probably next weekend, I'll let you know."

"Cool."

He left the stock room and I gathered my boxes to take out. It was hard to believe I was about to start hanging out with my former nemesis. Big Baby was cool, but I never thought we would get to the point where I hung out with him, without Dawn.

Tonya and I were the last two in the shop after closing. It was a long day and I was tired. This family stuck together, and everyone was on deck helping. To my knowledge, no one said anything about Melody being MIA for the day.

I stared out the window onto the busy street while I waited for Tonya to finish up in the back. Music with drums and horns I didn't recognize started playing loudly in the shop and the lights dimmed. It was still light outside so it wasn't completely dark.

Turning around, I watched as Tonya danced from side to side with one hand on her stomach and the other holding the shop microphone. She belted out the words along with the familiar voice of Shirley Brown, singing *So Glad to Have You* as she moved toward me performing like she was on stage.

I smiled wide and shook my head as she danced around me singing about how glad she was to have me. I laughed at the part about her being a horny hen.

She took my hand and I danced with her as she continued singing to me. She had a nice voice, I was impressed.

When the song ended we stopped dancing and I leaned down to kiss her.

"You're sticking beside me?" I asked smiling.

"You mine now."

"I better be," I said. "You're Shirley today? I thought you preferred to be Barbara?"

She laughed. "I know how Shirley feels now, I might check somebody over you."

"Oh, you're knocking people off the board now?"

"Damn right! I'm the Queen and nobody is messing with my King."

"Baby, your King is always safe."

She smiled. "Seriously, I appreciate you helping today, and everything you do for me."

"I got you, whatever you need. You might have to hire my mom, though."

Her eyes widened. "Your mother is a beast. Did you see how she was explaining the products to the people?"

"Yeah, I saw her, it's like she created them herself."

Our attention went to the door as Melody walked in with her ex-husband. She stopped when she saw us.

"Oh, hey, I didn't know anyone was here."

My truck was parked next door at the barber shop so it did look as if no one was here.

Tonya unwrapped herself from me and placed a hand on her hip.

"I know you didn't bring his limp-dick ass in here! After you didn't tell us about the Kinloch ladies or answer your phone!"

Melody covered her mouth. I looked to the side and wiped my face because I felt bad for dude.

"All the mean stuff you say? You're clutching your pearls?" Tonya yelled.

"Tonya, I'm sorry. I forgot about the Kinloch ladies. I just listened to my messages from Lois."

She didn't have any of the steam from last night. She seemed to be on the verge of tears.

"You forgot because you're too busy being mean to everybody except the person standing next to you! The one that fucked you over in the first place!"

Damn, this was uncomfortable as hell. I guess he thought the same thing. He whispered something to Melody and walked toward the door.

"Yeah, get on outta here! And you can go run behind him! I can't believe you, Melody! Do you know Mama and Brock had to help today because we weren't prepared? Even Dre's mother was here! And you're out with him! How much more does he need to do before you leave him alone!"

Melody dropped a few tears. Now I felt sorry for her. I put my arm around Tonya.

"Baby, calm down."

"Naw, she doesn't get sympathy because she cries! This whole business was supposed to be fun! I did this for you and Lois! And you're out with him while we slave! I'm done! You lock up! If you can remember to do it!"

She grabbed her purse and phone and walked toward the door.

I followed behind her. I stopped and put my hand on Melody's shoulder.

"I'm sorry," I said.

She nodded and dropped a few more tears.

By the time we were inside the truck, Tonya was fuming.

"Can you believe she's with him! I assumed she was off alone or whatever! But she was with him!"

I recalled my conversation with Brock about not getting in the middle of the ladies. I didn't say anything.

"And she has the nerve to not like you! Do you know he wanted alimony from her?"

"What?" I frowned. I didn't know he was weak like that.

"Yeah, that's right. He got mad because she filed for divorce for infidelity. He didn't want it on record as the cause and said he would make her pay alimony if she didn't amend it. He didn't want the kids to know he cheated."

"She pays him alimony now?"

She shook her head. "No, she doesn't. It's only because Dale threatened to hack into his computer system on his job and ruin him. She doesn't know that, she thinks he changed his mind about the alimony."

Her brother, Dale, had an IT company that was supposed to prevent hackers from infiltrating systems. I guess if he knew how to stop it, he knew how to do the opposite.

I started the truck and drove to the spice shop parking lot. I pulled in a few spots over from the ex. He was still inside his car.

"Why are you parking over here, let's go home."

"Baby, go back in and talk to her."

She squinted. "You feel sorry for her after all she's said about you?"

I shook my head and took her hand. "I'm thinking about you, too. We've had a good day and I know how you get when you're mad at her. I don't want the rest of our day uncomfortable because of this argument. Go on, go back in and do whatever sisters do."

"Umm, ok Brock Junior." She smirked and slowly got out.

"Don't say that again, that would make me your brother."

Her eyes widened and she closed the door.

On the way in she kicked dude's tire and went inside.

I shook my head. "These damn sisters ride hard for each other."

"Thanks for helping the sisters at the store last weekend," Donald said.

"No problem, whatever she needs I got her."

I was sitting on the deck at Brock's with Donald and Macon. We were supposed to be on the grill, but Brock wasn't home and Calvin, the next-door neighbor, wasn't here either.

"Whatever she needs?" Macon questioned.

I was wondering when the work-over session was coming. Guess it would be today.

"If I can give it to her, then yes," I answered.

"I've been listening to the women talk and from what they say you've never been in a real relationship," Macon said.

Donald cut in with, "And you rotate the women around like underwear. I've never seen you with the same woman."

"Until now," I countered. I sat back in my chair and waited for them to finish.

"Yeah, we see you with our sister for now. But how long is that going to last? How do you turn it off and date one woman after a lifetime of rotating?" Donald asked.

I took a swig from my beer. "It has been easy since the right woman came my way."

They looked at me and didn't speak. I needed to plead my case a little better. I had one sister that hated me, I didn't want to add two brothers. Tonya and I were good but their family was too close for me to have enemies. Besides, I saw how they treated Dale's ex-wife. I had no idea how she lasted in this family for twenty years and no one liked her.

"Real talk, fellas?" They looked at each other then me. "I'm forty-seven and I've never even thought about settling down until..."

Macon cut me off with, "You decided you wanted my wife."

Damn, I guess he hadn't let that go.

"Man, come on. You know Dawn is my girl. Has been since we were ten. Shit, you're married to her. Think about someone else coming in and taking her away."

He frowned. "Ain't happening, period."

"I admit I didn't handle it like I should have but at the time...look, I'm not going down that road again. You know the story and it's over. What I have with Tonya is real. Never thought it would happen to me but she's the only woman I want. She's all I think about."

Brock walked out on the deck. "Hey, boys! You all are early. We didn't plan to get started until a little later."

I looked at Macon and then Donald. I didn't say anything because I knew what they were doing.

Brock patted my shoulder. "I hope you two weren't trying to haze Andre."

"Pop, we are too old for that," Donald said.

"Exactly," Macon added.

Brock looked at me and I shook my head. "We are just choppin' it up."

"Good, because no one needs to point fingers! Let us not forget every woman has a family, including the ones you didn't quite treat right."

"He's not talking to me," Macon said.

Donald wiped his face.

"Macon, you haven't always been married," Brock added. "I'm talking to everyone, including myself."

"I knew I would find you all back here!"

Everyone turned to the voice of a dude I didn't recognize climbing the deck steps.

"Rio?" Donald said and looked to Macon and then to Brock.

"What's up? It's been a while," he said, once he was standing near us.

Everyone stood and slapped hands with him.

"How's it going? Good seeing you again. Excuse me for a minute," Brock said and went inside.

"Andre," I said and shook his hand.

"Rio, good to meet you, Andre."

Macon and Donald kept looking at each other, but neither of them would look my way.

Rio took a seat across the table from me.

"What brings you to St. Louis? I thought you were out of the country," Donald said.

"I was in New Zealand, but I'm here for now. Business has me all over. I came to see my mother. I need to get her moved into something a bit more manageable."

Macon nodded. "So you're here for a few weeks, days, what?"

Rio smiled wide. "I'm hoping if things go my way, I might stay and only travel when needed."

Donald and Macon looked at each other again.

A text came through on my phone. I smiled at the name Tonya programmed in my phone for herself.

B's Suga: How is it going with the brothers?

Me: I can handle them ;)

Rio kept talking. "I was hoping one of you could give me a little insight on things before I make my move."

"Yeah, man, we will get up with you later," Donald said, pushing his chair back.

"We are about to get on this grill with Brock. You know how we do," Macon said.

B's Suga: I was just checking ;)

Me: I'm good, Baby. I'll pick you up later.

B's Suga: See you at six.

"I'm on my way over to surprise her now. She doesn't know I'm here yet."

"Yeah, you might want to call first," Macon said and stood from the table. "Dre, let's go down to the pit and get it started."

Rio chuckled. "What's going on? Is Tonya with someone or something?"

I stopped moving and turned to Rio and said, "Yeah, she is."

Macon and Donald were looking between the two of us, but my eyes were on Rio waiting for him to respond.

"Oh, are you? I assumed you were a cousin I never met or a family friend." He laughed a bit and looked from Donald to Macon.

"And who are you?"

"Tonya and I were together for a long time. I was almost part of this family. Isn't that right, D?" He hit Donald on the arm.

He was cocky and arrogant. This must be the guy she said she wanted to have the baby with, and he moved out of the country. They were together for four years. She said he broke her heart, but she never told me the full story.

"What's your name again?"

"Rio Hendrix. You've probably seen me in a few business segments. I'm a financial analyst."

"You don't look familiar, and I've never heard of you," I returned.

"Welp, I have an important stop to make, so I'll leave you all to the grill. I better get going."

He slapped hands with Macon and Donald. "I'm sure I'll be seeing you all around soon since I'm back." He moved toward the steps. "Tell Lady B I said hello. Good meeting you, Andre."

"Same here," I said.

Once he left the backyard, Donald and Macon turned to me.

"Do you need to go over to the shop?" Donald asked.

My mind was racing but I had to play this right. I couldn't show up at the shop because her ex was in town. Weak men did that shit. Tonya knew what we had and she wouldn't let him come between us. As hard as it was, I had to let her deal with him.

I shook my head. "Naw, Tonya and I are good."

Macon slapped my shoulder. "You're a better man than me. If Dawn's ex showed up right now I wouldn't be calm and we're married. I can't imagine if we had just started dating and the man she used to be in love with came back."

Damn, now he was in my head. But I had to play it cool.

"Like I said, we're good."

The two of them looked at each other and Macon shrugged.

Chapter 9 ~ Tonya

The door chimed and I had to force my mouth closed. After locking eyes with him, I was immediately nervous and excited as a jolt of recognition, familiarity, and all the memories of our past together flooded my mind.

He moved closer to me while I stood frozen in place. My heart began to race. I felt as if I was about to explode with emotion. Along with the excitement, a wave of sadness and regret quickly crept in.

As he gently touched my cheek, the nostalgia slowly faded and the bitterness, anger, loneliness, and resentment entered my mind.

Why was I allowing him to touch me? He didn't deserve me.

"You are still beautiful as ever. I've missed your face," he said.

Stepping back, I replied, "Why are you here?"

He held his arms open. "You can't hug me?"

"Why are you here, Rio?"

Now my emotions were honing in on the feelings I felt the last time I thought about him. The abandonment, the rejection, the hurt, the lost time. I was pretty sure I hated him right now. But again, there was curiosity as well. Why was he here? Why after four years of radio silence was he in my space?

"I came to see you, catch up." He smiled.

Rio was attractive and overly confident. I didn't realize until after we broke up that he was arrogant.

His milk chocolate skin hadn't aged one bit in four years. The neat thin locs were a lot shorter than I remembered, but still tied into a single bunch at the back of his head. He was starting to gray around the temples, but it looked good on him. Rio was muscular and stood right at about six feet. The new thing about him was the perfectly lined beard and crisp edges around the perimeter of his locs. Years ago he wore his hair a little more natural, but now they appeared to be freshly twisted and groomed.

Melody and Lois walked in; they had gone to get coffee from Kahawa Coffee across the street. They both stopped talking when they saw Rio.

"Damn, look what the cat drug in," Lois spat.

Never taking an insult to heart, he smiled flashing his teeth. "What's up, Sis? I'm sorry to hear about Wayne's passing."

"Keep my husband's name out of your mouth, the time for condolences would have been a year ago."

His smile faded. "I deserve that and I'm still sorry. Wayne was a good guy. Hey, Melody."

Melody walked away without speaking.

"Damn, tough crowd."

After Lois walked away, he turned back to me. "Can we go somewhere and talk? Or maybe have dinner?"

"No," I said quickly.

He jerked back a bit in surprise. "It can be later, doesn't have to be today. I want to catch up with you and talk about your new business venture. You could have called me and asked for help planning, considering my career."

I frowned. "Why would I ask you for help? I haven't seen or talked to you in four years."

He blew out a breath and said, "That's part of the reason I want us to have dinner. I need to explain what was going on with me back then. There's a lot you don't know."

Now I was even more curious, but my pride kicked in and I said, "If you couldn't share it with me when we were together there's no need for me to know now. None of it matters."

"Is this because you're dating Andre now? I met him at your parents' place before I came here."

"What! Why were you there?"

Was that the reason Dre was short with me when I sent him a text earlier? I didn't need him around Dre. I could only imagine what he was thinking. Dre didn't play well with other men. And neither did Rio. Neither of them minded an occasional pissing contest.

"I wanted to stop by and say hello. Tonya, your family was good to me. Are you serious with this Andre fella?"

"Yes, we are serious and exclusive." I crossed my arms over my chest.

He smiled and licked his full lips. "I'll call you later. Give you some time to get used to me being back in town."

I shook my head. "Rio, it's not happening. I'm sure you've been in St. Louis plenty of times in the last four years and I have not heard from you. Let's keep it that way. Like I said, I'm taken."

He smirked. "Until I see a substantial-sized ring on your finger, I say you're available."

He reached to hug me and I stepped back again but was stopped by a table.

He was less than an inch away from me. He leaned down and whispered in my ear, "I want you back. Do you remember how I used to make you feel?"

I looked at him and nodded. "I do remember how you made me feel when you broke up with me after I mentioned having a family."

If he thought he was going to come in here and talk about how he made me feel physically and forget about how he ripped my heart out, he had another thing coming.

He stepped back and stared at me.

"Tonya, there's a lot you don't know. Let's talk and I'll explain everything."

"Why are you still here!" Lois yelled from behind me.

He put both hands up. "I'm leaving now. Lois, it was good seeing you again."

Lois walked over and stood next to me and folded her arms the same way mine were folded.

"Hey, I know not to mess with the James sisters. Tonya, be on the look out for my call. We will talk."

He turned around and left.

Lois turned to me. "What do you want me to do? Have him beat up, cut his locs off, what can I do?"

I laughed. Rio loved those locs, he would die if someone cut them off.

"Thanks, Lo. I'm going to ignore him. He's already met Dre today. Not sure what happened there."

"I know, Donald was trying to call you but I guess your phone is in the office. He called while we were at Kahawa and told us. I didn't know he would get here before we came back."

"Does Dre know he's my ex?"

"Yep, and according to Donald he wasn't happy about it but said he would let you handle it."

"I'll talk to him when he picks me up. I was hoping I wouldn't have to talk about it at all."

"How are you feeling about him? Honestly? You guys did have a four-year relationship."

"I know. I loved Rio and thought we would eventually get married and start a family. But he had other plans. I won't let him interfere with what I have with Dre."

She smiled. "Good, because I like Dre."

I moved to finish stocking my shelf. I hated that Rio was able to bring up all those old feelings. I was over him but there was so much left on the table when it ended. We never had the typical break-up conversation or any of the typical back-and-forth. We were in a good place one day, or so I thought, and then it was over. I was left in the dark about everything. He cut off communication and moved away. I hated him for what he did to me after four years. Never again. I promised I would never give another man that much time without marriage unless I decided marriage wasn't for me.

"Are you okay?" Melody asked from behind me.

I turned and smiled. We made up after I yelled at her last weekend.

"I'm fine, Mel."

"Is there anything I can do to him that would make you feel better?"

I laughed. My sisters didn't have a problem coming to my aid if needed. I guess we all did the same for each other. I know I wanted to fight her ex on several occasions.

"Not right now."

"Let me know when and I'll cut his locs off. You know how he is about that hair. Your phone was ringing in the office." She handed me the phone.

"I'll let you and Lois know, keep the clippers on standby," I said, as I unlocked my phone.

I had a missed call from Donald and one from Brock. Both probably wanted to warn me about Rio being in town.

I went to the office and called Brock.

"Hey, Tonya. Wanted to give you a heads-up that Rio is in town. He came by and Andre was here."

"I heard. He stopped by here, too."

"Your mama is upset; you know she doesn't like him. I had to go inside and keep her from going outside. She never knew he was here until she saw him walking in the front to his car."

My mother was a true mama bear. She didn't play when it came to her kids. She saw how devastated I was after he left and promised to give him a Franklin Street cussing the next time she saw him.

Franklin Street was in Vicksburg, Mississippi. Apparently, people cursed on that particular street when she was a child. All I did know was that if you were on the receiving end of a Franklin Street cussing, she didn't like you.

"I'm sure she's going to call me later."

"You better believe it. I hope things went well and you put him in his place. I see a bright future with you and Andre. I never cared for Rio."

"Really? Not even when we were together?" I was surprised. Brock never said anything bad about him while we dated.

"He thinks he's more than what he is. And he never made you smile the way you do with Andre."

I smiled. "You're right about that, it's easy with Dre. I don't think I've ever dated anyone that makes me feel comfortable telling him anything."

"That's what I know. You keep that in mind when he comes back to sniff around."

"I will. I have to go help out front. I'll talk to you later. Love you, Brock, and thanks for always being there for me."

"I'm always here, anytime. Love you, too. Bye."

"Look at me," he whispered.

My eyes were shut tight, and my arms were stretched out above my head. Dre was on top of me pulling in and out slowly. I felt every inch of him massaging my walls as he pulsated inside me.

"Tonya, look at me," he said again.

Slowly opening my eyes, his brown eyes came into view.

"Are you with me?" he asked.

"I'm with you, Baby," I whispered back.

He released my arms from above my head and wrapped me up in his arms without losing our connection. His mouth found mine and we kissed while he slowly rolled over, leaving me on top.

This kiss wasn't like our usual. His tongue swirled against mine slowly while he tenderly held my head in place by holding my cheeks. I'd never felt more cherished than in this moment with him.

I moved up and down at the same slow pace until I felt my core tightening.

"Dre, I'm about to..."

He held my face so that we were eye to eye.

"I know, I'm right there with you," he said.

The look on his face was so intense. His eyes were trained on me with his forehead slightly creased.

The moment I exploded he closed his eyes quickly and opened them again. He stopped moving and let out his release. This was the first time we were both silent and staring into each other's eyes during an orgasm.

If his goal was to clear my mind, he did it. I could only see and think about the man in front of me. I blinked a few times and smiled.

"Why are you smiling?" he asked. His large hands were massaging my behind.

"Because you make me feel good."

"Are you relaxed now?"

I nodded. "I am. But I'm hungry. Did you bring any food home?"

"I did. You want some?"

I was hungry but we needed to talk about Rio at some point. Donald told me that Rio mentioned he was coming by the shop in front of Dre. I didn't want him to think I was hiding it from him. And by the intensity of what just happened, I knew he was more than a little concerned. Dre was always a pleasing and passionate lover, but tonight was elevated.

"I'll get some food for us. I heard your stomach growling," I said.

I moved to get up but he held me by my waist and kissed me. Not a quick kiss, but a long kiss. Our tongues danced around until he finally ended it and kissed my cheek and then my neck.

Dre was not shy about touching but this was more than usual. Like he was telling me how he felt through touch instead of talking.

He finally let me go and I went to the kitchen to warm up the grilled shrimp and broccoli he made with the brothers and Brock earlier.

He came into the kitchen wearing nothing but boxer briefs and sat at the island. Once I sat next to him, I said, "I had an uninvited visitor at the shop today."

He popped a shrimp in his mouth. "I'm sure it was the same one that was uninvited to your parents' house."

"Yeah, I haven't seen or talked to him in four years. I know what he said over there and I want you to know it's you and me."

He nodded. "I'm not worried."

I side-eyed him. "Is that why you put it on me tonight? That was intense."

"Just thought I would switch it up a bit," he said and took a bite of his food.

"Well, I only wanted to clear the air because if this was the other way around I'd be feeling a certain way."

I didn't know why I expected a man to admit to anything. They usually acted up instead of admitting their feelings.

"Baby, look at me." I turned to face him. "Why would I think you would leave all of this after waiting thirty years?"

I laughed out loud. "I swear you get on my last nerve! I hate that Mel told you that."

He laughed too. "I'm just saying. You would have never told me yourself?"

I shook my head. "Nope! Or if I had it would have been years from now."

He shook his head. "You disappoint me. I'm glad I know, it makes me feel good."

I laughed. "Hurry up and finish eating. I want a repeat of what just happened."

He smiled wide. "I have all kinds of tricks, that was nothing. But I can't give you everything all at once."

I laughed and continued eating. Seeing Rio after four years had given me a brief moment of nostalgia, but I had my man sitting beside me. Rio broke my heart into pieces, and I would be damned if I let him back in my life.

The next morning, I had the day off from the shop. Melody decided she would give Lois and me each a day off after the Kinloch ladies debacle last weekend.

"Baby, let's go!" Dre yelled from the kitchen.

"Here I come!" I yelled back from my bedroom.

We were on our way to the Black Taste of St. Louis and then grocery shopping for the week. I grabbed my keys and paused when my doorbell rang. My building was locked and the elevator didn't work without a key. It had to be one of my neighbors.

My eyes widened when I made it to the top of the stairs. Dre and Rio were standing face to face.

I quickly walked down the steps. "Rio, what are you doing here?"

Dre didn't move, his back was to me, and Rio was standing in the hallway.

"I thought you might be free to talk today."

"Baby, did you know he was coming over here?" Dre asked without turning to face me.

"No, I did not."

"You need to leave. Don't come over here again," Dre said.

I finally inched my way next to Dre to see Rio and I added, "You need to go."

Ignoring Dre and me, he asked, "He's living with you?"

"ARE YOU HARD OF HEARING!" Dre yelled, and I jumped.

Rio held his hands up and stepped back. "I see you're thugging now, I'll catch you later."

"Thugging? Man, don't make me jeopardize my security clearance."

Rio looked at me and then walked away. I closed the door and turned slowly to look at Dre.

"That motherfucker is disrespectful!" he said loudly. "What happened at the shop yesterday? Why does he think he can show up over here?"

I honestly didn't understand what Rio was doing or why.

"Baby, relax." I grabbed his hand.

"I'm fine, Tonya. How did he get in the main door and up the elevator without a key? He's on some stalker shit. Go pack a bag, you're staying with me this week."

Okay, he was taking this too far. Rio wasn't a stalker; he was very persistent, but not crazy.

"Dre, I've known him for years, he's not crazy like that. Yesterday he said he wanted to talk to me, and I told him I didn't want to, and he left."

"So, you tell him you don't want to talk, and he responds by showing up at your door the next day? Didn't you say you haven't talked to him in years?"

I nodded. "It's been four years. I haven't seen or heard from him."

He stared at me and finally let out a breath. "Baby, I'm sorry, I didn't mean to yell. Come here." He pulled me into a hug and rocked back and forth. "If you haven't seen him in four years this is not the way to get your attention. This is weird to me. Please come stay at my place this week."

I knew Rio wasn't crazy, he was more of a bully, and he wanted what he wanted by any means necessary. However, from Dre's perspective, I could understand how this looked. It was a lot in less than twenty-four hours.

I puckered my lips and waited for him to kiss me. "We will stay at your house this week."

He smiled and kissed me again.

Instead of protesting I relented because we usually only stayed apart once or twice a week. I had a few things to do around here but I understood his point of view. If Big Ass would have shown up at his door while I was there, and he didn't come home with me I would be angry. So, I went back upstairs and grabbed clothes for the week.

By the time we were finally on our way to the Taste, Dre asked, "Why do you think dude is coming around after all this time?"

"I don't get it. He's the one that broke up with me."

"What happened the last time you saw him?"

Four years ago...

"Tonya, we need to talk."

I was a little annoyed because we had a long conversation about my clock ticking and wanting to have a baby a few weeks ago. Marriage was important to me, but I wanted a child even more. He hadn't said much about it since.

"Ok, what's going on?"

We were at my condo on the sofa. Rio seemed stressed over the last few weeks. I assumed it was work. Every once in a while, he would be overwhelmed from the traveling projects.

"I have a new assignment for work, it's in New Zealand."

I frowned in confusion. This was the first time I'd heard about a new assignment. "Ok, how many weeks this time? I can come with you for a week or so like we usually do."

He was quiet. He stared at me.

"Rio, what's wrong?"

"It's permanent," he said quickly.

"What? I thought you had to request to be transferred permanently."

After a minute of silence, he said, "I did make the request."

My eyes widened. "Excuse me? You requested to leave the country permanently?"

"Yeah, it's the best move for my career. International analysts are paid much more because the focus is on worldwide economics and not just the domestic economy."

"I get that, but what about us? How did you make the request without talking to me?"

More silence, then, "I'm not ready to have a family right now. I need to make a few more career moves. I don't want you waiting on me to get ready."

I squinted. "You're breaking up with me? Like this? After four years?"

He covered his face with both hands and then finally rubbed them over his locs.

"Tonya, I'm not ready for kids and a wife. I'm not sure if I'll ever be ready, it's not how I see my future."

"You BASTARD!" I yelled. "Four years! We've always talked about a future together and you drop me like I don't mean anything to you?"

He tried to hug me, but I pushed him away.

"It's not like that. I love you. I just can't be tied down right now."

"You love yourself! You don't love me!"

I began to cry from the pain and confusion. He hugged me after I stopped pushing him away.

"Tonya, I do love you."

I cried into his chest. "Why? Why would you do this to me if you love me?"

He kissed my forehead and left me crying in the middle of my living room.

"That was the last time I saw or talked to him until yesterday," I said.

Made me kind of sad to retell the story. I was in a lot of pain for months after he left.

Dre kissed the back of my hand.

"I really want to kick his ass now," Dre said.

I smiled. "The way I see it, he did me a favor. If you can hurt me like that for your career, I don't need you."

We were in the parking lot waiting to go inside the Taste.

"Damn, Baby. I'm sorry that happened to you. Are you sure you want to go in? We can go home and relax the rest of the day."

I'd shed my last tear and wasted too many days crying over Rio. He wouldn't get any more of my time.

"Nope, we are going to have a good day. We both finally have the day off and I'm hungry."

"Your ass is so greedy," he said.

I laughed and reached to hug him. "I can't help it, somebody had my legs wide open this morning."

He smiled. "Let me feed you, because it ain't over."

My mouth opened wide, and he laughed out loud. No way we were having sex again tonight. I couldn't hang.

Rio hadn't tried to contact me or stop by in two weeks, and I was relieved. Even though I was a bit curious, I didn't want to hear it.

We had our family reunion last weekend, so I was pretty busy. He wouldn't have been able to find me with all the family around anyway. The upcoming extended weekend was our family cruise. I was looking forward to getting away with my family and Dre.

"Mel, I'm going to get something to eat from across the street, ok?"

"Ok, we will hold it down while you're gone. Lois is leaving early but I'll be fine, take your time."

Melody had been a lot calmer over the last few weeks. She was still going though it with her ex but I refused to ask questions. The whole thing irritated me.

I walked into Kahawa and was met by Greenwood's senior citizen chess players, plus one that wasn't a senior but hung with them anyway, Star City.

"Hello, gentlemen," I said.

"Hey, Tonya! You're just the person I wanted to see," Mr. Gil announced.

I walked to the table where Mr. Gil and Mr. Kid were playing a game of chess. The youngest of the trio, Star City, smiled wide, showing his missing side teeth. He had a little crush on me and always smiled and stared at me until I spoke to him personally.

I put him out of his misery and said, "Hey, Star City..."

He finished off with, "... where all the ladies are pretty."

Star City graduated high school in the same class as Lois, Dawn, and Dre, but he got caught up in the streets. He never really made too much of himself once he aged out of the street life. Now he roamed the streets of Greenwood daily. He never hurt anyone and most of the businesses in the area took care of him. The guys at *Fade* trimmed him up once a month. I assumed it was free because Star City didn't work.

I smiled and asked, "Mr. Gil, what did you want to see me about?"

"Well, you know Kid and I, plus a few others are retired. Most of the businesses here in Greenwood have a place for us to play chess. You and your sisters have been open a while now and I don't see any tables and chairs for us."

"Would be nice to smell some of those fresh spices you all sell over there while we play chess," Mr. Kid added.

Mr. Kid had a baby face so everyone called him Kid.

"Our shop isn't big enough for tables and chairs inside. But you guys are always welcome to stop by."

"We don't mind sitting outside," Mr. Kid added.

Hmmm, maybe they were on to something. The rear of the building had a large space. Maybe we could build a deck and use it for people to lounge around and listen to music. Maybe even include heat lamps and an outdoor fireplace for the cold season.

"Let me talk to my sisters, I'll see what we can do," I said.

Mr. Gil smiled wide. "Your daddy would be so proud of you girls."

Mr. Gil and Daddy worked together before he passed.

"I appreciate you saying that."

"Can I come too, Tonya James? This is my city, where all the ladies are pretty," Star City said.

"Of course, our place is for the community, everyone is welcome."

"Thank you for your hospitality, Tonya James. On that note, I'm gone. I'll see you all later." He grabbed his briefcase and left the store.

He carried a briefcase and called everyone by their full names. He said it would make people think he wasn't a fool based on his former drug sales and drug use. Star City always made clear he was a high school graduate and held an associate degree from the community college and while he may be a fool, he was an educated fool.

I said my goodbyes and moved to the counter.

Kahawa Coffee was owned by Kalmin Ousman. He had the best coffee in town. Kal was a nice guy from a country in east Africa near Eritrea. He had a thing for my hair stylist, Nuri.

"Hey, Kal!" I announced when I saw him coming out of his office.

"Hello, Tonya! How are you today? You want me to have them make your usual?"

I smiled. "I do, but is Chef Al here? I'm hungry."

He nodded. "He is here, I'll have him make something special for you today. Do you have time to wait a few minutes?"

I took a seat at one of the high boy bistro tables and crossed my legs. "For Chef Al's food, I will wait all day."

"Good, I'll be back in a bit."

I scrolled through a few emails while I waited for the food and my coffee.

After a few minutes, the sun beaming in the window was blocked. Before I looked up I had a feeling it was Rio standing at my table.

"Hi, Tonya," he said softly.

Finally looking up I asked, "Rio, what is it? Are you watching me?"

"Can I sit?"

"No," I said quickly.

"Five minutes and I'll leave you alone if that's what you want."

Reluctantly, I said, "Five minutes, that's it."

He smiled and stared at me for a minute. I didn't feel anything.

"I've been driving by hoping to catch you alone. I promised I would not go to your home again, so I've been randomly coming by the shop to see if you were there. Every time I see you, Andre is either picking you up or dropping you off. I wouldn't have thought you would be with an insecure man."

I shook my head. "Aht–aht, you won't insult him. He's too good to me. And for the record, he's been picking me up and driving me around since we started dating. Get over yourself." I rolled my eyes

He chuckled. "Okay, I stand corrected. But do you love him?"

I wasn't sure where my love meter was with Dre at the moment, but it was none of Rio's concern.

"You don't get to question me. State your business with me so that I can go on about my day."

"Fair enough. First, I want to apologize for the way I left. I know it's been a while and I've wanted to reach out to you so many times. I've been following you on social media and to be honest I have not stopped loving you, Tonya. I tried to let you go, but I couldn't."

I frowned. "None of this makes sense. You broke it off with me."

"Okay, okay. When I told you I was moving to New Zealand I wasn't being completely honest."

I crossed my arms over my chest and blew out a breath.

He continued with, "My plan was to propose to you and give you a baby, but life got in the way."

I frowned. "Instead of proposing you ended things? Yeah, that makes sense," I said sarcastically.

"Tonya, I was sick, I was diagnosed with prostate cancer."

My heart dropped and I covered my mouth.

"What? When?" I asked.

"I went for a routine checkup and my PSA numbers were off. I went to the urologist and they told me I had prostate cancer. They said it was aggressive but curable, but it would most likely leave me sterile."

"Why didn't you tell me?" I had a million questions.

He shook his head. "I loved you too much to put you through that. I didn't know how it was going to go and we had talked about having a baby. I knew how much you wanted to have a child and I couldn't take that away from you."

I was in shock. "Rio, I wouldn't have left you because you were sick. Is that what you thought of me?"

"I know you wouldn't have, that's why I did it. You didn't deserve a husband that couldn't give you what you wanted. They also told me I wouldn't be able to perform sexually without assistance. That was a big part of you and me, how could I take sex and a baby from you?"

"Are you okay now? What happened?"

I couldn't believe I was sitting here talking to Rio about cancer. My heart went out to him, I couldn't imagine what he was going through.

"When I left St. Louis, I went to the Mayo Clinic in Arizona and got treatment. I was there for almost eight months until I went into remission. Instead of coming back home, I went to New Zealand on assignment."

"You're cancer free?"

"Yes, I have been for over three years."

I didn't want to ask if he was sterile or impotent, but I did want to ask a more important question.

"Why come back now? Why not call me after the first year?"

He shook his head and wiped his face. "Tonya, it was a lot for me back then. I'd love to talk to you more in private or over dinner to explain everything. But I will tell you that I never stopped loving you. I tried to let you move on but I couldn't. I need you in my life. If you give me one sign that we can start over, I'll be in St. Louis permanently."

I sat there staring at him. I didn't know what to say. I couldn't believe he went through cancer treatment alone. Dre's handsome face appeared in my mind. I was finally happy with a man that appeared to want what I wanted in life. But life was now throwing Rio in the mix.

He stood. "Think about it and I'll call you in a day or two. I'm sorry I had to drop all of this in your lap but I still love you."

He leaned down and quickly kissed my cheek. His familiar scent flooded my senses, and I closed my eyes. Rio had my heart for four years and broke it. Now, here I was rethinking everything I thought I knew to be true.

"I'll be in touch. I love you, Tonya."

He walked out of the coffee house and I sat quietly as Chef Al placed a large box of food in front of me. I wasn't hungry anymore; I had a lot to process.

I paid my bill and slowly walked to the door. Mr. Kid was humming the music while Mr. Gil sang the lyrics to *Used to Be My Girl* by The O'Jays.

Chapter 10 ~ Dre

I answered my ringing phone. "Hey Baby, what's up?"

"Hey, I'm going to Donald's after the shop closes, so you don't have to pick me up."

I frowned. She sounded sad. "Okay, you good?"

"Yeah, I'm fine. I'm going to hang out with him for a while and then go home."

"You're not coming to my place?"

"It will be late so I'm going to go home. I'll see you tomorrow."

Something wasn't right. She put me to bed at five in the evening. I'd let it ride though and not ask her about it.

"Ok, I'll see you tomorrow." She was quiet so I asked, "Are you there?"

"Yes, I'm here. Ummm, on second thought, I'll come to your place when I leave Donald's, my car is there. It will be late though."

"That's cool, you have a key. I'll see you later tonight then."

"Ok, I'll see you tonight, bye."

"Bye."

I ended the call and dropped my phone on the table.

"Tonya alright?" Rob asked.

I was at his place catching up with him and Serena.

I shrugged. "I'm not sure. I bet it has something to do with that ex."

Rob nodded. "The one you said showed up at her place or the one from the grand opening?"

"The one that came over."

My mind was about to venture off into new territory. This was the first time I was worried about another dude. I didn't like him at all, and I didn't understand that odd phone call. She didn't even sound like herself.

"You think she's been talking to him?"

"Before that weird conversation, I would have said no, but now I'm not sure. Tonya is very decisive, and that call didn't even sound like her. She's going to her brother's house instead of coming home."

Rob chuckled. "Okay, your house is home now? You're really into her. And you wouldn't usually be concerned about where a woman was going in the past. What's the big deal with her visiting her brother?"

"We've stopped by his house plenty of times. Now she's going without me and she doesn't have her car. If she was driving herself, I wouldn't think anything of it. But something is up, plus she sounded like she was in a daze or something."

"Let it go until she tells you differently. I'm surprised you even noticed it from a phone conversation. You're in the deep end now."

I would argue with him, but he was right. I loved that woman. I hadn't told her yet, but she had me.

"Not sure I can let it go," I said.

"Hey, Rena!" Rob yelled. "Come in here, our boy is having a love problem."

I stared at Rob. "Man, cut that out. You know how the girls talk. She'll be talking to Tori, Dawn, and Janae."

Serena came in smiling. "What's going on in lovers' paradise?"

"Your husband is running off at the mouth as usual," I said sarcastically.

"Tonya's ex showed up after four years a couple of weeks ago. They were together for four years too. Even came to her house unannounced. She's been cool until today. Dre said she didn't sound right when she called a few minutes ago."

I wiped my face. This dude talked too much.

Serena looked at me. "Tell me how the conversation went. Wait, do you love her?"

I didn't say anything, I looked to the ceiling instead and Rob let out a long whistle.

He slow-clapped. "Damn, my boy is in love. I'm proud of you, Dre. Serena, our boy done grew up on us."

"Be quiet, Rob," Serena scolded. "Dre, have you told her?"

"Nope."

"Why not?" she asked.

"I will, but things are going well. I didn't want to rock the boat."

"Tell me about the call."

Serena was sitting across from me on the couch with Rob staring intently and nodding as I told her about the ex-encounters and the brief phone call.

"Ok, you're right. I agree it may be the ex, but you could be reading too much into it so don't say anything to her about it. Just be normal. Either way, let her work it out and you continue to be yourself."

"So don't ask her what's wrong?"

"No, you can ask her if she's ok but don't harp on it. From what you told me, they never had closure. And if he's told her anything other than what she thinks happened in the past she's going to need to process it."

I frowned. "You think she's talked to him or seen him?"

She threw her hand. "Of course, she's at least talked to him. If he came to her shop and house without calling, he's definitely made contact by now. Put yourself in his shoes. If you want your woman back and you're bold enough to go to her house unannounced after you met her man at her parents' house, why would you stop trying?"

She did have a point and I wasn't cool with it. *Was she talking to him on a regular basis?* It had been about two weeks since he came to her place unannounced.

"Dre?"

"What's up?"

"Don't get in your head with this, let her have a moment with whatever is going on."

"I would say something if I was you," Rob added.

"Ignore him, he'll have you single. She likes you a lot. We talk when she comes to my Pilates classes, but those old flames will make you think."

When would she have seen him? Did he come by the shop again? Did he call her? This shit was going to drive me crazy.

Serena continued. "Dre, I'm telling you to keep cool on this one. Let her close things out with him if that's what she needs. And do not expect her to tell you about it. Not right now anyway."

I frowned. "Why wouldn't she tell me?"

"Because no man wants to hear that another man put something on his woman's mind. You all have that ego thing going on. Do you think Dawn ran and told Macon what you said to her as soon as you told her you wanted to be with her?"

"Why do you have to bring that up?" I asked.

"Because your ass ain't never been in love and you don't know what you're doing. You're about to be classic Dre and stake your claim with her. And I'm telling you if you do it, you'll run her off. Give her some breathing room."

My gaze shifted to Rob. "Why are you finally quiet?"

"Because I haven't loved but one woman and she's sitting next to me. If it was me, I wouldn't be sitting here talking, I would be waiting at home to question her. I wouldn't allow her to talk to him."

Serena laughed. "See what I mean? You don't know what you're talking about. He can't tell her what to do, he's not her father. And if he tries it, things won't work out."

Rob twisted his lips. "Man, listen to your boy. Go home and put it on her. That always works."

Little did he know I already did that and it didn't work.

Serena cut back in. "Why do men think they can screw a woman into submission? It's ridiculous. Give her space and you'll be fine."

"I didn't give you space in college when that nerd you dated before me tried to come back. If I can recall, I'm pretty sure I put it on you and you got rid of him."

I laughed. I remembered Rob trippin' out over Serena's ex that returned to the yard after leaving for a year.

"I can't believe you even remember that!" Serena said with a wide smile. She pushed his arm.

"He was hurt up," I said.

"You breaking bro code?" Rob shook his head.

I shrugged. "You've been married since we graduated from school. I assumed she knew."

"I did know!" Serena quipped. "I did almost go back to my ex though."

Rob sat up straight and yelled, "What!"

"The only thing that saved us was I had to leave school for two weeks when my dad got sick. I had time to think it through and I wanted to stay with you. If I had never left, I'm not sure what I would have done because you refused to leave my dorm room. You were all over me. I couldn't think straight."

Rob shook his head and looked at me. "See how these women are? I've been with her a hundred years and now she tells me she almost didn't choose me."

"It was about processing my feelings and thoughts. I knew I loved you but I'm not a robot. I had to think about it."

Serena was making a lot of sense. I would try to give Tonya space if she needed it. But if she was seeing that ex behind my back, that shit wasn't flying with me.

"All I know is when Dre leaves, I want some selfish sex. You're doing all the work. You owe me after this information."

Serena stood from the couch and laughed. "I'll take care of you, don't worry. I didn't have an exercise class today; I need some cardio anyway."

I laughed at Rob's mouth hanging open.

"See how she is? Now, she's going to use me for cardio instead of making love to her husband."

Serena stretched her arms while walking to leave the room and said, "Take it how you can get it. See ya, Dre."

I chuckled. "Later, Serena."

Rob shook his head. "Don't listen to me because clearly, I don't even know my own wife. Take her advice."

Chapter 11 ~ Tonya

rang the doorbell and waited. Today had been extremely emotional and I didn't know how to rationalize it all.

"What's up, Sis?"

I walked right into his arms and rested my head on his chest.

"That bad?"

"Mmm-hmm," I mumbled and nodded at the same time.

He hugged me tight and kissed the top of my head the same way he did whenever I had man trouble over the years.

"Am I listening or does Rio need to disappear tonight?"

Finally cracking a smile, I replied, "Listening."

"Ok, come on back."

I followed him into the two-story great room and connecting kitchen. Tori was in the kitchen moving around. She'd done an amazing job of redecorating the house since they were married. It didn't look like the same house.

She walked in with her arms outstretched. "Hey, Sis, do we need to posse up?"

I smiled and hugged her. "I need to talk, that's all."

"Ok, I made a little charcuterie board for you two. I'm going to go upstairs and let you have your brother."

My brothers had the best wives. I loved all three of my bonus sisters.

"Thanks, Tori. But do you mind staying? I'd like a woman's perspective too."

Her eyes widened and her mouth opened wide. "Of course, anything you need. I got wine, brown liquor, white liquor, chips, whatever you need."

"I'll take some whiskey."

Donald's forehead stretched and he turned to Tori. "Baby, let me help you."

I went to the restroom and then plopped down on the sofa, curling up around one of the plethora of extra-large fur pillows.

When Donald first moved in, the walls were painted contractor white. Tori added her touch and had the room painted dark steel gray with bright white crown molding and matte gold metal accents. The oversized modular sofa was black suede fabric. Brown fur pillows, white fur pillows, and metallic gold and white pillows were placed around the modular seating unit. It was beautiful, I felt like I was in a high-end swanky hotel with the gold accent tables and wall sconces.

The statement piece was the erotic abstract painting by the renowned Gavin Gray. If you paid attention long enough, an image of a man and woman having sex could be seen. As your eye made its way slowly across the painting the couple would appear to be in motion.

The canvas was black with different shades of metallic gold paint on its surface and a matte gold floater frame added a sophisticated touch.

Tori came in with a charcuterie board filled with cheese, fruit, crackers, and chips. Donald followed behind carrying a bottle of *Uncle Nearest 1856* and three tumblers.

"Y'all drinking brown liquor too?"

Tori shrugged. "Liquid courage. You have to get some stuff off your chest, right?"

I smiled and nodded as I took my glass from Donald.

"You also need some raw advice, right?"

I nodded again and swiped a few crackers from the board.

Swirling her glass of whiskey, she said, "This is how we get into it."

"Right!" Donald added. "Spill it, Sis, so I can decide for myself if Rio needs to go back to where he came from."

I took a few sips from my tumbler and waited for the amber-colored liquid to soothe me. I told them everything about Rio including the background story for Tori since she wasn't married to Donald back then.

"Oh my," Tori said and sipped her drink. "This is like a book or movie script."

"That's what I said too." Turning to Donald, I asked, "Well?"

"I don't see the problem. Aren't you with Dre now? He was at the family reunion with a t-shirt on."

"What does that mean?" Tori asked.

I was curious as well, so I added, "A t-shirt?"

"Before you pass out a family reunion shirt you better be sure about him."

"Really, Don?"

"Ok, listen, Rio was sick. I feel bad for him but he's still here and has more hair than me. If he had come back after a year, I would give him some weight but it's been too long. Dre had the family reunion shirt on, he's in."

I turned to Tori. "See why I asked you to stay? Although I wasn't expecting this type of ridiculousness from him."

"Babe, she needs to think about this, it's a lot all at once. She's not saying she wants to break up with Dre, she needs to put it all together in her mind."

"Put what together? I get what Rio did and it's admirable, but he should have come right back. I'm sure he hasn't been single and crying over her for all these years."

I hadn't thought about that. A thought came to mind. "But I don't know why he didn't return. Maybe he's impotent, that would be hard for him."

Donald shook his head. "His shit works, trust me. If it didn't, he would still be gone. And if there's a slim chance it doesn't work, is that what you want?" He lifted an eyebrow, then continued. "And stop making stuff up. If he didn't tell you that then why are you saying it?"

My usually laid-back brother was hyped when he had some of that brown oil in him. But he was always honest and gave it to me straight.

"He's right," Tori added. "However, I understand needing to at least hear him out."

I nodded. "I think I should at least listen to him; we were together four years."

"Go ahead and see where that gets you. Tori can tell you about secret dates."

Tori's head swung to Donald. "Give me that glass!"

"What?" he asked innocently.

I shook my head. Tori and Donald had major drama and almost didn't make it when Tori went out with her ex and Donald happened to see her out with him.

"I can't believe you are bringing that up. And don't you act all innocent as if you weren't contemplating Lena."

"I wasn't contemplating Lena. I knew I wanted to be with you."

"Lies! You told me yourself you thought about going to her place that night!"

My head was going from side to side, listening and sipping.

"I was! But I was contemplating sex, not a relationship, there's a difference."

I giggled. At least they cleared my mind.

Tori stared at him with her mouth open.

"I'm sorry, Baby. Give me a kiss, you know how I get when I drink brown liquor."

She smirked and accepted his quick pecks.

"I love you," he added and put his arm around her.

"I love you too, and he's right. We actually both contemplated sex with other people that night."

"Now why did you have to bring that up?" Donald asked with a frown on his face.

"You started it," she sassed back.

"Okaaay, well, now that we have that settled," I said.

"Damn, we're sorry, Sis. Tori can't ever act right in front of company."

"Me? Yeah, we're sorry. Your brother and I are both reformed hoes so we might not be the best people to give you advice."

I had to cover my mouth to keep from losing the liquor I had taken in. I grabbed a napkin from the table.

"Y'all are crazy!" I laughed out loud. "But I do feel better."

"What are you going to do?" Donald asked.

He leaned back on the sofa and Tori snuggled up next to him. He toyed with her hair while she ran her fingers across his leg.

"I don't know. I feel so bad for Rio going through that alone away from home."

"You are trippin'! I need some more testosterone in here. I'm calling Dale."

"I don't feel like telling the story over again tonight."

"Didn't you tell Lois before you left the shop?" he asked.

"Facts! Call him."

I told Melody and Lois about Rio when I went back to the shop. And whatever Lois knew, Dale knew.

"Are you sure she told him already?" Tori asked.

"You'll see," Donald said and tapped around on his iPad.

After a few rings, Dale answered with, "What it do, D?"

"What's up, what's up? I got Tori and Tonya in here."

Donald propped the iPad up on a pillow so we could all see Dale. They were seated across from me.

"Hey, Sisters, what are y'all up to? Tonya, you cool?"

"Told you," Donald noted, turning to Tori.

"What's your take on this?" I asked Dale.

Di-Di came into the frame. "Hey, everybody! Tonya, I'm sending you a big hug."

I looked at Tori and she shrugged. This family grapevine had no limits.

"Thanks, Sis. I appreciate it."

"You are welcome to come out here with us if you need to get away to clear your mind."

I loved my bonus sisters. "You are so sweet, thank you for that."

"Why does she need to clear her mind?" Dale asked.

"THANK YOU!" Donald said in dramatic form by slapping his knee. "These girls are saying she needs to think. There's nothing to think about."

"Are you breaking up with Dre?" Dale asked.

Palming my forehead I replied, "That's not what time to think means."

"Oh ok, I was about to say he had on a t-shirt at the reunion."

Donald looked at me, then Tori with a look of pure satisfaction.

"What is it with y'all and the family reunion shirts? Y'all act like it's a fraternity."

"Aye, this is more, this is family. You can't be tossing around family reunion shirts to just anybody. It ain't right," Dale said.

"Y'all are turning into Brock. He's the only one I thought wore that shirt like a badge of honor," I said.

"Tori is the only woman that I ever gave a family reunion shirt."

"You know I've only had two people wear one," Dale added, referring to his ex-wife and current wife, Di-Di.

All eyes were on me. "Okay, okay! Dre's the first guy that had a shirt!"

Tori and Di-Di both sucked in air with their eyes wide.

I hadn't thought about it, but Rio was usually traveling for work during our reunions. He came to the first day of the reunion one year and the last day another year. Other than that he wasn't in town.

"Rio never had a shirt?" Tori asked.

"That's what I'm saying. This dude ain't worthy, send him packing. If you can't come to a full reunion when you date for four years, you ain't about this family for real," Donald said.

"Preach!" Dale yelled.

"Y'all a rough crowd," Di-Di added.

Donald was indifferent when it came to Rio during our courtship. He was nice to him but not overly friendly. This was the first time he'd ever spoken against him.

We chatted it up a bit more and sobered up before Tori and Donald dropped me off at Dre's place.

On the way to the door, I received a text message from a number that wasn't in my contacts.

314-388-2368: Hey Love, it's Rio. I've been wanting to use this number for four years. I couldn't wait any longer. Can we meet this week? I have a lot more to tell you.

And just like that, he was back on my mind. Of course, I removed his contact information and everything that reminded me of him from my phone years ago.

Me: I'm leaving for a family cruise this week. I'll think about it when I return.

314-388-2368: Take your time. I promise I will wait patiently for you. I still love you and I always will. Think about me making sweet love to you while you're away.

I guess Donald was right, his shit did work. He wouldn't bring that up otherwise, pun intended.

I decided not to reply. I waved to Tori and Donald then went inside Dre's place.

<h1 style="text-align:center">Chapter 12 ~ Dre</h1>

 had gone out for a run after I left Rob's, then swung by to see the folks. I hadn't heard from Tonya, but I assumed she was at Donald's like she said.

Instead of going to bed, I decided on a swim. Aside from the tub filling from the ceiling, the in-ground pool was the second reason I purchased this house. It was a lot of upkeep, but I enjoyed it. Especially, my mother, she and her friends would use it for water aerobics a few times a month while I was at work.

The previous owners did a nice job with the backyard. My house sat on an acre and the pool area was like a resort. There was a round jacuzzi attached to the right of the pool and a stone waterfall in the center that flowed into the water. The pool was surrounded by a light-colored brick patio. The patio area also included a small outdoor kitchen and barbecue area outside the patio doors that led to my great room. The patio doors ran along the entire back wall of the great room and opened up to connect the patio to the inside of the house.

I tossed my towel on the lounge chair and eased down the steps into the water. It was midsummer so the cool water was refreshing. I dropped down in the water, fully submerged myself, and came up on my back. As I floated around slightly moving my arms, I thought about Tonya. If I lost her to that ex, I doubted I would have another chance at love.

She was special, she understood me. She had a quick wit, a great sense of humor, and a great business mind. In addition to her little tight body that had me sprung, she was humble. She would do anything for her family and me if I asked. Naw, I'd fight his ass over her. Tonya was mine now. He didn't get to circle the block on her.

The patio door opened and she walked out wearing a towel wrapped tightly around her body.

I swam over to the edge.

"Hey," she said.

"Hey, how was your visit with Donald?"

"It was fine."

I didn't ask another question because she dropped her towel, revealing her nude body. I'd seen her in the nude plenty of times, but I never got past how beautiful and free she was with her body.

She stepped down into the pool and swam to me. I watched as she gracefully moved through the water with the dark blue LED pool lights highlighting her curves.

When she was in front of me, she wrapped herself around me and I quickly kissed her puckered lips.

"Mmmm, you've been drinking whiskey," I said. I held onto her and moved so that her back was against the pool wall. We were on the shallow end of the pool, the water was up to my chest.

Nodding, she replied, "Just a little."

The sweet taste of the whiskey mixed with her natural sweetness required further attention. I kissed her lips again, moving my tongue past our connection and savoring her taste.

She matched my eagerness by pulling my head closer to her and sliding her body further up my chest.

Her nipples hardened as they grazed back and forth across my wet skin creating a bit of friction.

"I need you," she whispered.

That's what I needed to hear. My girl needed me. I was the one she came home to. I was the one that could make her feel good. I was the one that was readjusting his swim trunks to get inside of her.

Once I made the connection, she stilled and held her head back. I pushed in further.

Finally lifting her head, she caught my lips. Neither of us had to do a lot of moving because the buoyancy of the water naturally gave us a slow rhythmic pattern.

Damn, she felt good. As our bodies moved up and down with the flow of the water, her canal contracted, massaging every inch of me. She was made for me, no one else.

She finally ended the kiss, throwing her head back. Closed eyes and a strained face had never looked more beautiful. I watched as her nipples shrank even more and pebbled into small balls on her large swollen breasts.

Holding onto her wet body I continued to watch as she reached her peak and finally let go. It was beautiful and would be etched in my mind forever.

Dropping her head on my chest and wrapping her arms around my neck, I held on tight as I released and lost our connection.

Without talking, I slowly walked up the pool steps with water pouring from our bodies and walked inside with her wrapped around me.

It didn't stop there because she needed me. I washed her from head to toe in the shower and massaged oil across every inch of her body.

"Thank you," she said.

She was on her stomach with her arms folded under her head.

I was still massaging the oils on her back. When I reached her slim thighs and curvy butt, I couldn't help but run my tongue along the perimeter and leave a few kisses.

"I got you. Turn over."

She exhaled and turned over to her back. She watched me oil up her arms and breasts. I had to leave kisses there too. I drug kisses down each leg to her feet, making sure to pay special attention to her toes.

When I finally finished, she smiled and said, "I missed you today."

"I missed you, too. Can't you tell?"

She nodded with a big smile. "Get in the bed, I'm tired."

I was on my knees on the side of the bed. I ran a finger across her clit and she shivered. It was glistening with moisture.

I smiled. "We can't waste this, you're wet." I held my finger up.

Covering her face with both hands, she said, "You've been rubbing and kissing all over me, I can't help it."

"I'll let you rest but I need a quick taste." I sucked my finger clean.

"Dre, I..."

Her words were cut short when I dipped my head between her legs and licked the sweetness from her warm mound.

"Mmmm," she moaned, opening her legs wider to give me better access.

I chuckled. "I thought you were tired," I said, as I ran the tip of my tongue on her swollen clit.

Before she could respond, I sucked her in and gently dragged my teeth across her sensitive spot.

Her thighs immediately clamped my head between her legs.

"I'm sorry!" she said and loosened up her legs.

I kissed her lower lips a few more times and lifted my head.

"I'll get you during the night, don't worry," I said and laughed.

Whenever I hit that nerve just right, she would tighten her legs.

She laughed. "It's a natural reaction."

"Oh, I know. I forgot to pin your legs up. Like I said, I'll take care of you during the night or in the morning."

She slid into our regular spooning position. "Good night."

I kissed her puckered lips. "Good night, Baby."

After reaching to turn the light off, I wrapped her up and settled my hand on her stomach.

She had been quiet and needy tonight. I didn't know what that meant, but I would wait for her to tell me if there was anything I needed to know. Hopefully, I was overreacting, and she had a long day. However, my instincts told me she had something on her mind.

"Are you ready for the cruise? This is our first trip together."

I nodded. "I'm ready, but I'm glad we took off the whole week. I wouldn't have had time to pack and work."

We were leaving for Miami on Tuesday. The cruise left the following day.

"You're right about that, although I'm still working on this sugar."

"But this is what you love to do, so it's not really work," I said.

"That's true. Oh, can you open up my laptop and look at the video I'm going to post on our social media accounts? Tell me what you think. It should be on screen when you go in."

"Sure, ok. Let me see what you got." I opened the laptop and started the video. D' Angelo's song *Brown Sugar* played as the background music while she created her famous brown sugar.

"You like it?" She smiled wide.

"It's nice, Baby. Graphics on point but ummm, you sure about the song?"

"Huh? That's the perfect song, I mean it says brown sugar. He's talking about a woman but it still works."

I chuckled. "Baby, the brown sugar he's talking about is not a woman. It's a metaphor, he's talking about smoking a joint. The same way your cousin, Rick James, talked about Mary Jane."

She rolled her eyes and laughed. "First of all, stop calling Rick James my cousin just because we have the same last name. Second, I've listened to *Brown Sugar* for years. I know the words, it's about a woman; she might be a little edgy but he's talking about a woman."

I shrugged. "If you say so. I'll play the song. Listen to it carefully."

The song played and I stopped it during the first verse and said, "Exhibit A, he says his eyes are bloodshot."

"Naw, he's just saying he is getting high off of her," she countered.

I started the song up again, stopping it again during the second verse. "Exhibit B, the older sister is Chocolate Thai."

Her eyes opened wide. "Hell naw! Chocolate Thai is cannabis!"

I chuckled and started the song up again and stopped at the third verse. "Exhibit C, ménage a trois, he's defining smoking in a group."

"I can't believe I didn't know this! I never paid attention. I doubt if anyone else knows that. I'm still using it."

I shrugged. "Yeah, okay." I chuckled and closed the laptop.

"Come taste this," she said.

"I can't keep tasting all of this sugar. I can't be one of those dudes with the big tight belly."

She giggled. "It's just a tiny taste. Besides who else are you trying to look good for other than me? I like you how you are."

Leaning over to taste the sugar, I responded, "I can't let the people down." I sucked the sugar from the spoon and then kissed her. "Tastes even better now."

"You like it?"

I squinted. "Damn, it's good but tart. I can't think of what I would add it to."

She smiled wide. "It's for rimming glasses for drinks."

I nodded. "Okay, I could see that with the girly drinks. That's a good idea, Baby."

Tonya's ideas for the business she allegedly only started for her sisters were amazing. She constantly came up with innovative ideas.

"I had a few bartenders come in the shop looking for specialty sugars for rimming. I decided to create a special line and test it out."

"I see. That's a good idea. I like it."

"Thanks, this will be a small batch line. I'm naming it my *Rim Shot* line."

"How many flavors?"

"Three to start. I have watermelon-lime, cherry-habanero, and pomelo-cranberry."

"That's good, let me taste the others."

She gave me a side-eye. "Thought you wanted to get your body together?"

"You like it, so I'm cool."

There was a small spoon in a bowl of sugar so I picked up a bit on the spoon. This one had larger pieces, it wasn't like the others.

"Oh wait..." she said.

I had the spoon in my mouth before she finished. I immediately opened my mouth when the big pieces popped loudly in my mouth, scaring the hell out of me.

"What the hell? Was that Pop Rocks candy?"

By now she was doubled over laughing.

"I'm sorry." She laughed again. "That's something I'm working on, it's not ready."

I frowned. "You can't feed that to people without telling them."

"I didn't know you were going to eat it. The samples I want you to taste are over here." She pointed to two small bowls.

After the initial shock from the popping, the flavor was pretty good. "It tastes good. I could see the young crowd liking that."

"I know! Same thing I was thinking. I'm trying to test it to figure out how to prevent the candy from popping on the rim before you drink it. You need moisture for it to stick to the rim but that same moisture will make them pop."

"Hmmm, that's true. I didn't think about that. What about a thick gel, like Mel's honey?" I asked.

"Ohhh, you might be on to something." She pulled her phone out and started tapping on the screen.

I thought about the little surprise I had waiting for her on the cruise. She had a way with the sugar. Watching her in her element confirmed the surprise.

She also seemed to be out of the daze she had been in so maybe she was tired and it wasn't about the ex. I was thinking too hard.

But my mind always went back to the conversation with Serena and Rob. Serena was certain that the ex had seen her or talked to her. I would put that to the side and enjoy our upcoming vacation.

This would be my first time traveling with a girlfriend and family. In the past, it was one or the other.

I watched her move around the kitchen with an apron on that read, "Nothing but Sugar" across the front. She was wearing her multicolored-rimmed glasses and focusing on whatever she was jotting down on her notepad. Her curly hair was held back by a thick dark green band that matched her green-fitted joggers and tank. She was so beautiful; I couldn't keep my eyes off her. The sugar she spilled on her arm earlier had her brown skin shimmering under the rays of sunlight peeking through the window.

"I feel you watching me, Nerd," she said while pouring something into a measuring cup.

I chuckled. "You mine now, I can watch you when I want to."

She grinned but stayed focused on what she was pouring.

I was one hundred percent gone. I loved her. I wasn't ready to tell her though because I'd never been in love. I wanted to make sure it was real. My gut told me it was, but time would tell.

Chapter 13 ~ Tonya

Miami was cool, but only because I was there with my family and Dre. It was a little too crowded for me. We didn't even attempt to go to South Beach to avoid the crowd. Instead, we opted to have dinner in Brickell once everyone had arrived.

Mama was elated to have all six of her children plus all of the grandkids present. Calvin and Janae were with us as well, whom she counted as her children too. We were a live bunch, and I couldn't wait to get the party started once we were on the ship.

Dre came out of the bathroom with a towel around his waist, brushing his hair, looking like a whole snack.

"Come on, girl, get moving. Brock said we need to be in the lobby in thirty minutes."

"I'm moving now."

He disappeared into the bathroom again.

The last couple of days I tried hard to get my mind together about Rio. Dre tried to play it off but I knew he was wondering about it. I would have too if I were him. An ex showing up at my parents' house, the shop, and my house would leave anyone wondering.

After talking to my sisters and then Donald and Tori, the one thing that kept coming up was that if Rio wanted me, he should have come back sooner.

I specifically asked him if he was cancer free and he said three years. It didn't add up and as much as I loved Rio in the past, I had Dre now. He was everything I wanted. He was kind, loving, attentive, and everything in between. The way he looked at me was enough to make me melt. I knew I was in love with him but it still felt too new to have such strong feelings. I wanted to be sure it wasn't infatuation from all the years of crushing on him.

Maybe if Rio had come back before Dre and I got together, I may have entertained him for a while. But I doubt if I would have ever fully trusted him with my heart again. His leaving made complete sense from his perspective but to ghost me for four years was a lot to forget. Even if I had forgiven him, I would have always been fearful that he may leave again when life was difficult.

As new as it was with Dre, I didn't doubt him. With all the women he'd dated in the past, I'd never questioned his loyalty to me. He had become my rock and I was finally happy.

However, I would extend the courtesy to Rio and hear him out. I felt like I needed closure with him. But I'd deal with that after the cruise. Right now, I was going to enjoy the next five days with my man and my family, living the island life.

By the time we made it to the lobby, everyone was milling around chatting.

"I like the braids on you, real sexy," Dre announced as we rolled the luggage from the elevator.

"Why thank you," I said and blushed.

All of the ladies had braids. Tori's shop had our entire family as patrons over the last seven days.

My braids were black and transitioned to a caramel blonde at the midpoint. I didn't get them too long, they were to the middle of my back. Just long enough to make a bun.

"Good morning!" Brock announced. "There are a lot of us so I booked two shuttles to take us to the port. Honey, do we have everybody?"

Mama was smiling so hard you couldn't see her lips.

"Yes, all of my family is here! I'm so excited everyone was able to come."

"It's not like we had an option," Lois whispered to Dale and Di-Di.

Including the six of us, Dale, Donald, Macon, Lois, Melody, and me, plus our significant others it was a lot of people. Not to mention Calvin and Janae. The icing on the cake for Mama was the grandkids. Macon's three: Major, Chloe, and MJ. Dale's three: Dexter, DJ, and his new son and Chloe's boyfriend DJ2. Donald's son and my baby, Elijah. Lois' two: Anise and

Jasmine. Melody's two: Zyon and Zorya. Needless to say, two shuttles were necessary.

"Let's go to the shuttles," Brock announced.

Our group took up most of the lobby and everyone was so loud.

The kids were in front as we moved outside.

Zyon and Zorya were off to the side. I stopped moving when I realized they were talking to their dad, Zy, near the sidewalk. Melody's ex was super tall and thin as a rail, there was no mistaking him.

The loud chatter came to an abrupt stop among the adults. I turned to find Melody with knitted brows and a scowl on her face. I guess that answered my question, she had no idea he was here.

Zorya was a daddy's girl, she was smiling and chatting it up with him. Zyon was smiling too.

"Baby, is that old boy?" Dre asked.

"Yep," I quipped. I tried to catch Donald's eyes but he had a death stare on Zy. Dale and Macon were staring too.

Brock got in front of us and said, "Everybody listen up! All grandkids go to the first shuttle bus with Gram right now!"

"But, Pop, we can't all fit!" Chloe announced.

"Yes, you will! Go on now!" He ushered all the kids to the bus and then yelled, "Zyon and Zorya, let's go, get on the shuttle."

The rest of us stood still and said nothing.

Dre finally whispered, "Are y'all about to kill ol' boy?"

Once Zyon and Zorya boarded the bus, Brock came over to us.

"Melody, did you know Zy was coming?"

"Absolutely not!" she slightly yelled.

Brock continued, "Do you want him here?"

"No!"

Brock clapped his hands together. "In that case, I trust that my children will figure something out that won't land them in jail. If your momma misses this cruise, it will crush her. But..." he paused. "Most importantly, that is my grandkids' father, and I don't want Zorya and Zyon upset over this. I'm going on the shuttle with the kids and your momma. Put your heads together and figure this out." He turned and waved to Zy and then hopped on the shuttle.

Zy was standing at the curb like a bad ass kid trying not to look at us. All eyes were on him. Melody made a move to go over to him and Macon stopped her.

"He came this far, he can come another twenty feet."

"Yo, Zy!" Dale yelled.

He had the nerve to turn around like he was surprised his name was called.

Dale lifted his head quickly, silently instructing him to come over to the group.

"What's up everybody?" he asked, once he was in front of us.

No one said anything until Donald asked, "What the fuck are you doing here?"

"I'm not trying to create a scene. Melody, can I talk to you in private for a minute?"

"No!" Melody spat.

"Hell no!" Macon said.

"I was trying to surprise you. The kids said you all were going on a family cruise and I thought it would be nice if I came along. I didn't know it was the whole family, I thought it was just you and the kids."

Melody blew out a breath. "So, now I have to be bothered with you during my family vacation? I made it clear last week that I didn't want to deal with you anymore."

"I WANT MY FAMILY BACK!" he yelled.

"Who do you think you're talking to!" Lois yelled.

"Take it down, Zy. I will fold yo' long ass four ways," Macon said calmly.

Dale stepped up to the front. "Zy, did you tell the kids you were going on the cruise?"

Reluctantly he replied, "I didn't get a chance to tell them before they got on the shuttle."

"Good, because you ain't going!" Dale announced.

"Naw, I already paid and I'm here. Melody, you better talk to your brother!"

Melody folded her arms and stared at him.

Dale continued with, "She doesn't have to say anything to me. I'm talking to you! Do you remember what I promised I would do to you if you didn't retract that alimony request?"

Zy stared at Dale with squinted eyes but didn't say anything. His chest rose and fell a few times.

"Wait! What?" Melody asked. "You told me you were acting out of anger and when you calmed down you withdrew it. My brother had to threaten you?"

"Mel, baby, it wasn't like that."

"Y'all kick his ass! I'll figure out something to tell the kids! I hate you!" She lunged at him and

Macon grabbed her with one arm before the rest of us could catch her.

"Take her to the shuttle," Macon instructed.

"I got her," Dawn said. She put her arm around Melody and went to the shuttle with Janae and Tori in tow.

"Now, as I was saying, you aren't going. You're going to get on the shuttle and go to the port with us. You'll tell Zyon and Zorya you came down here to see them off because you're here for whatever reason and then you leave. Understood?"

"You think you can tell me what to do? Threaten me about what's mine? Those are my kids!"

Dale lifted his sunglasses. "Man, we all have choices. You can go if you want, but I promise by the time you get home you'll have some serious issues. I will make your life a living hell. That's a promise, no threats from me. You got about ten minutes before we get to the port to make a decision. Let's roll, y'all."

Dale turned and walked toward the shuttle.

"Damn, so y'all like the Gangsta' Bunch instead of the Brady Bunch?" Dre whispered, referring to the old television show.

"Really?" I chuckled and he shrugged.

The short ride was lively. Zy sat near the front of the shuttle and didn't say anything.

"Hey, everybody," I said loudly and waited for them to look my way. "The song Brown Sugar, is he talking about a woman or weed?"

"Weed!" they all said in unison.

They all turned back to their conversations. Melody was to my right and Dre was to my left.

"Mel, did you know?" I asked.

"Yeah, who doesn't know that? It's similar to *Mary Jane* by Rick James."

"I told you everyone knew except you," Dre said and laughed. He turned back to his conversation with Calvin.

"Did you know Dale threatened Zy?" Melody asked.

"I did. And I didn't tell you because you were so upset about everything. And Dale swore us to secrecy."

"Lois knew?"

"You know she doesn't tell Dale's business."

"I wish I had known. I would never have gone back to him, or maybe I would have. Who knows, I'm all jacked up."

I hugged her. "You'll get better, Sis. I'm just happy you ended it with him."

"I made an appointment with the marriage counselor we used. I stopped going a while back but it's time. I need to sort myself out."

"Aww, Mel. I'm so proud of you. And I'm glad you apologized to Dawn."

She nodded. "Yeah, we are sisters for real now. We hit each other below the belt and made up."

We both giggled. "You got that right."

"I've been wanting to tell you; I really like Dre. I've never seen you this happy, not even with Rio. I thought he was going to have a lot of women."

I poked my lip out and cupped my hands into a heart. "Thanks, Baby Sister."

She hugged me. "I love you, thanks for putting up with me. I'm pulling it together. Getting rid of Limp Dick was my first order of business." She angled her head in Zy's direction.

I laughed out loud. "I'm sorry I said that. Ok, well not really."

She nudged me and smiled. "Don't be, it's the truth." She leaned over and tapped Dre on the shoulder. He was still in a full discussion with Calvin.

He turned to me. "What's up, Baby?"

I smiled and pointed to Melody. "She tapped you."

He looked from me to Melody then back to me.

"I wanted to say hi," she said.

"Hello?"

I nudged her and she continued with, "You want to have coffee with me one morning while we are on the cruise?"

"Without Tonya?"

"Yes! Just you and me," she explained.

With a straight face he replied, "Naw, I'm good." He turned back to Calvin.

Melody's mouth opened wide, along with mine.

He turned back to us. "I'm just playing." He laughed out loud. "I'll go with you. You feeling ya' boy now, ain't you? See, Baby, I told you. The people can't pass on all this."

Melody tried not to laugh but couldn't hold it in.

"This is going to be an interesting trip," she said.

"I think we already started," I added.

Once we made it to the port, the kids, Momma, and Brock were waiting for us.

Zy got off the shuttle first and made a B-line to the kids.

Melody stayed with us and let him have his privacy with them. A few minutes later we all watched as he hugged the kids and rolled his luggage across the parking lot away from the cruise port.

I guess he took Dale's advice after all.

"That's what I thought," Dale said to Lois.

"He doesn't know us, does he?" Lois returned, and high-fived Dale.

Dre shook his head, and mumbled, "Gangsta' Bunch."

The process for getting onboard was pretty long because there were so many of us. After dropping our luggage and checking in we had lunch as a family.

A couple of hours later, the ship was in motion. We all stood on the top deck and waved to the people at the port and took lots of family pictures before heading to our cabins.

On the way to our cabin, I wanted to check on Melody one more time. She was rooming with Lois.

"I'm going to stop and check on Melody, I'll be down in a minute," I said to Dre.

I upgraded our cabin to a larger suite with a balcony. Mel and Lois were on the same floor as us.

"Take your time, Baby."

I kissed him and said, "I hope you like the suite, I thought we should have something nice since this is our first trip."

He smiled wide. "Look at you taking care of your King."

"That's right! You mine now!" I said playfully.

Dre had been so good to me I wanted to do something nice for him. All the help at the shop was more than I expected and was very much appreciated.

"See you in a minute."

I cut the corner and went to the sisters' room. Hopefully, that was the last of the drama and Zy didn't double back and get on the ship. I didn't put anything past him.

Chapter 14 ~ Dre

The scent of fresh flowers invaded my nose as soon as I walked into our suite. My girl had this set up nicely for us.

After moving our luggage into the bedroom, I went to the balcony to let in some fresh air. The balloons, fresh flowers, chocolate-covered strawberries, and champagne were on the coffee table in the seating area. I took a strawberry from the container and opened the envelope on the table next to the goodies.

Hey Love,

Thought I would send you off right on your family vacation. Wish I could have been with you. I'm counting the days until you return, and I get to touch you again. Your skin and scent haven't changed a bit. That kiss was like adding fuel to my fire. It reminded me of what I've been missing. I could go on forever about you. But you already know my name means River and I never stop flowing when it comes to you☺. See you when you get back. The strawberries and champagne are a reminder of our first time making love. I hope you remember; I sure do ;)

I love you, Rio

My body was hot all of a sudden. I had to reread the letter because I know good and damn well this muthafucka didn't say he touched her!

I hopped up from the couch and walked around trying to figure out what to do because I had no outlet. I was surrounded by her family and the ocean. My forehead was moist, and I couldn't control my anger.

"Chill, Dre, chill. Tonya ain't playing you like this. Or is she?"

I punched the air a few times. This was the reason I didn't do relationships. People always on the bullshit!

Serena told me she had seen him! And she came home talking about how she needed me when she had been with him! I had to get out of this room.

I checked my phone and there was no signal; I couldn't call Rob to talk me down. Dawn was with Macon; I didn't want to bother her.

I sat back down and put my head in my hands to try and calm myself.

My eyes went to the door as it opened. She walked in with a big smile and then squinted her eyes.

"What's all this?" she asked, referring to her little gifts from Rio, River, or whatever the fuck his name was.

I didn't say anything. I just watched her and sat back on the couch.

"Dre? What's wrong? Why are you looking at me like that?"

I tossed the card on the table.

She kept her eyes on me and picked up the card. Her eyes widened as she read it.

"Ummm, okay. Can we talk about this? This is not the way it seems from what he wrote."

After staring at her a little longer, I asked, "What part isn't the way it seems? The fact that he knows where you are? Or the part where you kissed him and added fuel to his fire? Or is it the part where he's expecting to see you when you return?"

She sat on the couch a few feet away from me. "Dre, I can explain, I..."

I cut her off. "Are you playing me? Have you been seeing him behind my back?"

She frowned. "You're accusing me of playing you? Really, Dre? When would I have the time? We are always together."

I chuckled. "You're getting an attitude with me and I'm on a cruise with your family surrounded by fuckin' Valentine's Day from your ex? You got me out here looking crazy!"

She grabbed my hand. "You're right. I apologize. Let me explain. I did see him."

That shit hurt.

She continued. "I only saw him once. I was picking up lunch from Kahawa and he came inside while I was there."

I told her he was a stalker!

"He asked if he could talk to me, and I agreed to give him five minutes. He explained that he broke up with me four years ago because he had prostate cancer and went for treatment in Arizona. Long story cut short; he's trying to win me back."

"Where did the kiss come in?"

"He kissed me on the cheek when he left the coffee shop, that's it."

"Why didn't you tell me you saw him?" That was the bigger issue.

"It was a lot to process," she said, and shrugged.

Same thing Serena said. I kept quiet. I dropped her hand and ran my hands down my face.

"I didn't want you to think I wanted to go back to him."

"Then why the secrecy? Why not tell me like you did when he came to the shop?"

She blinked a few times. "Maybe because I was confused about what he said. I had no idea he was sick. It was a lot to digest and I didn't want what's happening right now to happen."

"This wouldn't be happening right now if you had told me."

"I can't explain it, you've never loved someone and have them leave you."

That comment made me angrier. "What does that have to do with you being honest? All I'm saying is this dude is out of pocket. He snuck into your building after you said you didn't want to talk to him. Now he sends all of this shit to our cabin. And you're talking about processing, but you got me out here looking like a clown."

"That wasn't my intention. I just needed to deal with it on my own. I didn't want to put my stuff on you."

Shaking my head slowly, I replied, "You think I'm not in tune with you? That I didn't know something was up? I know you, Tonya! I know your body! I know your facial expressions! I know that when you don't finish your food something is up! I know that when you have a glass of wine after work you had a good day, but if you have dark liquor it's been a rough day! So when you're dealing with stuff on your own as you call it, I know about it. And what do I do? I give you what you need—my time, gifts, dinners, sex, whatever you need I give it to you! Because I'm always looking out for you! And in return, you're processing the man that broke your heart."

She wiped the lone tear that finally dropped. I had to get out of this room. The walls were closing in.

I got up from the couch and stepped around the Valentine's table.

"I need some air," I said, and left the room.

∞ ∞ ∞

I probably walked the whole ship. I wasn't even mad at her anymore, but damn that shit hurt my feelings. I wasn't speaking on it with her though. I'd walk this ship five times before I copped to some hurt feelings.

Actually, I didn't know if it was hurt feelings or a bruised ego. I was in love with this girl and she was out here "processing" his ass.

I didn't have one woman from my former squad on my mind, hadn't thought about them since I was with her. I was all in. I'm wearing family reunion T-shirts, stocking shelves, going on a family cruise, and what was she doing? She was "processing". What did that even mean?

I found my way to an outside area facing the water and sat in an Adirondack chair.

There was an open-air lounge behind me with music playing and people eating.

Out of my peripheral vision, the biggest of the Gangsta Bunch, Big Baby, was heading my way. *Damn, I hope he kept walking.*

"What's up, Dre?"

"Not much, what's happening?"

We slapped hands and he sat in the chair across from me. There were five Adirondack chairs in a semicircle facing the water.

"You got it," he responded.

He kept quiet and focused on the water. The sun was bright but was on its way to set in the distance. The dark blue ocean water rippled as the large ship cut through it seamlessly.

"A few years ago, I met the woman of my dreams. I knew she was meant for me, but she had this male friend that I didn't care for..."

This damn family told everything! Now everybody knew what happened.

He continued. "You know what I did? I followed her lead. Because our relationship was between the two of us, it didn't involve him. However, as a man it bothered me, but I had to put my ego to the side if I wanted her. I couldn't go off on him or say much to her about him because I was new in her life. So, I said nothing and let her deal with him. He eventually showed his ass and she put him in his place. And I had nothing to do with it."

I shook my head. "The only flaw in the story is that I wasn't an ex she was in love with," I said.

"Nope, you weren't, you were worse. You were her best friend and had been in her life for thirty years. Women aren't like us, they have to evaluate everything, especially when it's someone that matters to them, like a best friend or ex."

"I hear what you're saying, but I'm telling you this is different," I emphasized. I wasn't intimate with Dawn. There was no touching and past sex.

He nodded. "Okay, let me take it a step further. Rio sent a Hallmark store to your cabin, right?"

I turned to him. "Way to push the knife in further, Brutus."

He shrugged. "It was a lot of stuff. I'm just saying. But anyway, I understand why you're mad and you were able to tell Tonya how you felt about it or whatever, right?"

I nodded, waiting for him to get to the punch line.

He continued. "I couldn't do that with Dawn. I had to take it and not say anything. The day after your car accident we were supposed to go to KC together to see my kid's game. She didn't go with me because she wanted to check on you. Imagine how many names I called you on the four-hour drive alone. So what I'm saying is a room full of flowers versus her leaving you to go to him ain't bad."

I sat quietly and thought about what he said. Maybe I did need to forget about the ex and let her process it.

The rest of the family trickled in, but they all went to the open-air lounge. Dale, Donald, and Calvin came to the area with Macon and me and grabbed a chair.

"I hear we got a problem with another ex," Dale said.

I wiped my face. I was embarrassed. I was an only child, and not used to this many people in my business all at once.

"It's all good," I said.

They all laughed out loud.

"Man, we have all been there. Ain't shit good in your mind right now," Donald said.

"I'm cool," I tried to say convincingly.

"Yeah ok, same thing I said when I watched Tori on a date with an ex while we were seeing each other," Donald admitted.

I'd heard a little about it but not the whole story.

"Yep, that shit was painful to watch and that was almost it for us. But I had to put my pride to the side because I loved her."

"Same thing for me," Calvin added.

"I know Janae didn't do anything," I said.

Macon laughed. "Janae broke in Hollywood too."

We all laughed. They called him Hollywood because he was a child television star.

Calvin smiled. "First date, I'm at Janae's house and the ex shows up while she's in the shower."

"Ohhhhh," we all said in unison.

"He walks in and goes to her bedroom door. Luckily, the door was locked so he couldn't get into her bedroom."

Dale fell over laughing. "What did you do when you saw him going to her door?"

"What could I do? It was the first date. I didn't know he was an ex at first. When I opened the door he came in like he was familiar with the house. When she came out of the room, she played it off though and he left."

Donald cut in, "Was he tripping with you?"

Calvin nodded. "Hell yeah, he was arrogant as hell. I took my shoes off and sat back on the sofa like I was familiar too. When she walked him to the door, I played *Don't Leave Me This Way* on her speaker system. You should have heard how Teddy P came in singing."

We all fell out laughing.

I added, "Brian was a trip. I forgot he showed up at Macon and Dawn's reception uninvited. I had to lie and tell him her father wanted to talk to him."

Calvin laughed. "Good thing you did because I was about to ruin the party. He had his hands on her."

We had a good laugh, I was feeling better about the ex. This love thing was new to me, but apparently, my situation wasn't new.

"See, we've all dealt with some other dude trying to block at some point. It goes with the territory," Macon said.

"That's how you know you got a good one, other men want her," Donald added.

"I'm glad y'all can bond over this. I didn't have this problem. My lady was mine from the jump, no confusion." That came from Dale.

Everyone stared at him.

"What?" he asked.

"Bro, you deserved an easy ride after your crazy first wife," Donald said.

We all laughed out loud.

"Y'all are some haters!" Dale quipped playfully.

"Moral of the story, ignore Rio and whatever he's doing. You wouldn't be on this family trip if Tonya wasn't into you. She's not like that," Donald said.

"Not to mention you had on a family reunion shirt last week," Macon said, and the rest of them nodded in agreement.

"Not just anyone wears one of those," Donald supplied.

"And Tonya never gave one to Rio," Dale added.

Dude was around four years and didn't get a family reunion shirt? This talk that I dreaded made me feel a lot better about our relationship.

"Hello, hello! Welcome to Karaoke at Club Bliss!" someone announced over the microphone in the lounge area. "Coming to the stage first is Tonya James singing *Long As You Love Me* by Shirley Brown."

My head snapped around quickly to see her walking up on the small stage.

"Ok, Sis!"

"Go 'head, T!"

The fellas were saying something, but I was focused on the strapless flowery sundress she was wearing. The bright yellow and orange colors were beautiful against her dark brown skin. Her braids were hanging down her back and moving as she adjusted the microphone stand.

"Hello, everyone. I chose this song because it has a bit of an island vibe to it. But I also want to dedicate it to the man I love in the back wearing the blue shirt. So here goes. Mr. Brown, this one is for you."

The fellas were patting my shoulder and trying to get my attention, but I couldn't look away from her. The music started and she began singing about her patience and that as long as I loved her she would be alright.

I moved closer to the inside of the lounge. My eyes were locked with hers. My heart was pounding or doing something I'd never felt before.

Lady B and Brock went to the dance floor. The fellas were talking behind me.

"Macon, damn, why do you always have to dance?"

"Now we all have to dance if you go!"

"Sorry, bros, I dance with my wife as much as I can. See ya."

Macon followed by Dale, Donald, and Calvin each took their wives to the dance floor.

I continued watching Tonya sway to the music and point to me singing about how she was wrapped up in my sweet love.

My girl had me. Rio could go to hell, Tonya was mine. I would have to figure out how to put my ego to the side like the fellas said, but today wasn't that day.

Tonya finished my song and placed the microphone on the stand. Everyone clapped as the music continued.

She left the stage and made her way to me. Facing each other, I said, "I love you, Baby."

Jumping up, she put both arms around my neck. I held onto her tight and closed my eyes.

"I love you, too. I'm sorry."

"I need lips," I said.

She moved her head back so that we were eye to eye and I kissed my girl.

"I want to wrap my legs around you but I have on a dress and my ass will be out."

Chuckling, I said, "Stay decent right now, because later it's definitely going to be out."

She smiled again and placed kisses all over my face.

∞ ∞ ∞

It was something different about confessing my love for her. It felt a little crazy. I couldn't stop kissing and touching her.

We returned to our cabin after dinner because Tonya wanted to talk. I had another idea so we hadn't quite talked yet.

"Dre?"

"Yeah, Baby?"

"Can we talk now? I've had two orgasms and I'll be sleeping soon."

"That's what lovemaking does to you," I said and kissed her forehead.

I didn't want to talk about Rio or anything associated with him until after I made love to her properly. He wasn't about to take up any more time on this trip after this conversation.

I was also happy to see that none of his little gifts were in sight.

It was pretty dark in the room except for the moonlight coming in from the balcony and a small light on the desk.

She crawled on top of me and rested her chin on her folded hands.

"I know you don't understand why I need closure with Rio, but I do. I shared four years with him, and he snatched it away without warning. As a woman, it made me question if there was something I did wrong or could have done better. Not necessarily for him but for me and future relationships."

Rubbing her back, I replied, "You're right I don't fully understand it. But as long as you and I are solid, I'm good. But in the future, I can't be blindsided like that again. You have to tell me what's going on. Can you imagine if he said any of that shit he put in the card to my face?"

"Dre, I'm not running to tell you every little thing that happens. You have to trust that I love you and that I want to be with you. Besides, he's the only ex that ended without closure, this won't happen again."

I blew out a breath. "Good. Are you going to hear him out when we get back?"

She stared at me and nodded. "There's not much to hear out from him, but I will tell him he needs to move on. I would ghost him like he did me but that's just not who I am, especially considering he had cancer."

"Do you think he was really sick?"

She smiled. "He's a lot of things but he wouldn't lie about having cancer. He lost his father to cancer."

"I love you," I said.

She laughed. "I know you do! You say it like every ten minutes."

She was right, but I couldn't stop saying it now that I told her.

"You opened the floodgates."

She puckered her lips and kissed me. "I love you, too. Let's get some sleep."

"You're right, I have to meet my sis for coffee in the morning," I said.

"I'm so proud of Melody. I knew she would come around."

"You know I'm irresistible."

She laughed out loud. "You are impossible! Go to sleep."

∞ ∞ ∞

"I thought you were going to stand me up," Melody said, after I sat across from her at the table.

I almost overslept. "Nope, I'm here. So what's up?"

She sipped her coffee. "I wanted to formally apologize to you for the way I treated you. I was in a bad place. Well, let's say I'm getting out of a bad place."

I nodded. "Is this part of a twelve-step program?"

She smirked. "Okay, I see you're not going to make this easy for me."

Chuckling, I answered, "Naw, I'll go easy on you since I'm going to be in the family and all."

Twisting her lips to the side and widening her eyes in surprise, she asked, "Oh really?"

I frowned. "I have a family reunion shirt."

She laughed. "What is it with Brock and the brothers and those family reunion shirts?"

"Hey, I'm in now, plus I love your sister."

Covering her mouth and tilting her head to the side, she responded, "Ohhhh, I'm so happy for you two. Tonya so deserves it, and I will say I was wrong about you."

"I get it. You see these good looks and muscles and you think I play around."

"Correction, I saw you with different women every time you were around."

I nodded. "You're right, I did keep a rotation going in the past. Your sister is all I need now."

She smiled. "You know when I knew you were a good person?"

"When?"

"The day Tonya yelled at me about the Kinloch ladies. I felt so bad and I was embarrassed that she did it in front of you. That was when I knew I had hit the bottom. After all I said to you, I couldn't believe you extended that amount of grace to me. You also made her come back in and talk to me. That was huge, you could have said nothing and let us deal with it. Thank you for that."

Listening to Melody apologize felt good. I wanted to have a good relationship with everyone in her family.

"Ain't no thing. I couldn't kick you while you were down, that's not my style."

"I appreciate it and I appreciate your help in the shop. The other thing is, I was next door at the barber shop getting my sides trimmed up after I got my braids and Ced was cutting Star City's hair. After he left, I asked him how Star City could afford that expensive haircut. You know how much they charge over there, it's not twenty bucks. He told me that you paid for all of his haircuts."

Ced ran his mouth too much. That wasn't something I wanted other people to know about.

"Star City isn't a bad dude, he made bad choices. It could have been any of us."

"But that's really nice of you to do it on a regular basis. I bet he appreciates it."

I shook my head. "He doesn't know."

"Wait, Star City doesn't know you pay for his haircuts?"

"Nope."

"Why not?" she asked.

"I've known Star City since we were kids, graduated together, and everything. I can't snatch his pride like that. He's always been a street hustler. He thinks if he cracks a few jokes and slick-talks the barbers they will cut him up for free. It's what he's used to doing and people aren't going for that on a regular. So, I asked the fellas to cut him up once a month and I'd take care of it. He has a couple of grown kids and grandkids that he sees from time to time. He needs to be decent when he sees them."

"You are a good guy, Dre. That's very nice of you. But what about the clothes? Ced said you bring clothes to the shop too."

I cocked my head to the side. "You had coffee with Ced too? Damn."

She smiled. "You know this family is nosey."

"They have a lot of young dudes and older ones that come through the shop and need clothes for interviews or whatever. I got a few of us in the loop and put a little closet together at the shop for the fellas in need. We replenish it when they run out. Just a little something to help out."

"Dre, that's cool. I had no idea they were doing that in the barbershop."

"Everything doesn't need to be on blast. Just trying to help out where we can in the community. Again, one wrong move, and that could be any of us at any given time."

She smiled and nodded. "I see why my sister is into you. You have a good heart."

"Thanks, because I'm into her too."

"I know you are, and don't you worry about he who shall not be named. He's a bastard. He better not let me catch him snooping around the shop."

Sis was cold-blooded. Better him than me on the receiving end of her wrath.

"Damn, Mel, you don't believe his story?" I asked. *I know I didn't.*

"Naw, I'm sure he had cancer. However, if he loved her the way he says he did, he would have come back after he left Arizona. But he's lying about something, he likes to manipulate."

Same thing I thought, but as I said last night, I wasn't giving him any more time on this cruise.

"Alright, I'll let you handle him." I chuckled. "Thanks for the coffee but I have to get back to the love of my life."

Melody laughed and rolled her eyes playfully. "I can tell you are new at this! Last night at dinner I heard you over there telling her you loved her a million times."

Standing from the table, I replied, "Gotta let her know. She's my first love, she's getting all of it."

"Go 'head, Lover Boy, I'll see y'all later."

I hugged her and said, "That would be Mr. Lover Man."

Chapter 15 ~ Tonya

I did not expect to have so much fun on my family cruise. Day one wasn't the best, but we made up for it. We went on two island tours, snorkeled, zip-lined, and jet-skied. Dre was a pretty boy, but he was extremely masculine when it came to sports and activities.

I had no idea he rode motorcycles in his twenties and thirties until I watched how he handled the jet ski so well. Even Donald commented. Donald was the family rider; he'd been riding for years.

Today was the last island before the last day at sea and return to Miami. I was excited to tour St. Kitts because this was my first time here.

The kids separated from the adults today. They left early in the morning to go on a mini speed boat excursion followed by a dune buggy excursion. That was a bit much for us so we chose to do an island tour and hang at the beach for the day.

Dre said he had a surprise for me.

"What are you daydreaming about?" he asked.

We were on the tour listening to the guide explain the history of the island.

"I'm listening and wondering when I'm getting my surprise."

He chuckled. "You'll get it soon enough, be patient."

I poked my lip out pretending to be mad. He kissed me quickly.

"I feel better now."

The tour bus slowed down and stopped in front of a huge sugar cane field. It was beautiful. In the distance, the old sugar mill sat in the middle of the field.

"Before we get off the bus and take a closer look at the sugar cane, I hear there is a person who specializes in sugar on the tour."

I turned to Dre and he shrugged. The rest of the family turned to me.

"Ms. Tonya, can you come off the bus with me?" the tour guide asked into the microphone.

"Is this the surprise? What does he want me to do?" I asked Dre quietly.

"I don't know, maybe Lady B or Brock told him."

"Come with me."

I walked to the front of the bus with Dre behind me.

"Look at her, she can't do anything by herself now," Lois whispered, and then snickered.

"They are all in love now," Dawn added playfully.

I eyed both of them but couldn't help but smile.

Once we were off the bus, I noticed a man with a camera around his neck standing nearby.

"Ms. Tonya, we have a quick photo shoot set up for you in the sugar cane field. According to Mr. Andre, you own a store where you make customized sugars. He thought it would be nice to have pictures of you in the field in your store."

My mouth opened wide. Holding my chest I turned to Dre. "You thought of this for me? When?"

"When we first booked the cruise. I knew they had sugar cane fields here and thought you would enjoy having the photos on the wall at the shop."

I began rapidly blinking my eyes to stop the tears from welling up.

I grabbed him around the waist and hugged him tight. "Ahh, Baby, this is so sweet and thoughtful. Thank you so much!"

Puckering my lips and standing on my toes, he kissed me, and the photographer snapped a picture.

"You're welcome, go take your pictures. We will get a few with your sisters with you too."

Could this man be any sweeter to me? I wanted to cry so badly but didn't want to ruin the moment with him consoling me.

"Okay, okay," I said and ran off with the photographer behind me. I jumped up in the air and he snapped a few photos.

The field had very tall sugar cane, so I didn't go between the cane. I stayed on the perimeter. The tour guide took a large machete and cut a few canes down and then I cut one down. I was able to trim the stalk down so that I could suck on the raw cane. I was delighted. I had Dre taste some and then cut a few pieces off for the rest of the family. The photographer took plenty of pictures of me while I cut the cane and pictures of my sisters and me. This was a great idea, and the pictures were going to look good on the wall of the shop. Even looking at the cane when the bus arrived the thought of photos never crossed my mind. Dre was good for me, and I didn't plan on letting him go.

Once we were finished and back on the bus I nuzzled under Dre and smiled.

"You love me, don't you," he said.

"I sure do! Thank you for this. You don't know how much this means to me."

I couldn't quite express how much a thoughtful gift meant to me. It was a perfect surprise.

"You want to show me later?" he asked.

"Oh, you get whatever you want for the rest of the cruise. I promise!"

"Bet! We are skipping dinner tonight."

I laughed. "Agreed!"

∞ ∞ ∞

If I could have stayed on the cruise with my family and Dre, I would have been there another two weeks.

I was well-rested and back in the groove of things. It had been almost two weeks since returning and the family was still riding high from all the laughs and fun. I know I was still on cloud nine.

Standing in the shop, admiring the pictures from the sugar cane field was a constant reminder of our vacation. Instead of choosing one photo, I framed about six of my favorites and Dre hung them for me.

My favorite was the simple kiss we shared with the sugar cane as a backdrop. My other favorite was one with my sisters and me holding hands in the air and laughing. I hung it next to a picture we took as children in the exact pose. That was Lois' idea, and it turned out great.

The photographer was also able to capture a great picture of me inspecting a raw piece of sugar cane. And another of my eyes lighting up after tasting it. I loved those photos.

"You still admiring the photos?" Melody asked.

I smiled wide. "I am. That was so nice of Dre."

"It was. I've been wanting to ask if you've heard from Rio?"

Lois butted in, "Same thing I want to know."

I couldn't figure out why I felt the need to hear him out. After I returned from the cruise it finally clicked. I felt bad about him going through his cancer treatment alone.

I realized that it was his choice and he did what was best for him. While he assumed he was sparing me, he still did what was best for him at the time. I had to respect it. Deciding to go through something that life-altering without the person you love means that maybe we weren't true partners.

I put it in the context of my relationship with Dre. If there was anything that happened to me, I would want him by my side. I would never push him away because I thought our relationship was built on what I assumed our life should be.

I also realized that I was not one hundred percent all in with Rio. He broke up with me and I never tried to call him or make contact after that final conversation. If Dre broke up with me right now, I would be at his house the same day trying to talk to him. That's how much I loved him and believed in what we had. He's mine and...

"Tonya?"

"Oh I'm sorry, Ummm, yeah, I heard from him. He called and I told him I'd moved on. I'm not interested, and I don't feel like I owe him anything. It's been too long."

Lois smiled. "That's what I'm talking about! You don't owe his ass shit! Rio was cool but he's not down to earth like Dre. We want Dre," she chanted.

I laughed. "I want Dre too. I just love him so much."

"We know," they twinned.

"Am I that person I used to hate? The one that's always talking about her man and how good he is?" I looked back and forth between the two of them waiting on an answer.

"Who's going to tell her?" Lois asked.

I covered my mouth. "Do I talk about him that much?"

I honestly didn't realize it.

Melody unlocked the door. It was noon on Saturday and time to get the day started. The door chimed a few minutes later.

"Well, hello ladies."

"We are going to the office," Melody announced and grabbed Lois before she could respond.

I watched Rio approach me slowly.

"Hello, Beautiful, how have you been?" he asked.

"I've been well, how are you?" I returned.

He stared at me for a moment. I was standing behind my sample table prepping taste cups for my *Rim Shot* line. I had about six bartenders coming by today to test them out. Rod and Haven also wanted the Pop Rocks sugar to be exclusive for *Solstice*. I was still working on that idea, but I promised them it was theirs. I was close to coming up with a solution.

"Not so good," he replied.

My eyes went to his and I squinted. "Is everything okay, health-wise?"

He blew out a breath but kept his eyes on me. "I was disappointed that you chose not to speak with me. I tell you I had cancer, and you tell me you've moved on. I thought you would at least hear me out. We did spend four years together."

"Rio, I'm sorry about you being sick, but we can't go back in time. You chose to exclude me from that part of your life. I respect your decision, but we can't go back," I said.

"Wow, I would have expected a little more empathy from you. Tonya, what we had was special. I'd hate for either of us to miss out on the type of love we shared."

I shook my head. "What we shared was in the past. It wasn't sustainable through thick and thin. Is that not why you left?"

He moved closer. "I did that for you! That's how much I loved you. I sacrificed my needs for you! Can't you see that?"

"Ok, I respect that, and if this was one year post break-up I would have run back to you. But it's not! It's four years later. Why didn't you come back for me after you were cleared by your doctors? Why three years later?"

The door chimed. We both turned around and a lady walked in with her eyes glued to Rio. He was fine so I understood the attraction, but she looked angry. She was very pretty; we could have been sisters. Same size and same brown complexion. Her hair was in a long straight bob style. I usually wore mine in a natural curly tapered style. Her eyes were a little smaller than mine and of course, our clothing styles seemed different. She was a bit homely.

I stepped around the table to greet her. "Hello, welcome to the SHE-iS spice shoppe."

She finally looked at me and smiled. "Hello, nice to finally meet you, Tonya."

"Oh, I'm sorry. What's your name?"

She held her hand out. "My name is Lesley." When I took her hand, she continued with, "... Hendrix. As in Rio's wife."

Whaaaaat? I slowly turned to Rio and he had a death stare on Lesley.

"Soon to be ex," he clarified with venom.

I took my hand back and looked between the two of them. *Rio was married?* Stunning.

"Yeah, he's right. We will be divorced soon, but I thought I would come to get a glimpse of the woman whose shadow I've been living in since I married him three years ago. I'm guessing by the look on your face he failed to mention me. And our son."

My head whipped back to Rio. *He had a child?*

"Ummm, can't say that I knew about either of you," I said, still looking at Rio.

Rio said nothing. He stared at me.

"When his evil ass mother sent him that news video of you dancing in the street, he decided he couldn't live without you anymore and he asked for a divorce. It was time. He called me by your name when he was supposed to be making love to his wife."

My mouth slightly opened. I was speechless. Lois and Melody gasped. They were supposed to be in the office but I now knew they were in the hallway listening.

Lesley walked toward the door. "Nice meeting you, Tonya. Rio, our son is at your mother's house. I'm leaving tonight. I expect you to have him back in Arizona in three weeks per our agreement." The door chimed and she was gone.

"Tonya, baby, I can explain. That's what I've been trying to tell you."

I chuckled. "Wow, Rio. You are a piece of work. I can't believe I almost jeopardized my relationship to talk to you. You have a whole family?" He moved closer to me and I held my hand up. "Don't!"

"You wouldn't talk to me; I've been trying to explain."

Frowning, I said, "But you were able to explain about your being sick but didn't include your family? You always did massage the truth, not sure why I'm surprised."

A flash of anger appeared on his face. Squinted eyes, flared nostrils. "I have never lied to you! I left you because I was sick! Do you know how badly I wanted to tell you? I couldn't do that to you because I loved you! Lesley was a nurse at the Mayo Clinic who was there for me when I went through my treatment. They didn't think I could have kids or even get an erection without assistance! She came to my place looking like you and out of the blue I was standing at attention! One slip-up, the one time I was weak and missing you I slept with her! I was coming back here! I was coming! I swear I was, and I found out she was pregnant! What was I supposed to do? I couldn't leave her pregnant! So I did what I thought was right and married her. We moved to New Zealand, and I tried to make it work for three years."

He paused and then continued. "My mother sent me that news clip of you dancing and that was it. I couldn't do it anymore, I had to try to get you back. Tonya, I love you. You have to know that. I don't care about who you're with now, we can figure it out. I'll wait for you, I don't care!"

I was in shock. I stared at him and all the memories from our past rushed into my mind. Memories of our good times. Memories of us laughing, making love, all of it.

As I turned my head, the photo of Dre and I kissing in the sugar cane field caught my eye and my heart melted. That's where my heart belonged. I once loved Rio but that was in the past. Right now, and for the foreseeable future, my heart belonged to Dre.

"I'm sorry, Rio. I can't be with you, I'm in love with Andre. Not to be cruel, but the way you say you feel about me is the way I feel about him. I can't live without him."

He stared at me for a while longer. "If what you feel for him is what I feel for you then I don't have a chance."

He moved closer to me and touched my cheek. "He's a lucky man. I love you."

He backed away from me and left out the door.

Lois and Melody slowly walked in from their ear-hustling station.

"Oh, Rio left?" Lois asked.

I cut my eyes at her. "I heard you two in the hallway."

"I told you she heard us!" Melody scolded.

They both walked to me with their arms opened wide and hugged me.

I smiled and took in my sisters' warmth and affection. "I love y'all nosey asses."

They both laughed. "That was a heavy conversation, how are you feeling?" Lois asked.

"Right!" Melody added. "I almost felt sorry for him. But he was still being sneaky by not telling you everything a few weeks ago."

I exhaled. "Honestly, I feel relieved. It was hard not knowing. But now I know why we ended and why he stayed away. I hate that he feels the way he does, but he will find love the same way I did. My heart was broken when he left me. I healed and found an even deeper connection with Dre. He will do the same one day."

Lois looked at Melody and nodded. "Alright, Sis. So do you see yourself marrying Dre?"

"I gave him a family reunion shirt, you tell me."

They both laughed out loud. "Not the shirts again!" Melody yelled.

"Seriously, I love Dre. If he asked me to marry him today, I would say yes."

"Ok, Sis, we hear you," Lois said. "We thought you were going to need to take the day off. But since you're fine, you can stay and work."

I smiled. "The bartenders are coming by today to sample the *Rim Shots* and Dre drove his parents to Chicago for a party. I would be bored if I left."

"Oh, that's right. Why didn't you go with them?"

"I wanted to go but the bartenders are coming and remember we closed for the cruise. It's been busy since we've been back. But I miss my baby." I poked my lip out.

My phone pinged.

Dre Bae: We made it to Chi-Town. Last trip I'm doing without you.

I smiled.

"That must be Dre," Melody sang.

Me: Agreed! How am I going to sleep?

Dre Bae: You want to catch a flight up here tonight?

I laughed out loud. "Y'all, he's asking if I want to catch a flight up to Chicago tonight."

Melody laughed. "Y'all are sickening! He will be back tomorrow night, right?"

I nodded with my lip poked out. "But I miss him."

Lois cut in with, "What time are the bartenders coming by?"

"About two."

"Go see your man, you have plenty of time. It's like an hour flight," Lois said. "My husband is gone; I wish I could fly off to see him. Baby, life is too short. You tell him yes. Mel and I will handle the shop tomorrow."

I bounced from one foot to the other. I snatched my phone up.

Me: YES!!!

Dre Bae: booking it now, your flight is at 6:30. I'll pick you up from Midway.

Me: I'm so excited! Thank you! I love you!

Dre Bae: I love you more, see you later.

I was so excited, and I literally saw him this morning.

"Okay, my flight leaves at 6:30!"

Luckily my hair was still braided, and I only needed an overnight bag.

"That's what I'm talking about!" Lois high-fived me.

Dre Bae: Macon and Dawn are taking you to the airport.

Me: You take care of me ;)

Dre Bae: ALWAYS!!!

"Macon and Dawn are taking me to the airport."

"You text them that quick?" Melody asked.

"Nope, Dre did!"

"Go 'head, brother-in-law! That's how you do it!" Lois yelled, and we laughed.

The rest of the day went by quickly. The bartenders along with their proprietors loved the *Rim Shot* sugars and asked if I could sell to them exclusively. That was music to my ears because now I didn't have to worry about coming up with new packaging. In return, they would put our shop name on their drink menu.

Lois and Melody were in full agreement. We agreed to work up a contract next week.

My day had gone well, and I couldn't wait to see my man!!

∞ ∞ ∞

Chicago was lit! Dre and I danced for two hours without sitting down.

"These old people know how to kick it!" I yelled over the music.

Wiping his brow, he nodded. "Let's go sit for a minute."

As we approached the table Mrs. Barbara smiled and waved us over. "Tonya, I want you to meet a few people."

Dre shook his head and sat down next to his father.

"Ok, this is my daughter, Tonya. Isn't she cute? Look at this perfect figure."

The ladies hugged me like I was a small child while I smiled.

"When is the wedding?" one of them asked.

"Oh, honey, you know how these kids are. Who knows."

"Think you might have a baby for him?" another asked.

Luckily Mr. Larry stepped in with, "This girl is too young to be caught up in a hen session. Leave her alone!"

"Shut up, Larry!" they fussed.

"Barbara, how do you put up with him?"

He grabbed my arm and ushered me to my seat.

"So you left me to the wolves and didn't save me?" I asked Dre as soon as I sat down.

"I got one word for you."

"What's that?"

"Cruise."

I laughed and said, "You're right, you did a great job with my family."

The beat to our song kicked in and we locked eyes.

"Let's go!" he said and grabbed my hand.

D'Angelo's *When We Get By* blasted through the speakers as we hit the dance floor. We were even more in sync with each other than we were the first time we danced together. Maybe it was because we were in love. Either way, we moved along with the rest of the Chicago steppers like professionals.

By the time we finished dancing, we were exhausted, so we went upstairs to our room.

We had a beautiful room with a great view of Lake Michigan.

"I'm so glad I came! Thank you for inviting me up."

"You're welcome. Where I go you are always welcome."

We were snuggled up in the fluffy bed wearing our white hotel robes.

Looking around I said, "You would have been lonely without me, this suite is nice. And that view."

"I would have been fine in the standard room I originally booked. I got this room because you were coming. Only the best for my girl."

He was so good to me that it felt like a dream.

"You are so sweet, thank you." I kissed him.

"You want to stay an extra day?"

"Ummm, yes. But what about your parents?"

"They are retired, they won't mind. I'll call them."

Five minutes later, we were snuggled back up with our stay extended for an additional day. Mrs. Barbara said if it got her closer to getting a grandbaby, she would stay the week.

I sat up and crossed my legs facing him. "I have to tell you something." He shifted his eyes to me. "I had a visitor at the shop today."

"Please don't tell me dude showed up again after you told him you moved on."

I nodded and he continued with, "He's a stalker, I'm telling you. The one day I leave town and he shows up. What did he say?"

"He wasn't alone."

Frowning, he asked, "Who was with him?"

"His wife," I dropped casually.

"HIS WHAT!" He sat up in the bed. "He's married?"

"He also has a son," I further revealed.

"WHAT!"

I nodded and ran down the story in detail.

Dre shook his head. "That's crazy. So did the wife look like you?"

I nodded. "She really does, she could be a fourth sister. But guess what? I saw her in the airport on the way up here."

His eyes widened. "Did she see you?"

"Yep, she came over and talked to me. She gave me a little more detail than he did. She said they really did start well for the first year and then things got rough. She showed me all kinds of pictures of them together smiling and having a good time. The baby looks exactly like him, I mean he literally looks like a small man."

"You were cool talking to her?"

"It was awkward when she first came over but I think she was relieved that I wasn't with him. I told her I was on my way to you and she started telling me everything. I didn't know what to say so I listened until it was time for me to board."

"Damn, Baby, I'm sorry all of that happened and I wasn't there. But you know what's messed up? He knew who I was on the deck that day because he saw the news clip."

My mouth opened wide. "I didn't think about that. I guess he did because they announced our names."

"It doesn't matter anyway, you mine now."

"That's right, Baby!" I leaned over and kissed him.

"Let's get some sleep. We can go hang out tomorrow."

We took off our robes and got into our usual spooning position.

"Tonya?"

"Hmmm?"

"Thanks for telling me about today."

"Of course, I love you."

"I love you, too."

The End

Epilogue ~ Dre

Three months later...

Your boy was about to do the damn thing! Yeah, I was proposing to my girl. I opened the shop door and was blown away by the setup the girls did. All I said was to set up something nice and they went overboard. Tonya would love it though, and that's all that mattered. It was her birthday, and I was proposing.

"Hey, Dre," Dawn said and clapped her hands. "I'm so happy for you. Can you believe we will be married to siblings?"

"That is crazy, but I wouldn't have it any other way. My best friend and my wife are in the same family. D, I love her, I mean like for real, for real."

"I know you do."

"No, I like really love her," I emphasized.

Dawn playfully rolled her eyes. "Everybody and their mama know you love Tonya."

"I'm just saying, do other people feel this happy?" I asked teasingly.

"Somebody come get him!" Dawn yelled.

The rest of the girls came from the back.

"What is he doing? Telling you how much he loves Tonya?" Melody asked.

"You know it!" Dawn said.

"All of y'all are haters! Y'all supposed to be happy that we are happy."

"Everybody is happy, Dre." That came from Tori. "But give us a break. We know you love her."

"Wait a minute, do I say I love Tonya that much?"

"YES!" they all said in unison.

"Well guess what?" They all turned to look at me. "I LOVE TONYA!!" I burst into laughter.

"I can't stand him!" Janae said playfully.

"Where is she anyway?" Melody asked.

I shrugged and they all stared at me. "What?"

"You don't know where Tonya is?" Melody asked.

"No, she had errands, she'll be back. What's the big deal?"

"Because you stay up each other's tail," Lois added.

"Don't shake the foundation, Lois, that ain't cool," I said.

I moved around the shop. There were large photos of us blown up all around. Starting with a still from our very first dance at the intersection. That seemed like ages ago and it had barely been a full year since that day.

The next photo was a still of us dancing at *Solstice*. That was the day we officially became a couple and Tonya was wearing that orange dress and shoes with the butterflies. The other pictures were candid shots of us at the family reunion in our matching shirts, the two of us on a jet ski, and of course her favorite, the kiss in the sugar cane field. My favorite was the photo I'd never seen until recently. Dawn gave it to me. It was a photo of Tonya on stage singing to me while I watched intently. The look on my face summed up my feelings for her. I was in love with her.

"Dre, why did you choose the shop to propose?" Janae asked.

"Honestly, I thought it represented our relationship. Although it's new, this spice shop established enough steam during a short period of time to become a pillar in the community."

"Damn, Dre, you're going to have us in here crying," Lois said.

"Okay, I'm going home to get her. Make sure y'all are gone within the next thirty minutes. Melody, don't forget to call her."

"We got it," Melody said.

"Alright, I'm out. Thank you, ladies, again for setting this up. I wouldn't have known where to begin. I also wanted to let you all know..." I put my head down.

"Ahh, Dre are you crying?" Tori asked.

The four of them walked over to me and I lifted my head. "I wanted to let y'all know that I LOVE TONYA!" I laughed out loud and left the building with them groaning.

Once I was in my truck, reality set in again. I was nervous. I knew she would say yes, but I was nervous about the actual marriage. I didn't want to mess anything up.

When I asked Lady B and Brock for her hand in marriage, I also asked for tips. Brock told me the key to a successful marriage was communication, compassion, and coins. He said if you can talk to your wife, understand her point of view, and provide for her, everything else would fall into place.

I took that to heart. After being single and childless for so many years, I had plenty of money to provide for her. After that thing with Rio, our communication improved. The one thing I was still working on was understanding her point of view. That would probably take a lifetime to figure out.

By the time I made it back to her place and picked her up, it was almost time for the proposal.

She looked beautiful in her red strapless dress. The plan was to have dinner, but I was waiting for Melody to call her.

"Did I tell you how beautiful you look tonight?"

"You did, but I don't mind you telling me again." She batted her eyes.

Her phone rang; hopefully, it was Melody because I was driving extra slow trying to stall.

"Hey, Mel, what's up? Hold on, let me put you on speaker."

"Hey, Brother," Melody sang.

"What's up, Sis?"

"Go ahead and ask him. She's trying to cut into my birthday dinner."

"What's going on, Sis?" I asked, as if I didn't know.

"Can you run Tonya by the shop? I think I left my honey pot warmer on. I know you are going to dinner down the street. It will take me thirty minutes to get over there and I'm in bed."

"Ain't no thing, we got you, Sis."

Tonya shook her head.

"Thanks, Brother. You're the best. Tonya, I'll call you tomorrow, enjoy the rest of your birthday."

"You call him brother, but you call me by my given name? Wow! I might be jealous."

Melody laughed. "Sorry, Sis, love you, bye."

"Bye, talk to you tomorrow." She ended the call.

"Are you trying to take my sister away from me?" I asked.

She laughed out loud. "You two are ridiculous. You can have her crazy behind."

We laughed as I pulled in front of the shop and killed the engine.

"Oh, Baby, you can sit here, I'll run in. Her honey pot is in the front on her sample station."

"Since when do you open doors and I'm around? Especially, as good as you look tonight. Sit tight, Birthday Girl."

She smiled wide and blushed. "Okay."

I rounded the truck and opened her door. Once she unlocked the main door and disarmed the alarm system, she turned on the low lights.

Her mouth opened wide when she took in the room full of our large-scale pictures.

"Dre? What is all of this?" She didn't know where to look. She turned to me then the pictures, then back to me.

"Happy Birthday, Baby."

She tiptoed to me in her heels with her arms opened wide.

"Thank you! This is beautiful! Can I look at the pictures?"

I hugged her and kissed her. "Of course, go look."

She went to each picture and inspected them one by one.

"Dre, this is so nice! It's like a timeline of our relationship. I love it!"

When she finally realized I didn't answer she turned around. I was on one knee holding her ring box.

Epilogue ~ Tonya

*M*y eyes were wide open. He was on one knee in his crisp black suit and tie, looking just as handsome as the first day I saw him my freshman year of high school.

Holding my hand to my chest and fighting back tears, I slowly walked to him.

"Tonya Lila James, you are an extraordinary woman. You are intelligent, beautiful, and full of life. I love your sense of humor, your wit, and even your smart mouth. You keep me grounded and you are my peace. I need you and I want you in my life. Will you marry me?"

I nodded and finally let out the tears I'd been trying to hold back.

"YES!" I said loudly. I hugged him and gently kissed his lips.

He stood up and swung me around. "I'm getting a wife," he whispered.

I nodded and held his face. "Thirty-plus years later I am marrying that boy I crushed on at orientation my freshman year."

He kissed me a few more times and asked, "Baby, do you want your ring?"

"Oh yes, I'm sorry! I completely forgot that part. I have what I want." I pecked his lips.

He smiled while taking the ring from the box. "I'm glad you feel that way, but you're wearing this ring. The people need to know you're off the market."

I held out my hand and watched as he slid the ring on my finger. It was absolutely beautiful!

"Dre? This ring? I love it!"

"Only the best for my girl."

The round center stone was set in a white gold pavé setting. The stones in the pavé setting were chocolate diamonds that looked like... "The setting looks like brown sugar!"

He smiled wide. "It does. Oh, read the inscription."

I took the ring off, the inside of the ring read *Brown's Sugar*. I was speechless.

"Do you like it?"

"I love it, Baby! This is perfect!" I said. "This is the best birthday I've ever had! I love you!"

"I love you, too. Are you ready for your birthday dinner!"

"I am, let's go!"

By the time we made it down the street to *Solstice*, I was on cloud nine. My ring was shining, and I couldn't keep my eyes off my fiancé.

"Can we skip dinner and go home?" I asked.

"You want to?" We were sitting in the parking lot of *Solstice*.

My stomach growled. "Maybe a quick bite."

"That's what I thought. You know your greedy behind can't miss a meal."

"Stop insulting your fiancée," I teased, as we walked to the door holding hands.

Dre opened the door, I stepped inside.

"CONGRATULATIONS! AND HAPPY BIRTHDAY!" everyone inside yelled.

My mouth was wide open as I surveyed the room and saw the faces of our family and friends.

Dre put his arms around me and whispered, "Happy Birthday, Baby. I love you."

I didn't want to let him go, but we needed to greet our guests.

"Happy birthday, Tonya! Let me see the ring!" Mrs. Barbara said.

"Yeah, let's see the ring!" Lois added.

Dre rented *Solstice* for the evening. It was wonderful being surrounded by the love of my family and friends. Dale and Di-Di surprised me as well, I did not know they were in town. We took pictures, danced, and ate.

"Congratulations, Auntie," Elijah said as he held his arms out.

Out of all the nieces and nephews, Elijah and I had a special bond. He was Donald's only child and I was there with him every step of the way during his childhood visits.

I hugged my first baby and shed a few tears.

"Thank you, Elijah. I know you're grown and working now but you'll always be my baby."

His smile resembled Donald's, along with his hazel eyes.

"I'm glad you're getting married, I worried about you all the time."

Before I could respond, Donald walked up and picked me up. "Happy Birthday, Favorite Sis."

Laughing, I responded, "You better not let Lois hear you saying that."

Donald tossed his head to the right. "Are you kidding me? Look at her, she's with her favorite now. She and Dale have been talking nonstop since we got here. She's not worried about me."

"You know I should have known something was going on because Lois would have called me a few times on my birthday, and I haven't heard from her but once today."

"She got her buddy with her; you know how she is about Dale."

"You peep Melody over there with Macon? Those two get on my nerves too. Look at them."

"Yeah, I see them," Donald said.

"You two are doing the same thing!" Elijah emphasized.

Donald and I looked at each other and fell into laughter.

"Get outta here so I can talk to my sister!" Donald said playfully.

Elijah kissed my cheek. "Happy Birthday, Auntie. I'll catch up with you before I leave town."

Once Elijah left, Donald asked, "How are you feeling about everything? You look happy."

"Don, I am so happy. I love him so much. The only regret I have is that I didn't get a life with him when I was younger. But I plan to make up for lost time."

"There you go, Sis! It wasn't your time back then. You'll appreciate each other more at this age. Trust me, I know."

My eyes scanned the room until they landed on Dre in an animated conversation with Dawn. He appeared to be re-enacting the proposal.

"I know you're right."

I was over the moon with my birthday and engagement. I also couldn't believe not one family member slipped and told me about the party. They got me good this time, but little did Dre know I had a surprise for him when we got home.

Later that evening, after we danced the night away, Dre and I were at his house snuggled up on the sofa.

"When do you want to get married," I asked.

"Baby, I'm the man, that ain't my area. That's all you. You tell me when. All I do is pay for everything and show up where I'm told to be."

I laughed. "You're not helping at all? Not even with the date."

"Nope, because my only job is getting you moved in here and settled."

Moving into Dre's house was a no-brainer. He obviously had the most space and we both loved the area since my condo was around the corner. I'd have to sell my condo because they didn't allow renting.

"Thank you again for today. I loved every minute of it." I puckered my lips for a kiss.

"Anything for you, Baby. You do understand the full responsibility of becoming a Brown, right?"

Playfully rolling my eyes, I responded, "Would you stop! I am hyphenating my name."

"Okay, go ahead and do it, but I want you to say it out loud." He had a satisfied look on his face as if he knew something I didn't know.

"My new name will be Tonya James Brown." My eyes widened as I realized how that sounded.

Dre laughed. "See! Do you want to be nicknamed James Brown by your family? Because you know it's coming. Lois would be the first to say it."

"I never said it out loud. That is an awful name for a woman, I can't do that!" I stared at him and continued with, "Why didn't you tell me how ridiculous that would sound?"

"Baby, you've been out in the streets and independent too long, you're feral. It's going to take some time for me to break you in," he said with a straight face.

"If I'm feral, what are you?"

"In love with you," he said and kissed me.

Our kiss deepened once his hands started roaming inside my robe.

Stopping his hands, I ended the kiss. "I have something for you."

He placed kisses on my neck. "Mmm-mmm, later, I have what I want."

"No, really. I have something for you. I planned to give it to you at dinner."

He finally sat up and frowned. "You have something for me on your birthday?"

I nodded and hopped up from the sofa. "Be right back."

I grabbed the small box from my purse and handed it to him.

He put the box next to his ear and shook it. "What is it?"

"Open it!" I sat next to him and waited while he opened the box. He looked at the two small images and then at me.

"Baby? You're..."

I nodded and smiled.

"I'm going to be a husband and a daddy?"

I nodded again as he inspected my ultrasound pictures from earlier today.

"But when? How long have you known? How do you feel? Come here." He kissed me again and hugged me.

"I found out today. I went in for my annual exam and the doctor told me. I had no idea. Are you okay?"

His mouth was open. He stared at me. "Yeah, I thought one of us couldn't produce because we have a lot of sex. I'm surprised but I'm happy. How are you feeling about it?"

"I've gone through a wide range of emotions today but I'm happy too."

He quickly opened my robe and placed his hands on my stomach. "We made a baby, Tonya."

Covering his hands, I nodded. "I know, we did."

"Can we have another one after this one?" he asked. "I want our kid to have a sibling."

Dre was a planner; I knew I would have to keep him focused on the current before he went off into the future.

"Can we have this one first and see how it goes? I'm not young, Baby. Are you sure you're okay?"

"Yeah, I'm fine. I have a thousand things running through my mind right now that I need to do. Do you want to stop working? You can if you want to. Do we need a different house for the baby? We can move. I have to get more life insurance and start a college fund for my daughter."

Here he goes. "Baby, relax. Let's get through the pregnancy. I'm okay working, the house is fine, you have plenty of insurance, just breathe."

I held on to his face and rubbed his beard until he calmed down. "Okay, now, why do you think it's a girl?"

He frowned. "I know she's a girl, my little king will come after her."

Ok, whatever, there was nothing I could do with him right now. He was in planning mode.

He was up on his feet walking around.

"Are you sure we don't need to move? We have this pool out here. Is that safe? Let's just look around and see if we see something better."

"Dre, you love this house..."

He waved me off. "I have a family now. I have to make sure my wife and kids are safe. You want a ranch like this or a two-story?"

I walked over to him with my arms outstretched. "Come here, please."

I hugged him and then led us back to the sofa. "Listen, I know you got us, okay? We don't have to move, people live with pools around kids all the time. We will be fine. If we decide to move later, okay. But right now, can we enjoy the last few minutes of our engagement day?"

He let out a breath and smiled. "Dre about to be a daddy!!!"

He seemed to be coming out of planning mode. "You want to tell our mothers?" I asked.

"Let's wait until morning, mine will be up all night. Like you said, let's finish celebrating."

I nodded. "You're right!"

I glanced at my brown sugar engagement ring and smiled. It was such a beautiful and unique ring.

He slowly removed my robe and dropped kisses on my shoulder.

"What's your name going to be?" he whispered.

"Tonya Brown," I said breathlessly as he sucked that sensitive spot on my neck.

"And what is my name for you?"

Holding my head to the side to give him better access, I answered, "Brown's Sugar."

"That's right, Baby. You mine now."

The End

Music Inspirations

The heroine, Tonya James, was inspired by the music of Shirley Brown. I grew up listening to the strong women around me sing her sultry lyrics as our St. Louis legendary radio host, DJ Lou 'Fatha' Thime, played her songs on Saturday mornings. Listening to her music today is nostalgic— it brings back good memories of my mother and childhood. Her featured songs in the story are:

Woman to Woman
Between You and Me
So Glad to Have You
Long As You Love Me

The hero, Andre 'Dre' Brown, was inspired by the music of D'Angelo. My college days and twenties were filled with music by D'Angelo. His music seeped into my life in 1995 and spanned from college parties on the sundeck to after-work traffic jams on the Beltway. The music of D'Angelo continues to blast in my home on a regular basis. His featured songs in the story are:

When We Get By
Spanish Joint
Nothing Even Matters (Lauryn Hill ft. D'Angelo)
Brown Sugar

I hope you enjoyed the music selections and the inspiration they provided in developing Tonya and Dre's characters and storyline.

Shirley Brown and D'Angelo thank you for delivering music that continues to inspire decades later.

Thank you for reading! I hope you enjoyed Brown's
Sugar!
Please consider leaving a review on Amazon!

SHE iS series
Brown's Sugar
Honey Pot ~ Coming Soon!!!

The Love Movement
Slick
Wet
Ride

Something About Love Series
Book 1 ~ Something Old? Something New?
Book 2 ~ Something Borrowed? Something New?
Book 3 ~ Something Blue? Something New?

Mingle with Marlee!
Facebook: *Marlee Rae*
Facebook Group: *Mingle with Marlee*
Instagram: *@marleeraewrites*
Email: *marleerae45@gmail.com*
Website: *www.MarleeRaeReadsAndWrites.com*

Brown's Sugar

Marlee Rae

Brown's Sugar

Made in the USA
Middletown, DE
23 November 2024

65260836R00128